EROTICA SHORT STORIES FOR NAUGHTY WOMEN

A COMPILATION OF STORIES FOR ADULTS OF EXTREME SATISFACTION

THE ELEVATOR WASN'T MOVING
FAST ENOUGH

 The elevator wasn't moving fast enough. I watched the dull red numbers change from floor to floor, seven, eight... They seemed to be moving slower, almost like the building was getting tired. A four letter word caught in my throat. I would have let it loose if I were alone. There were two others on the slow ride, a rich gray suit and a bicycle courier. I swallowed the word and began tapping my foot, thinking the elevator may get annoyed and move faster.

The suit got off on nine, slowing me down even more. I moved over to the panel and smacked the close door button a couple of times which seemed to amuse the courier. The button was useless. The elevator doors closed in their own sweet time. After an interminable wait, it began to rise again.

"Running late?" The courier asked. I turned, about to snap at him. He was young, probably couldn't drink legally. He was fairly trim but rather sloppy in the hygiene department. It looked he lost his razor a few days ago.

"Yes," I replied, turning back to the console to watch the numbers slowly change. There was no need to bite his head off.

"Can you push twelve, please?" The courier asked.

"We just past it," I said and pushed the button.

"I'm not late," The courier said smiling. I turned back *q*uickly to the young man. Young was relative since I just had my twenty-fifth birthday. He stood confidently in his black knee length bike shorts, his windbreaker unzipped open to his stomach, revealing a taut blue t-shirt. It was the nicest thing anyone had done for me in a long time. He was not as shabby as I first thought.

"Thank you," I said as pleasant as I could. It was hard, as late as I was, to muster a smile, but I did. A lot of stress faded away at that moment. Here was a little piece of the world that wasn't out to get me. It would be nice if he was a few years older with a better job. Not that my job was anything to be proud about. My father's death had wounded me in heart and future. It created a legal mountain whose peak wouldn't be reached until my thirty-second birthday. I was rich, I just couldn't touch any of it.

"No problem," The courier replied, then he leaned against the far wall and looked away, seemingly uninterested in more conversation. For a moment, I thought I would have to fend off an advance. I looked down at my blouse and skirt to see if there was a stain. Nothing. Just me. A strange disappointment clouded my mind. I would have preferred a small flirtation.

The elevator doors opened on fifteen. I sighed and exited, the courier seemingly oblivious to my leaving. "Good luck," the courier said when my back was turned. I turned as the elevator doors closed. He smiled at me in a soft dreamy way. Unthinkingly, I smiled back, the doors acting as a comfortable shield for the brief flirtation. Life was good again.

"Ella, you're late again," Agnus Tremaine spat with hands on her wide hips. Her graying hair, glued in curled clumps atop her head, bounced to emphasize every word. I sighed. I had hoped to escape my step mother's notice. Life was bad again.

"Accident on sixth street," I stated as I moved toward the utility room. My utility room, held in trust.

"My daughters don't seem to have a problem arriving on time," Agnus continued with a grating tone. I hated these times. Seven more years of being under this woman's claws.

"They seem to be on vacation more than not," I returned with my own venom. Agnus had fooled my father into tieing up his assets until I was older. She, of course, became executor and, in turn, my jailer. I suspected she was a slut in bed. I could think of no other reason my father would screw me like he had. I loved him more than anyone, but he was a man and I knew he wrote that will with his dick.

"Business trips are not vacations," Angus defended Drizella and Anastasia. I was sure they got little done in Tahiti with my money. "I only wish you had their work ethic," she continued as if I didn't know the truth.

I ignored her continuing rants and pulled out the bucket and mop. My bucket and my mop. I was required to stay with Tremaine Marketing, Inc until I came into my inheritance. He just failed to say in what capacity. Agnus thought it best I was the night janitor. Seven more years and I can fire her. I began to fill the bucket with hot water. At least Agnus would go home soon. My home.

"The floors were done poorly last night," Agnus continued while pointing out some corners that held dust. There was a rider in the will that stated if I failed to stay with the firm, I would lose it to the next in line. Agnus was next in line. My only saving grace was that she had to answer to a board and the court. My life was miserable, but I still had hope.

I added a potent lemon-scented cleaning fluid to the bucket. At least it overwhelmed the perfume that Agnus liked to swim in. I ignored her other admonishments, knowing they were designed to get me to lose it and quit. That wasn't going to happen. I just had to stay out of trouble and in seven years, I get to fire the bitch.

I turned with my prepared bucket and smiled at Agnus. It was my you'll-get-yours smile. She never understood that smile. I think she thought I had a few screws loose. It always made her back away and lose her train of thought. The only attack I was allowed. I certainly couldn't yell at the CEO. That might be grounds for termination. It was a war and I had to let her win all the early battles.

"Good evening Mrs. Tremaine, Ella," Raj said, his olive-skinned smile leading the way out of the elevator. I smiled back, which irritated Agnus more. She had hired Raj as the night tech thinking I wouldn't be comfortable with an immigrant from India. The opposite occurred. He had become a dear friend and I adopted myself into his family. His wife Kiran and their daughter Aanya were such a lovely family.

"Mr. Vijaya, do think it is wise spending your time with pleasantries when there is work to be done?" Agnus asked. Raj lost his smile. His green card held him to his job as surely as the will held me.

"No, Mrs. Tremaine," Raj answered and moved quickly to the control room. I wanted so much to shove the end of my mop into Agnus's mouth to shut her up. I closed my eyes and let the image float away. Seven more years. Raj could stay. Agnus was out.

Agnus followed Raj into the control room. I was sure it was to give him an impossible list of tasks and remind him not to fraternize with the janitorial staff. The hallway seemed to brighten when she left. A devious thought entered my mind and I laughed to myself. The first sign of insanity, but it felt good. I began mopping. Mopping exactly where Agnus would have to walk in order to leave. Images of her falling on her ass were pleasant. I started humming Dancing Queen and used the mop as my partner. My thoughts were very pleasant.

Agnus didn't fall. I apologized for not thinking and starting at that end of the hall. It was humorous watching her walk in her high heels while holding herself along the wall. It was hard to hold my smile in, but I had a lot of practice at it. The corners of my mouth stayed low while my insides jumped with glee.

"Good night, Agnus," I called as she pushed the elevator button. She hated when I called her by her first name at work. I saw the anger in her eyes when she turned. I knew she wasn't going to walk back across the newly mopped floor again. Chalk up another one for Ella. Agnus just grimaced and stepped into the elevator. My body relaxed when the doors closed. The bitch was gone.

I pushed the bucket and mop into the corner. It was usually the last thing I did. I had a system. A series of steps that optimized the time it would take to clean the offices. Mopping first would just slow me up. Optimized work time allowed for optimized free time. I grabbed the large wheeled garbage can, vacuum cleaner and dust rag. Office to office, I *q*uickly dusted, emptied trash, and vacuumed then closed the door.

I had told Agnus it took thirty minutes to clean an office. She said I should be able to do it in twenty. It actually took less than five when I put my mind to it. Chalk up another one for Ella. I was done in under three hours, floors mopped and all the glass cleaned. They were my offices, so it wasn't as hard to do as Agnus thought. She was conniving, but a little on the dumb side. If she really wanted to get on my nerves, she should have me working during the day, with her.

I restored all my supplies and cleaned myself up a bit. I tossed a few dollars at the vending machines for a coke and chips. I went to the control room to see Raj. It was our nightly ritual. Raj worked and I kept him company. It was a somewhat boring existence, yet when shared, it lost its 'boring' status and become tolerable.

"Almost a record, Ella," Raj said, pointing at the clock.

"If she wouldn't have hung around, I would have broken it," I said. I raced myself every night. The quicker I got done, the sooner I could chat with Raj. I watched as he executed another batch process. The screen said he was updating the report server. A restructured database that allowed quick access for decision-makers. The two years I have sat with Raj had schooled me well on the inner workings of my company. I don't think Agnus thought I knew thing one about the goings one. Chalk up another one.

"Kiran wants you to come over Saturday afternoon," Raj said when he was sure the batch was executing. He spun in his chair to look at me. They were using me to try and become more American. I loved them, so I always agreed.

"I would love too," I agreed, "is Kiran making those potato things again?" They were to die for.

"Aloo kikki," Raj reminded me. I will never remember the name, "of course she will." Saturday seemed to far off. My social life was shit when I wasn't with the Vijayas. Working nights puts a huge cramp in one's mojo. I sleep when most people were awake and was heading off to work when they are getting frisky. I was sure that was part of Agnus's plan.

"I have to warn you," Raj continued, "Aanya has a new board game she wishes to play." I laughed. Aanya thought of me as a big sister. In truth, I thought of her as my little sister. She was more attuned to American styles than I and schooled me often. I helped her with the things a young girl couldn't talk to her parents about. Usually, boy things. Aanya was in the eighth grade and the drama had begun. The boys were just beginning to think girls weren't as useless as they thought. Girls, on the other hand, were separating the studs from the duds.

"Sounds like fun," I said. I had no plans that even sounded close to a good board game. Raj looked at me funny. I could tell he was thinking. His eyes always became still when his brain was working.

"I love that you come," Raj said, "it makes Kiran and Aanya very happy, but I worry we are stopping you from things." I smiled and decided to torture him.

"What kind of things?" I asked.

"You know...things," Raj said, using his hands to emphasize things.

"You mean like snorkeling?" I asked with humor.

"You know what I mean," Raj replied, trying to hide his blush.

"Ahh, you mean wild sex," I said, my eyes wide waiting to see if I could deepen the red in his cheeks.

"Well..." Raj stuttered, "I mean you're a pretty girl. You should be out on dates." Raj tried hard to clean up my words. I smiled at him.

"Agnus makes that difficult," I said, "my time is coming." Seven more years. Raj turned back to his terminal and began typing again.

"Kiran worries about you," Raj said *q*uietly. I felt my heart throb. Raj was worried about me. I loved him for it. I was in a hole right now and in seven years, I would climb out.

"You tell Kiran that all I need is aloo kikki," I said with a little laughter. That got me a chuckle. I certainly didn't want Raj sad on my account. I thought back to my last boyfriend. It had been before my father had past away. I would be lying to myself if I didn't admit that I missed the intimacy. Sex had its medicinal properties and was a ton of fun as well. Fried potatoes and board games were a poor substitute.

I changed the subject and asked Raj what he was doing. This is how I learned about my company. Raj, who had access to all the information, would instruct me in his tasks and I, in turn, would learn. I knew an awful lot about how the money moved, who moved it and why. I knew each employee, who were the slackers and who drove the business. In seven years, the board wouldn't find a naive girl, they would see a knowledgeable woman owner who knew how things worked. Agnus was digging her own grave. That was my solace.

I stepped into the bathroom before the end of my shift. I looked into the mirror and began to dishevel myself. I pulled a few strands of hair from my ponytail and let them float in a wispy mess. I smudged my glasses with fingerprints and pulled my shirt so it hung poorly, half out of my skirt. I had to look harried before Agnus arrived. There was rarely a need for her to be at work early. Her sole goal was to ascertain my level of misery. I gave her the answer she wanted to see. I girl on her last leg, about to throw away her inheritance. My secret defiance was my shield. Only seven years to go.

~

The drive home was miserable. Bands of rain ran across the windshield with a ferocity that made that wipers moot. I decide to pull over and let it pass. My first mistake. I ran over something that must have been placed there just for me. The telltale flapping and the steering pulling to the right let me know I had a flat. I went through my entire vocabulary of foul words. Then, I went through the litany again. The rain picked up. I made up some new words.

I waited for the rain to stop. I used the time wisely and pulled the owner's manual from the glove compartment. I had never replaced a tire on this car. I cringed when I saw the instructions. There was a bolt in the trunk, when turned, lowered a temporary tire. It was raining and I would have to retrieve it from under the car. The rain never stopped, but did change to something less than a deluge. I sighed and stepped out into the rain.

There were a lot of places I could have picked to pull over. I had to pick a spot where recent construction had left mud where rock should have been. The state had decided it would be good week to dig up the culverts along the side of the road and had deposited most of it on the shoulders. My white tennies sunk on contact. I slammed the door with anger as my only umbrella, I squished my way to the trunk.

I promptly squished my way back when I realized I had not undone the trunk hatch. The world was attacking and my mind was becoming traitorous. I gave up trying to walk carefully when I felt the mud ooze into my socks. Shoes ruined. Chalk one up for mother nature.

The bolt was stubborn. I had no idea which way to turn it as rain pelted my back. Finally, when I felt cold wetness find more private areas, I figured out it was clockwise. I gave up trying to do it quickly. I was soaked. It didn't matter how long it took anymore. I squatted down, my wet skirt fighting the movement, and saw the tire lying in the mud, almost two feet under the car. I tried to reach it, flailing at the edges. I sighed and dropped my knee into the mud. It found the rocks under the mud causing more wonderful words to escape my throat. I cringed as I shifted my knee and created a semi-unpainful spot to anchor it.

One hand on the trunk, I lowered myself, reached under the car and dragged the now muddy tire toward the back. My blouse was ruined by the time I figured out how to detach the tire from the cable that had held it under the car. I carefully lifted, trying to hold it away from my skirt. I turned and a wave of water, mud and whatever else was on the road covered me as a semi passed. I looked down at my clothes and lost it. I was tired, wet and now covered in mud. Swear words were no longer enough. Tears mixed with rain as I slipped and slid my way to the flat front tire. My throat was spasming as I went back for the jack and tire wrench.

Another bout of hard rain whipped through and my left foot slipped into the culvert. It came back missing its shoe. I leaned against the car, clutching the tools, trying to stop the horrid feelings coursing through me. I had no more anger to rely on, only hopelessness.

"You look like you could use some help," a male voice called. I looked up, my glasses blinded by rain. I didn't know who it was. I could only sob, covered in mud and show my tools. I didn't want to be helpless, but my mind was surrendering to it all. You can't fight the world.

"We'll start with the jack," the man said, and took it from my hands. He was taller than me, that much I could tell. He moved confidently to the front as another dousing came from the clouds. I followed him, my sock trying to leave itself in the mud. "Stand away from the side in case it slips," he said as he kneeled into the mud trying to find a secure place for the jack.

"Thank you," I said, remembering my manners. "Thank you," I said louder, certain that my first attempt was lost in the rain. He looked back at me and I saw a smile between the droplets running down my lenses.

"Wrench," he said, holding out his hand. I put the wrench in it and he affixed it to the jack. He began raising the car. "Crappy day for a flat tire," he observed. I nodded though he wasn't looking at me as he concentrated on the jack. I wiped my glasses with my wet finger. He had dark hair, soaked through. His shirt and pants were a mess now but looked expensive. The one shoe I could see was brown leather and not something found at Walmart. My savior was some kind of executive, probably on his way to work. I sucked in a breath and forced my helplessness away.

"That should do it," he said rising with the wrench. I took it from his hands, trading it for a smile.

"Thank you," I said again. I couldn't believe I had lost it. An executive doesn't collapse at the first sign of trouble. In seven years, I needed to be a rock of confidence. He smiled back, the rain running off his nose and past his strong chin.

"You lost your shoe," he said, pointing at my sock.

"It's been one of those days," I said, trying to ignore the loss. I moved to the tire and inserted the blade end of the wrench into the slot of the hubcap as the manual had said. It popped off and I pretended it didn't surprise me. He was there to catch it before slid into the culvert. He watched as I went at the first lug nut. I pushed down on the wrench and it didn't want to move. Hesitantly, his hand moved next to mine and we pushed together. The nut relented. He removed his hand and let me finish.

He stood there in the rain, holding the hubcap and collected lug nuts one at a time. To be honest, his presence gave me strength. His desire not to push the poor woman out of the way and do it himself was nice. He moved from savior to helper without a thought. I was smiling when I finished the last lug nut.

"I'm Ella," I said as I handed him the last nut. The rain was beginning to let up again.

"Peter," he responded.

"Thank you for stopping," I repeated again. I lifted the tire off the car and it bounced in the mud. I longer cared about the mud that splattered on my ankles.

"You said that already," Peter said. I looked up at him. He was smiling at me, almost laughing as I struggled to wheel the flat tire off to the side. He made no move to help, which was strangely helpful. I lifted the dinky donut tire and struggled it onto the bolts. He moved behind me. I suspected he meant to catch me if I started to slide into the culvert. Most helpful.

He handed the nuts to me, one at a time, and I screwed them on hand tight. The rain was beginning to cooperate and became more of drizzle. He handed the wrench back to me and I cranked the lug nuts tight. I turned to seem him loading the flat tire in the trunk. No communication, just optimized performance that limited the time we needed to be in the rain. I liked Peter.

I moved to the front of the car, inserted the wrench into the jack and began undoing what Peter had done. He met me there and watched as the car came down. "You handled that well," he said. I could hear the humor in his voice. He was having fun with me. I laughed.

"I am glad you stopped," I admitted as the jack slowly folded back to its rest position, "I was letting it get to me for a moment there." I looked up as I detached the wrench. He held out his hand and I put the wrench in it. I grabbed the jack and we carried them back to the trunk and threw them in. He closed the trunk and turned to me.

"I think you need to rush home, Ella," Peter said, with a sly smile. I wasn't sure what he meant. Was he giving me a command. I don't take well to commands. His smile changed when he saw my confusion. He leaned closer.

"I think you are a bit more beautiful than you intend right now," Peter said, his smile growing again. I stepped back as the realization hit me. I looked down and *q*uickly covered my breasts. The rain had made my blouse and bra see-thru. The cold rain had woken my nipples. Traitors. Peter laughed sweetly as he backed toward his car. "Absolutely beautiful," he repeated as he opened the door car. A sleek black Lexus that he seemed to fit into well. Red-faced, I headed back to my car and put my soaking wet muddy body on my clean seats.

I looked in the rearview mirror and saw him there. Peter was waiting to make sure I got back on the road. I smiled. Beautiful he said. He looked pretty good himself. I smiled to the world and waved to Peter as I got back on the road. Beautiful. I liked my breasts being beautiful. Thank God I didn't know him. I wouldn't have been able to ever face him again. That was, by far, the best worst experience I ever had. That smile of his was so honest. He wasn't just trying to make me feel good. He meant it. My breasts just got promoted to my favorite body part. Sorry calves, you just got demoted.

～

I had Kiran nearly in tears she was laughing so hard. My flat tire exploit was funny now that it was history. Lost a skirt, blouse, and one shoe (therefore two) in the incident. It cost me money I could hardly afford to get the tire repaired, not to mention the sleep I lost. At least my breasts were beautiful. That's the part Kiran thought was best. Thankfully, Raj and Aanya were in the other room while I helped Kiran in the kitchen. Raj would be embarrassed for me and not see the compliment I saw. Kiran understood. She had a wonderful sexy side that she usually only let Raj see when the lights were down. She trusted me, so I knew some of her secrets.

"I told you," Kiran said, between gasps, "you have it going on." Another bout of laughter caught her as she imagined me nearly naked on the side of the road.

"It was kind of nice, " I agreed, "embarrassing, but I think he really thought I was hot."

"You need more flat tires," Kiran laughed, "maybe wear a bikini next time." I tried to hold back my smile, but I just couldn't. It felt good to be admired, if only for a few minutes. I wasn't an exhibitionist, that I knew. It was just his smile and his words. "You should have gotten his number," Kiran added.

"No," I said, "I couldn't. I would die of embarrassment if I ever saw him again."

"He said you were beautiful, " Kiran countered, "and you said he wasn't hard on the eyes." I pushed Kiran's shoulder, lovingly.

"He's probably married," I argued, "what are you are trying to do? Turn me into a slut." Kiran gave me a sly smile.

"A man tells you, you are beautiful, you can at least see if he is married," Kiran raised her eyebrows up and down. Raj had his hands full with this one. I chuckled and held back my response. There was no arguing sex with her.

"You need to take some risks," Kiran continued, "I did with Raj and never regretted it. He is a good father and keeps the bed very warm." Her smile told me exactly what she meant.

"I think you took the last good man, Kiran," I said, half meaning it, "the rest are married, gay, or after only one thing." I wouldn't mind that one thing, but a possible future would be a requirement.

"You need to stop spending your Saturdays here," Kiran said, "you need to put yourself out there." She smiled, "maybe enter a few wet t-shirt contests." We laughed together as we began putting the fried potato patties on the serving tray. I had already forgotten the name of the things. My tongue loved them, it was my brain that refused to cooperate.

After a nice dinner, we all sat down for Aanya's board game. It was different from any other game I had ever played. It turned out to be a very enjoyable game. It was called Stone Age and you had to lead your people from a hunter-gather society to an agrarian one. You did this by gathering resources with workers and dice. You then spent the resources to buy huts and special cards. It was easy to learn and engrossing. Raj won the first game and we all agreed to play another. I thought I had the second game in the bag, but Aanya won by two points. She had amassed a good collection of cards. I would have been upset, but the look on her face was wonderful. She was young and needed the victory. It made the game all the better.

Aanya complained when her mother told her it was time for bed. I gave her a hug and promised to play her game again next week. I was actually looking forward to it. I think I had a strategy down that would lead me to victory. She kissed her mother and father goodnight. I watched the affection and was slightly jealous. I wanted what they had. I wanted crazy passion with a man followed by a family filled with love. I didn't think that was too much to ask for.

Raj broke out a bottle of wine. He and I were just entering our normal work cycle so we were wide awake. Kiran struggled to stay with us during the weekends. I always left when her yawns exceeded more than one a minute. We talked about American things. TV, thank the gods for the DVR, movies, books and anything that made them feel more like citizens. As the night wore down, the topic usually returned to work. That is when Kiran would begin to yawn.

"Your mother was especially upset last night," Raj said, remembering Agnus's tirade about the trash cans not being washed out. I just emptied them since they all had liners.

"She is just trying to wear me down," I said, "it will take more than trash cans to get under my skin." I took a sip of my wine. They both knew that the company was mine as long as I could hold out until I was thirty-two. "Why do you stick around Raj," I said and quickly qualified, "I would hate to lose my only friend there, but she treats you like crap." Kiran and Raj exchanged a look I didn't recognize. I was missing something.

"My staying here in America requires I keep this job," Raj said, "I don't have a choice."

"Is India that bad?" I asked. It didn't seem so horrible. I had even considered visiting there when I came into my inheritance. If Raj and Kiran were examples of the people there, I definitely wanted to make the trip. Kiran's face lost its happiness. I had asked something I shouldn't have.

"My family would not cherish my return," Kiran said, "they think I am dirty now." I saw a sadness in her. I didn't like how it looked.

"I am not the same caste as Kiran," Raj said. Kiran scooted over and leaned on Raj. I had asked something very sensitive. "she married below her status and it is just not done in her family." He paused for a moment before he continued. "Her family holds with the old ways. She and Aanya would be at risk if we were to return." I sucked in my breath. I didn't know there were places in the world where things like that still mattered.

"I didn't know," I said in a way of an apology.

"How could you," Kiran said with a forced smile. I had visions of Kiran and Aanya dragged off to some horrible family tribunal.

"To America," I said, raising my glass "and your quick path to citizenship." Raj smiled and Kiran's smile lost its fakeness. We tapped our glasses together and I quickly changed the subject. The rest of the evening went with less drama and returned to our own brand of humor. I needed them for my sanity and they needed me for a friend. It was a good arrangement. I left when Kiran's yawns exceeded the prescribed parameters.

~

I was early for once. It was nice to avoid Agnus's admonishments. I was surprised to not find her waiting for me with new degrading instructions on her lips. I took it as a gift and moved to my closet and began retrieving my supplies. I didn't see myself cleaning offices for the rest of my life, but it didn't take a lot of thought and allowed my mind to drift. Lately, it drifted to a man named Peter. Every time I saw that smile in my mind it sent champagne bubbles through my blood.

"What will I wear?" I heard it from my stepmother's office. It sounded like Drizella. I quietly moved down the hall. It was rare to find one of my step sisters at the office anywhere near closing time.

"We'll go shopping," Angus announced with an excited voice, "for both of you." I heard a duet of agreements and knew that both of my sisters were there. I walked into the office, my curiosity getting the best of me. Sure enough, what constituted my family was gathered in Agnus's office.

"Shopping?" I said. I knew it didn't mean me. I liked the tinge of guilt I could generate in them. They may be gold diggers, but they were human as well. I watched their expressions of joy dissipate as their eyes found me. Chalk another one up for Ella. It was going to be a good night.

"This doesn't concern you," Agnus threw back. She was using my inheritance so I felt it did.

"Sounds like a party," I said with an excited grin. I looked to my sisters and they lit up, foolishly thinking I was sharing with them.

"Charity cotillion," Anastasia blurted out. It was so easy to stir her red haired covered brains. I looked back at Agnus who was trying to feign disinterest.

"I suppose we are making a donation," I commented. I made sure the word 'we' was emphasized. Agnus looked flustered. I knew instantly that this was more a society play than a business decision. She had a high opinion of herself and her two daughters.

"It is beneficial for us to contribute back to the community," Agnus lied. She was trying to get her daughters married off to wealthy men. Maybe find another one for herself. More of my money down the drain. Anyone willing to marry those two, wouldn't be rich for long.

"Everybody who's anybody will be there," Anastasia added.

"What's the charity?" I asked. I almost threw my dust rag at Agnus when she had to look it up on the invitation. Beneficial for the company my ass.

"Children's hospital," Agnus read. At least my money wasn't being thrown in a ditch. I felt a little better. I decided I would make Agnus uncomfortable anyway.

"Where's my invitation?" I asked. It was fun watching her fumble with her mind. She was spending my money after all. She didn't see it that way, but I did.

"We need executives to represent the company," Agnus smiled when the answer came to her, "janitorial staff would not be how we would want to represent ourselves." I smiled back and watched her lean away. She hated my smile. Seven more years.

I left them, curses dying on my lips, and returned to my cleaning. It infuriated me that they were using my company to further their gold-digging plans. I almost swore at my father for leaving me in such a predicament. I sucked it back. He was only human and had little defense against a demon like Agnus.

Agnus and her daughters left shortly after. They were babbling about tomorrow's shopping. Executives my ass. I was in an especially dark mood when I sat down with Raj later that night. Even my glasses seemed to be steamed up.

"Why don't you go?' Raj asked me after I had explained my mood.

"Psst," I spat, "me at a formal dance. I couldn't afford to look in the front door. Agnus keeps the purse strings tight about my neck." Raj turned back to his terminal and began typing. He turned back around with wide eyes.

"$5,000 a plate," Raj said, "your sisters better have a good time."

"$5,000?" I exclaimed. Raj nodded. "That bitch. I will be lucky if there is anything left when she's done."

"Why don't you go?" Raj repeated.

"Where would I get $5,000?" I asked, waving at the atmosphere, "I could barely afford to get my tire fixed. Agnus certainly won't give it to me." Raj smiled and went back to his terminal. I moved behind him to see why he was so pleased with himself. His fingers were moving quickly as he fired off some program I had never seen.

"How many tickets do you want?" Raj asked. His voice was arrogant and full of pride. I saw a series of text prompts followed by commands I did not understand.

"What are you doing?" I asked.

"I am in the organizers database," Raj said, "I can slip in a ticket for you and no one would be any wiser." He was exceptionally proud of himself.

"You hacked the system?" I asked. The thought scared me. I took a step back as if that would make it less wrong.

"No one will know," Raj said, "I wrote a program that finds its way into networks." I stared at him. I thought I knew him. "I've never used it before, but it's untraceable." He chuckled to himself, "these people are good. Shark firewall, but I chewed through it in under five seconds."

"Raj!" I said, "you could end up in jail." He shook his head.

"They've never seen anything like this," Raj praised himself, "It travels through so many proxies it's untraceable. That's if they figure out I was in at all."

"Why would you write such a thing?" I had a whole new opinion of him. It was scarier.

"I toy with all sorts of code," Raj explained, "once I get my citizenship, I am going to need a resume. This will be the cornerstone. I am a master of network security. This proves it. Shark firewalls are the best in the business. The same ones the military uses."

"You're risking too much, Raj," I said, "you'll never get your citizenship if you get caught."

"I'm careful," Raj said, but I noticed he ended the code's execution.

"Thanks, but I prefer you out of prison, " I said with a smile, happy he turned off his hacking program. Raj smiled back with a bit of hesitancy. I don't think he thought the whole thing through. Writing the code was as far as his mind took him. He had such a brilliant mind. I think Kiran married up, not down.

The rest of the evening went as the hundred before it. I learned a little more about the company while sharing a nice conversation. The cotillion left my thoughts and hopefully Raj's.

~

My drive home was dry and without a flat tire. I arrived home to find my sister's already awake. It was odd to see them up before seven. I usually made it a point to be in my room when their alarms began to sing at seven thirty.

"Do you think he will be there?" Drizella asked. Anastasia was leaning on the counter in the kitchen sipping on a cup of tea nodding.

"Of course he'll be there," Anastasia replied, "his family runs the thing."

"Good-looking and loaded," Drizella smiled, "we should research him. Find out what he likes. I sure wouldn't mind walking down the aisle with him." My interest was pi*q*ued. I almost wanted to call the poor guy and warn him.

"You'll have to go through me first," Anastasia warned, her red hair waving from side to side as she bobbed her head. "You wouldn't have even known about him if it wasn't for me." Drizella looked like she might fight back, but instead, became thoughtful for a moment.

"We can't go upset with each other," Drizella reasoned, "he'll hate us both. No one wants bickering sisters." Anastasia's face softened. "he has to have rich friends. If we play nice, the winner can set up the other with his friends." A smiled grew on Anastasia's face. It was mirrored on Drizella's. I hated when they laughed together. It sounded like a clutch of chickens with breathing problems. I moved in to save my ears.

"Who are you two after now?" I said as I entered. Anastasia was startled, which pleased me. Drizella just smiled. It looked like her mother's smile. It displeased me.

"You wouldn't know him," Drizella said with a sweetness coating her bitter undertones.

"Try me," I said.

"You know the Charmings?" Anastasia asked, "the one's throwing the charity cotillion?" I nodded though I had no idea who they were. High society was lost on me.

"They have a son," Drizella continued, "he's single, wealthy, and not hard on the eyes." Anastasia chuckled. Another chicken chuckle.

"And you two are going to throw yourselves at him," I observed. Inside I was laughing. He would have to be a complete idiot to connect with either of my step sisters. It would almost be worth the $5,000 just to watch.

"Throw is the wrong word, dear sister," Drizella corrected, "we are not without charm."

"Certainly not," Agnus agreed. She came in behind me and made me jump. I hate when she does that. "and we have to go shopping to make sure he sees those charms."

"I thought this was business related," I said, my tone dropped to my disgusted level.

"Two birds, my dear, two birds," Agnus said. She moved to the coffee pot and poured herself one. "Would you like a cup, Ella?" She always offered me things she knew I would decline. I was on my way to bed and in no need of caffeine. I choose not to respond.

"You can't use company funds to marry off your daughters," I said. I shouldn't have, but she was spending my inheritance in the most irritating way. Agnus just smiled at me and sipped her coffee. She knew she could. "How does hounding the son of the benefactors improve Tremaine Marketing's image?" I was getting angry. I should have just gone to bed.

"It is all a little above your head, dear," Agnus continued. More chicken giggles from her daughters. "It's best to leave the complexity to those who understand it." My face began to heat up. I had to remind myself that she held the purse strings for seven more years.

"You look like you can use some sleep, dear," Agnus continued. She took a sip of her coffee and seemed pleased watching me stew. "Jealousy doesn't become you," Agnus added. It was all I could do to not scream. They were in my house, working at my company, and spending my money. There wasn't a damn thing I could do about it.

"Seven years, Agnus," I said slowly. I was grinding my teeth.

"That's a really long time, sweetie." Agnus's grin was unbearable. I almost let loose of the 'B' word. I knew it would be costly if I did. I took a deep breath and gave her the smile see disliked so much instead. At least it removed hers. I headed off to bed, my mind fuming at my father for leaving me in such a mess.

∼

I hardly slept at all that day. It is hard enough to keep your eyes closed when the sun is out. Add in a controlling stepmother that boiled my brain and sleep was the last thing my mind wanted to do. Instead of counting sheep, I thought of many wonderful methods of torture for Agnus. When it was time for work again, I was exhausted, angry, and less than friendly.

I stepped off the elevator on time. Agnus was waiting with a list of todos. I think she saw me near the breaking point. I kept to my smile and half listened to her demands. She became flustered halfway through, seeing that I wasn't going to lose it. We exchanged veiled unpleasantries and headed our separate ways. Without my surrender, the war would rage for another seven years.

"Bad day?" Raj asked. I had sat down rather hard and I think I was glowering.

"I am letting her get to me," I sighed, "I have to watch her trash my future and there is nothing I can do about it. Now she wants to trade some of my future so her daughters can fish for husbands." I chuckled when I thought about it. "It's not like they have a chance anyway."

"They do come off a bit needy," Raj agreed.

"A bit greedy," I corrected. Raj laughed then covered his mouth with his hand. He was never one to loudly disparage someone else. Anything above a whisper made him uncomfortable. His stalled laugh did make me feel better. At least someone in the world understood my troubles.

"I still think you should attend the cotillion," Raj said after he brought himself under control, "you need to get out and meet people and rescue your sister's poor targets." This time, I laughed while shaking my head no.

"Even if we could get away with it, I couldn't short the children's hospital $5,000," I responded. The thought of me running around warning men of my sisters approach was amusing. I could see Rag was disappointed in my choice. "You just want to use your new toy," I observed.

"For good. It must never be used by the dark side," Raj joked, "I can think of nothing more honorable than putting you on the dance floor where you belong." I liked how he could make me forget my step-mother. I smiled at his sincere humor. I needed more friends like Raj and Kiran.

∿

The weeks went by and I was confronted with new dresses, hairdos and shoes. My stepsisters seemed to enjoy modeling for me. My money, my house and they didn't stop to think I might resent it. I tried to ignore it all, but a small black pit formed in my stomach and I couldn't seem to fill it with happier things. I could forget my thoughtless family when I went to see Raj and Kiran, but I would eventually return to see my sisters all dolled up, practicing for the cotillion. As the dance neared, it only got worse. For the first time, I was truly happy I worked nights so I wasn't inundated all my waking hours.

"Two more weeks, Raj," I sighed as I sat down to watch him work, "I will be happy when this dance is over so I don't have to watch my sisters preening anymore."

"I've been thinking, Ella," Raj said quietly, "what if you paid for the charity tickets." He knew I didn't have that kind of money.

"Raj, I'm lucky to pay for the gas to get to work," I said. His smile was devious and he leaned closer.

"What if the company paid," Raj whispered, "it's your money anyway. Or it will be."

"You want me to embezzle?" I asked with a little shock.

"You would be stealing your own money," Raj justified, "my program will make it impossible to trace and you would be where you should be."

"There's not enough time," I wavered, "Agnus would see me there anyway and we would find ourselves in prison." The idea of attending the function did have a strong appeal. To see my sisters hopelessly flailing at men would be worth the entrance fee.

"Agnus only sees you as you are," Raj continued, "if you rid yourself of your ponytail and glasses, add some makeup and a new hairstyle, I would have trouble recognizing you." I shook my head.

"There's not enough time," I repeated. Raj smiled again.

"Kiran has a friend who is a seamstress. She does alterations for wealthy women," Raj argued, "you can borrow a dress for the night."

"Kiran is in on this?" I asked. Raj's smile was growing.

"She wants to see you all dressed up," Raj said, "she thinks you miss too much of life." I couldn't believe Kiran was in on the conspiracy. It made it seem more feasible.

"I can't see without my glasses," I conceded.

"Contacts."

"I can't afford contacts." I admitted. I would have to save up and a week wasn't enough time.

"Your company can." Raj was countering all my objections. "I can crack Coupon Crave's servers and get you in on a contacts deal as well as limo and hairdresser. I have to fit you in after the fact, but they will never know and I'll make sure you pay everyone." I stared at him. My friend was a master criminal and I never knew it.

"You owe yourself this," Raj continued, "you can't wait till you're thirty-two to start living. You'll get too used to being alone. Kiran and I don't want to see that."

"You sure we can't get caught?" I asked to reassure myself.

"It would take someone very skilled just to know they had been hacked," Raj replied, "even more talented to trace it back to the last proxy. No one has seen code like this before. They won't even know what they're looking at."

"It really is my money," I said, trying to convince myself. Raj looked pleased with himself. He knew he nearly had me over the edge and ready to say yes. "I would really enjoy watching Drizella and Anastasia bomb."

"And you might even meet someone," Raj added. In my dreams. Raj was already taken and everyone else works days. I questioned whether there was another vampire out there for me. A little flirting may not hurt, though.

"Kiran will help?" I had no idea while I kept piling requirements on. Raj just nodded. "Okay," I committed, "let's do it." Excitement replaced the black pit in my stomach. Raj turned to his terminal and went to work. He turned his chair around and handed me a phone.

"Type in a password, something unique," He said.

"Whose phone is this?" I asked, turning it over. It was just a slim black smartphone.

"Yours," Raj said, "present from Kiran and I. It's prepaid so it's not tied to your name." He always knew I was going to cave and say yes. I laughed softly. "Something somewhat long so that it can't be broken into. I have some encryption of my own invention running on it. Without cracking the password, it's contents are useless." I thought for a moment, then laughed to myself as I typed in the first memorable thing I could think of. It was fairly long but made me smile and I wouldn't forget it.

"What name do you want to use?" Raj asked as I handed the phone back to him. This was going to be completely cloak and dagger. I picked the first thing that came to mind.

"Cindy," I said, 'Cindy Thompson." Raj began typing. He worked for over thirty minutes with joy in his eyes. He was impressing himself as much as he was impressing me. He went back to the phone and began working on it, then back to his terminal. Finally, he handed the phone back to me.

"All set Cindy," Raj said as proud as one man could be, "you have an appointment for tomorrow at the eye doctors, it and all the rest are in the Coupon Crave app on the phone. Your ticket for the charity ball is in the email account I created for you."

"You are incredible," I complimented.

"Just toss the phone away when you're done," Raj added, "it's the only thing that comes close to tying you to the fact you stole your own money." I had no choice, I hugged him. It made him uncomfortable, but I needed too. He was smiling when I separated, so no harm done.

~

Kiran helped me choose a dress. Had I seen it in a catalog, I would have never picked it out. When it was on my body, I couldn't not choose it. A soft champagne pink fabric that was cut and sewn in such a way, it looked like it came over my shoulders loose and wrapped my breasts, then tied off in the back. Below the faux wrap, a pleated high shirt started and flowed ever more sheer to the floor. It was soft elegance. Kiran's friend, Samantha, altered it to fit snug around my waist and drop into my cleavage. Just enough showing, to tease, but not arouse. I felt beautiful.

"Now, no stains or anything," Mary reminded me, "and take care to not snag it when you enter or leave the car." It made me a little nervous. I knew it was an expensive dress.

"I'll take good care of it," I replied. I could see her apprehension. She was doing this as a favor for Kiran and didn't know me at all.

"It does look good on you," Mary smiled. Kiran agreed. I twirled a couple of more times in front of the mirrors. It was the best I had ever looked.

"You need to stop in and see Madam Winslet," Mary continued, "she would have the perfect shoes for that dress. She owns a boutique off Harlem."

"Sounds expensive," I said.

"You have to have the right shoes," Mary instructed, "she's a friend of mine. I'll call ahead and make sure she gives you her best price."

Mary was right. Madam Winslet sold me a pair of pink heels that really completed the dress. I would be paying them off of the next six months, but I did get a 50% discount off the $1,500 list. They became the most expensive piece of clothing I had ever purchased. Most likely, I would wear them only once.

~

I slept in the control room, the night before the cotillion, under Raj's watchful eye. It wasn't comfortable and I was only able to grab a couple of hours, but I needed them for the day ahead. I would add a few more hours in the morning then off to the hairdresser. I had an 11:00 AM appointment. The Limo was supposed to pick me up at five. It would be tight, but the hairdresser was close to home and Kiran was there to carry me through the final stages.

The hairdressers accepted my phone's Coupon Crave coupon without question. I was a little hesitant when I handed it to them to verify, but Raj had done his job well.

"My name is Daphne and I will be taking care of you." The woman said as she approached. I smiled as the blonde led me to a chair. Her hair billowed out near her shoulders and seemed to frame her face well. I had high hopes for my hair as well. "Beatrice will join us in a moment to handle the makeup." Daphne smiled to set me at ease as I sat down. "Now what are your looking for, dear?"

"I'm not sure," I admitted.

"Something elegant," Kiran jumped in, "she's going to a formal ball."

"That will be fun," Daphne stated as she fluffed my hair, "maybe a high braided bun with a few accents strands running loose. It would look divine with your skin tone." She tucked some of my hair up high on my head, "we'll have to add some highlights to make it pop." The last time I had a high maintenance hairdo was when I went to prom. I would have to take her word for it.

"That sounds nice," I said, looking at Kiran for help.

"Lovely," Kiran agreed. I felt better about my decision.

"My head is yours, Daphne," I directed. She removed my glasses and started with a warm wash that felt so good I almost nodded off. My light brown hair was then professionally highlighted with soft dirty blonde streaks that seemed to blend perfectly, almost like they had been there all along. Daphne knew her job.

"Your first big dance?" Daphne asked. She was trimming away my split ends and cleaning up hair by my neck.

"Prom was the last one," I answered, trying not to move my head.

"We'll make you the star of the ball," Daphne smiled, "you'll have men throwing themselves at your feet." I tried not to laugh, not wanting to disturb her scissors.

"I'll just be happy to not trip on my own feet," I said with a smile in my eyes.

"Nonsense," she continued, "you have wonderful bone structure and with a smile like that, they will be fighting for a dance." I felt my face blush. I don't know how much I had embezzled for her services, but it wasn't near enough.

"It's been awhile," I joked, "not sure I remember what to do with a man."

"It's like riding a bike," Daphne quipped, "but a lot more smiling comes with the sweating." I couldn't stop the laughter this time. Kiran's face wasn't helping. "You'll have to be still if you don't want to look like Medusa." I settled down, struggling to hold my smile in check as Daphne went back to work.

Daphne pulled my hair into a tight braided bun with a few small trailers that were curled down the side of my face. It felt strange not to have a ponytail hanging behind me. My head felt freer with nothing to resist my neck from turning.

"Absolutely wonderful," a large woman said as she moved toward my chair.

"This is Beatrice," Daphne said, "she'll take care of your makeup." Beatrice walked around the chair looking at my face, her fingers drawing shapes in the air almost like she was finger painting.

"What color is the dress?" Beatrice asked.

"I have it in the car," Kiran announced.

"If you could bring it in, it would help," Beatrice added, not looking at Kiran. Kiran ran off *q*uickly. "We don't want to do anything that would lessen the dress or the hair," Beatrice mumbled, "they should compliment, be friends and laugh together." I was a bit worried she might be insane. "I never try to build beauty, only bring it out. Gently steer the eyes in the proper direction, but never demand their attention."

"She's an artist," Daphne commented, "trust her and you will be pleased." I had little choice since I was already way out of my league. Kiran entered with the dress. Beatrice pulled back the plastic and held a small portion of the fabric under my chin. Her head moved wildly from side to side, then up and down. She was looking from every angle. She handed the dress to Kiran and wordlessly shooed her away.

Daphne brought over a large case and set in on the counter. The top opened down the center and it unfolded into numerous trays filled with all sorts of makeup products. Beatrice took one last look at my face, turned and grabbed a jar with acuity.

"Close your eyes, dear," Beatrice instructed. I did and relaxed as the chair lounged back. I heard a stool sliding up next to me. She went to work. She was humming some tune I almost recognized as she lightly applied something to my eyelids. Fingers, cloth, and brushes moved across my face with expertise. For all I knew, I would look like a clown, but she didn't seem to be making any deviations from her intended vision. She paused for a moment when I yawned. It was, after all, my internal clocks middle of the night. The work continued when my mouth settled.

I was almost to dreamland when Beatrice announced she was finished. I opened my eyes and saw three heads staring at me with smiles. Daphne raised my chair back into a sitting position and they all stepped aside. I could barely recognize the face in the mirror. Daphne's hair and Beatrice's face combined to give me sophistication with an air of fun. I smiled. The face in mirror glowed. I had never looked so good in my life.

"Camera?" I asked Kiran. She fished her phone out of her purse and captured my new look. It would only last for the night and I wanted proof.

"You're gorgeous," Kiran said as she examined the screen on her phone to make sure the picture came out. I turned to Daphne and Beatrice.

"Thank you," I gushed, "you're miracle workers."

"It's all in the raw materials, my dear," Daphne said, waving the compliment away.

"We did do good, though," Beatrice smiled as she nodded. I suddenly couldn't wait to get home and don the dress.

"4:15," Kiran announced, "we have to rush." I left a sizeable tip. I couldn't really afford it, but I haven't been this pleased with my looks since I figured out my parents were biased when I was five years old. I grabbed my glasses off the counter and headed out the door.

Kiran and I hurried to her house. I put in my contacts and stashed my glasses and a change of clothes in Kiran and Raj's guest room. When I came out of the room fully dressed, Raj gave me a wolf whistle. Kiran smiled and didn't even scold him. Aanya was wide-eyed, her expression said it all. I twirled, watching the hem of my skirt billow out. Everything was perfect. I had never been perfect before. Tonight, I would be a princess.

The doorbell rang. Our timing was perfect. Raj opened the door to two gentlemen in black chauffeur livery. "Elite Limousine at your service," the older of the two bowed. The younger, somewhere in his twenties was staring at me. He got an elbow from his elder. "I am Jaq, your driver," the elder smiled as he spoke, "and this is my son, Gus. He will be handling the doors."

"Pleased to meet you," I said and for the first time since a fifth grade play, I curtsied. It seemed so natural and the dress seemed to flow with it. Aanya giggled and I shared a smile with her.

"Are...are you ready, Ma'am?" Gus stuttered. His eyes were still taking me in. He made me feel even more beautiful. I smiled at him and his face went red. Yes, I was more than ready. Kiran giggled.

"I am ready, Sir," I said, moving toward the door. Kiran rushed forward with the small pink hand purse I had found at the store. The color was perfect for my dress and held my phone and some backup makeup. Everything else, I left with Kiran.

Gus held the door of the limo for me. He looked gallant doing it and had obviously been given instructions on how to stand. Jaq seemed proud of him. I thanked him as I entered which brought a smile to his face. There was room for ten people in the back of the limo. I was careful to tuck my dress carefully so it would keep its shape as I sat. Gus made sure my dress was completely inside before he closed the door and joined his father in the front seat.

"We should have you at The Fountains in twenty minutes, Ms. Thompson," Gus said and pushed a button which started a divider rising up behind the driver seat.

"Please," I said, startled at being closed in, "I would rather you didn't close me off."

"Of course, Ma'am," Jaq said with a smile and lowered the panel. He started the car and headed down the road. "It is a fine night for a dance," he commented, realizing I preferred conversation.

"I am so looking forward to it," I said with a formality that was born from the dress, "It has been a long time since I have attended one." I didn't tell them it was my high school prom.

"I think you will make *q*uite the impression," Jaq continued, "Grace and beauty always play well at these affairs." I felt my cheeks warm. Grace and beauty.

"I borrowed the dress," I admitted, to embarrassed to accept all the credit.

"A shame you can't keep it," Jaq said, "you wear it so well."

"I...thank you," I said, unused to the compliments.

"It's really pretty," Jaq added. My smile was becoming permanent. Jaq was turning in his seat, I suspect to face me. A stern look from his father had him cease and return to facing front.

"I don't usually go to these types of things," I said, as I realized the ball was becoming a reality. A little apprehension was sneaking in.

"You will have no trouble fitting in," Jaq countered, "Though I suspect you will be exhausted from all the offers to dance."

"I am afraid I don't know anyone there," I admitted. I would know my step family, but I was intent on avoiding them.

"It's all in the advertising," Jaq said, "just say yes to the first dance request and make sure you're seen on the floor." He chuckled almost to himself, "The single men will go into combat mode to get the next dance. I must admit, I find you brave to attend unescorted." I wasn't sure if I wanted to cringe at the thought or bask in the glory of being brave. I looked out the window, now wondering if I had made the right decision. I did it more to have a secret fight with my step mother. A battle she wouldn't even know we were having.

"Gus and I will be right outside," Jaq continued. I think he sensed my apprehension, "If you need to take a breather, thwart a suitor or leave early, we are at your disposal." I smiled at him. I could use a couple of brothers for emotional support.

"That is good to know," I said, "I might take you up on that breather. Any other pointers?"

"Just smile," Jaq said. "It's usually pretty stuffy at these things and you are going to be like a fresh breeze." I blushed, happy I chose not to drive alone to the event. I needed my embezzled pseudo brothers.

I spent the rest of the trip learning about Jaq and his son. Gus was learning to take over his father's business and he made sure I knew he was currently unattached. I was flattered with his subtle flirting, knowing that his father would keep it in check. He was a nice guy, but not my kind of guy. I couldn't really define what I was looking for in a man. I only knew what wouldn't work. I wasn't even sure a perfect partner existed for me. Given my current work schedule, he would have to be part vampire.

Gus deftly pulled the limo around the main fountain missing the other vehicles by inches. The building was called 'The Fountains.' Though I had driven past the front gate before, I could never see over the hedge grove that bordered the property. It was luxurious. Three story high roman columns stood sentry along the long stone porch. To each side of the grand entry steps, lay expertly trimmed bushes that were dotted with red flowers. Light shone through the tall windows, driven by elegant chandeliers that I could just make out since the main floor was raised a good ten steps higher than the drive. Finely dressed people, mostly couples were climbing the steps and heading toward the entrance.

Jag moved *q*uickly to open my door. He was smiling as I exited, happy that his father's eyes were finally pointed elsewhere. I straightened my dress as I stood and did a quick turn around. "How do I look?" I asked Jag.

"Beautiful, Ms. Thompson," Ja*q* replied, with a tinge of desire. More flirting. For his benefit and because I couldn't stop it, I smiled honestly. I saw his cheeks go red again. It was all the encouragement I needed. "We will be parked near the walkway," Ja*q* added, pointing off to the side where a brick walking path terminated.

"Thank you, Ja*q*," I replied. I took a deep breath, straightened my shoulders and started up the stairs.

There is something about walking into a new experience where past knowledge was useless and perceived scrutiny is high. It raises the heart rate and increases stupidity. My heart went into overdrive as I pulled my phone from my purse. It took three tries to type in the long password that I no longer thought humorous. A well-dressed doorman scanned the invite off the phone and waved me inside with a smile. I almost tripped over the threshold.

I bypassed the coat check table and walked slowly into the ballroom. I was a fish out of water. People were gathered in small groups around the rim of the dance floor. There were small waist high tables scattered about that most of the groups had gravitated to. Waiters and waitresses roamed taking orders and delivering drinks. I had thought myself lonely before. I was desolate now.

Standing in the entryway seemed conspicuous and the last thing I desired was to be seen as obviously lost. I fought off the idea of running back to the limo. I moved slowly into the room, fighting the fear I knew was irrational. I set a goal. Find the bathroom I would eventually need. It let me move with more of a purpose.

"What a lovely dress." The comment came as I passed one of the small occupied tables. I *q*uestioned whether it was directed to me and turned my head late in response.

"Truly lovely," A second speaker stated. She was a mature woman oozing sophistication. Her smile seemed honest though her posture was starched proper. Her friend, I suspected the initial speaker, stood a little more cavalier though her jewelry spoke of years of wealth. Both were in conservative, but appealing gowns.

"Thank you," I stammered. My feet stopped oddly out of sync with my turn. I was both happy that someone had spoken and nervous that I may enter into a conversation out of my league. The cavalier women smiled and covered a small chuckle with her hand.

"Stop it, Betty," Ms. Sophistication scolded, "she is nervous enough." She turned to me, gracing me with a warm smile. "You look like you may need a friend. Would you like to join us for awhile?" I had never heard kinder words in my life.

"Yes, very much," I said with more enthusiasm than appropriate. Betty's smile became inviting as she made room for me to slide up to the table. I saw they both had glasses of wine untouched in front of them. They may have just arrived.

"I am Ruth and this, of course, is Betty," Ms. Sophistication said, "and you are?"

"Cindy," I replied, happy that I had enough sense to not say Ella.

"I gather this is your first shindig," Betty said, ignoring the scowl on Ruth's face. Betty was a straight forward woman who didn't hide her intentions. She moved quickly to the point and wasn't overly concerned with niceties. I liked her.

"Yes," I said, more in my element with Betty, "this event is a lot nicer than I am used too."

"Well you certainly dressed for attention," Betty complimented. Another scowl from Ruth. "you'll have those boys eating out your hand." I suppressed a laugh.

"I'm not really here to find a man," I admitted, "it is more of a small revolt. I was told I couldn't go and I decided I could."

"Never let them tell you no," Betty insisted, jabbing her finger on the table to emphasize the point. "I like you already."

"But be pleasant when you do it," Ruth said softly, trying to counter Betty's aggressiveness.

32

"Would you like something to drink?" A waitress had snuck up behind me.

"Yes," I replied. At $5,000 a ticket, I should drink a few gallons. "some wine would be nice."

"Red or white?" The waitress queried. I had no idea how to answer. It depended upon how sweet the wine was. I was always partial to whatever was on sale and had a screw off top. I knew I was thinking too hard when Ruth jumped in.

"Why not try both," Ruth said, nodding to the waitress, "then you can decide your flavor for the night." I didn't even know that was an option. I looked up hopefully at the waitress, but she had already moved on, Ruth's suggestion taken as the order.

"Thank you," I said, smiling at her diplomacy.

"Excess is always the main theme at these things," Ruth instructed, "never fear to ask for what you want. It is expected."

"Ugh, those Tremaine girls are here," Betty said, her eyes pointing to the entrance. I took a quick look at my stepsisters and their mother. I had to admit they looked good. If they kept their mouths shut, they might attract a few men. "Those two have been hunting for gold the last four events," she continued. My face reddened. How much of my money were they using to fund their safaris?

"Hunting?" I asked, keeping my back to my sisters. I knew the answer, but I wanted to keep the conversation going. I enjoyed stepsister gossip.

"Husband hunting, my dear" Ruth replied quietly, "they aren't very good at it. Hard to get is not in their repertoire." I stifled a laugh. Betty didn't quiet hers.

"Sorry, Love," Betty apologized into Ruth's scowl, this time hiding her smile. I was surprised how she said it. It sounded like she meant it. "It's their mother that eggs them on," Betty continued in a whisper, "she was somewhat successful in her hunting," she shrugged her shoulders, "like mother like daughters." That was an astute observation. My stepmother was very successful. Too successful. Maybe I owed my stepsisters some slack. Like me, it's not their fault they were saddled with Agnus.

A waiter stopped by offering small plates with mixed hors d'oeuvres. Ruth accepted one for the table along with a set of cloth napkins. The waitress followed a moment later with my red and white wine. I sipped the red, cringed at the bitterness I wasn't expecting. The white was a lot sweeter with a nice fruity finish.

"Looks like the white appeals to you," Ruth said, smiling at my taste testing. I must have made quite a face when I tried the red.

"I guess my palette is uneducated," I said, trying to sound suave in my ignorance.

"Nonsense, " Betty said, "your tongue knows what it likes." I saw Ruth send a smile Betty's way. I began to notice they shared a lot of special looks. They must be friends from way back.

The snacks were to die for. All were finger food, the napkin your only plate. I watched Ruth bite into some kind of roll, holding the napkin daintily under her chin. I copied the movement when I bit into a cracker with some kind of seafood concoction. It melted in my mouth. A tangy mix with a hint of sweetness, crab I think, offering a soft texture against the cracker. The real problem with assortments of hors d'oeuvres, there isn't enough of the ones you really like. The seaweed and rice roll was pretty good, but the crab cracker was my favorite.

While we were sampling the food, Ruth and Betty were giving me an education about the families present. The Gildersons, old money made prior to the civil war in the slave trade. They gathered as a group after pushing three of the small tables together. The Wilkersons, newer money made by owning many local radio and television stations. They were a rather loud crew and seemed to be laughing more than talking. The list went on as I began to lose track of the names and occupations. Ruth and Betty were an encyclopedia of family knowledge.

"Excuse me, Miss," Betty said, waving down one of the roving waitresses.

"Yes, Ma'am."

"Those crab crackers, what are they called?" Betty asked.

"Crab on a Cracker, Ma'am," the waitress replied with a smile that wasn't insulting.

"Of course," Betty smiled back, "can we get a plate of those and another glass of white wine." Betty and Ruth were handling me. It was going to be a better evening than I thought. "and thank whoever is making the Crab on a Cracker."

"Yes, Ma'am," the waitress nodded before she headed off.

"Thank you," I said to Betty. Ruth beamed at Betty with pride. My mouth moved before my brain could stop it, "are...you two...a couple?" I wished I could take it back as soon as I said it. I was sure my cheeks were turning red.

"For thirty years, dear," Ruth said with a soft smile. I was so thankful I was right. Some might find the insinuation insulting. Ruth and Betty shared a look that only a couple would understand. I raised my almost empty glass.

"To thirty more years," I toasted. Ruth laughed and didn't scowl when Betty joined her. I was at the perfect no-pressure table. Our glasses clinked and we drank to their years. I was then treated to their history, difficult courtship, family trauma and finally the inevitable acceptance by all. It was a good tale that we were able to share many Crab on a Cracker over. More than once they had me laughing. The third glass of wine didn't hinder the amusements.

"Those are the Charmings, of the Boston Charmings," Ruth said, her eyes leading to the entryway, "Daniel and Rebecca. They are the ones who sponsored this ball. Lots of old money, railroads and stock-yards." I looked over at the man and women who entered with strong smiles. Many of the guests turned and greeted them as they entered. They seemed comfortable with each other, every now and again they would find a reason to touch each other, be it hand to hand or hand to shoulder during a chuckle. "That's their son Peter." I nearly spilled my drink.

Peter was my flat-tire Peter. My-breasts-are-beautiful Peter. I felt my face flush as I turned away quickly. I couldn't possible face him. He had seen me practically naked and he knew me as Ella. I tried to suck my breasts into my chest. I downed the rest of my wine and took a deep breath. I wasn't sure I could stay knowing he might see me. Damn he looked good, somehow taller out of the rain.

Thankfully, the band started to warm up. The sounds distracted the ladies from my obvious surprise at seeing Peter. The warm up sounded like the band tended toward a brassy swing. I wasn't sure I could hold my own with that kind of dance. That and Peter, I was as uncomfortable as when I first entered.

"Cindy," Ruth said, waiting for my eyes to acknowledge her "you're looking a bit pale. Are you feeling okay?"

"Fine," I said, after letting out the breath I was holding. I forced a smile to my lips, trying desperately not to look back at Peter. I was waiting for the shout 'Hey, aren't you the naked tire girl.'

"We have to find you a first dance," Betty said, "someone polite who will keep his hands to himself." Sisters - that's how I saw Betty and Ruth. I never really thought of Anastasia and Drizella as sisters. We never really cared what happened to each other. Betty and Ruth seemed to have adopted me as their own.

"George would be happy to do it," Ruth said, "and a nicer guy you couldn't meet. He might spend a few minutes describing his stamp collection, but he'll move on if he sees your bored." Peter's hair looked softer now that it was dry. I glanced back briefly to verify. His eyes met mine. I snapped my head back. "What do you think, Cindy, do you want us to fix your first dance?" George wasn't Peter so it was better than embarrassment.

"Ahh, sure," I agreed, half-heartedly, "I'm not sure if I can dance well to swing."

"Just smile, Dear," Ruth chuckled, "men just want to think you're pleased with them." Ruth headed off, I assume to gather George.

"Peter Charming is not hard on the eyes," Betty said, her eyes alive with humor. She saw right through me.

"Who?" I stalled. I couldn't believe Betty was putting things together so quickly.

"Mr. tall, dark and dreamy," Betty said with a laugh, "the guy who has you all flustered."

"He doesn't know me," I said *q*uickly. Too quickly. The ridiculous statement had a desperate tone to it.

"I could change that," Betty said, her smile turning evil mixed with teasing.

"Please don't," I begged. Betty lost her smile, examining my desperate expression. Her eyes softened and her shoulders relaxed.

"I'm only teasing," Betty said, her voice relaxed, "He's kind of a loner anyway." I knew she sensed my apprehension and was letting her kidding drift away.

"Loner?" I asked. Her statement surprised me. Loners don't pull off to the side of the road in a rainstorm and help people with their flat tires.

"He's some kind of computer genius," Betty informed me, "he isn't living off his trust fund like half the people here. Of course, building a personal fortune requires work and work requires time. From what I understand, he is married to it. Not that a lot of women haven't tried to change that."

"What's he doing here?" I asked.

"Hard to tell your mother no, I suppose," Betty chuckled, "she is still hopeful for grandchildren to spoil." I had to smile. My real mother, had she lived, would have wanted the same. My father would have been satisfied with happy and Agnus would prefer me out of the picture, something I meant to deny her.

"Here comes George," Betty said, pointing with her wine glass. I turned to find a well-dressed man approaching with a large smile. He was escorting Ruth, her arm entwined with his. His nose was speckled with prominent freckles that went well with his neatly cut red hair. More cute than handsome, his smile was welcoming. I found myself trying to copy it.

"Cindy Thompson, may I introduce George Gilder," Ruth said. George's eyes found mine, he held them with confidence.

"Ruth informs me you need a partner for the first dance," George said. His voice was unexpected. Deeper than his face advertised, more like a network anchorman. "I would be honored if you allowed me." Ruth was beaming. I assumed she had a special liking for George. I couldn't say no if I wanted to, and I didn't want to.

"That would be lovely," I replied, trying my best to assume the speech patterns from Downton Abbey. George's smile grew.

"How's the family, George?" Betty inquired in her trailer park way.

HIS EYES TRAVELED FROM FACE TO
FACE AS HE TALKED

"Wonderful, Betty," George said and moved himself to the table between us. His eyes traveled from face to face as he talked, seemingly including us all. "My sister had her baby. A girl she named Wilhelmina after our grandmother. So, I'm an uncle now." The conversation went deep into his family that Ruth and Betty seemed to know well. Normally, my mind would have drifted away, but George made it a point to include me and had me laughing at some of the histories. He was a charming guy.

"I think that's our cue," George said as the band started the first song. He held out his hand and I felt more than comfortable taking it. Luckily, it was a slower song, more big band than swing. The sax was nicely melodic. George led me to the floor, taking my right hand in his left and placing his right hand lightly around my waist.

"I have instructions to show you off," George said, "I am thinking I may just keep you for myself." I laughed at the humor in his eyes. "There's a lot of people wondering who you are."

"I'm nobody really," I said, my smile frozen to my lips. He spun me around so I was facing back the way we came. It was easy to follow his lead.

"Take a look at the girls," George said. I knew he meant Ruth and Betty. There was a small crowd around them. "See, your popularity grows. They're all wondering who the beautiful woman is." I looked back at George. He meant beautiful. My face heated up. "Blushing just makes it prettier," he added. His laugh was so forgiving I had to join him.

George was a wonderful dancer. He seemed to know when I might stumble and moved in a way to absorb the errors. He floated me around the floor as he pointed out people, warning me about some and complimenting others. His joke about my stepsisters was most amusing. We danced right by them and my stepmother without an inkling of recognition. Ella wasn't beautiful, but Cindy was.

"You're a wonderful dancer," I said as the song was winding down.

"All due to my mother," George said, "she insisted I take dance lessons for many years." He leaned in close to my ear, "I think she expected it would get her grandchildren *q*uicker."

"How's that working for you?" I joked.

"My tastes don't lean toward women," George said, without a hint of it being uncomfortable.

"Ahh," I said, "and may I say we women are most disappointed." I came to fancy dance and the first three people I meet are gay. It was strange and somewhat comforting. No pressure to be anything but friendly.

"Thank you, Cindy," George said honestly. He spun me around, making my gown billow out in a most wonderful way. "I can see why Ruth likes you." The music stopped and so did we. After a brief applause, he escorted me, arm in arm, back to the ladies. The people surrounding them drifted off as we approached.

"Thank you, George," I said, my smiling emphasizing the point, "I really enjoyed the dance."

"As did I," George replied, "I need to make the rounds, but I would love a repeat sometime later tonight if I may."

"Absolutely," I agreed. I felt so pretty with him leading. I wanted to feel like that again. He nodded with his smile and excused himself.

"George is such a nice guy," I said to Ruth and Betty, "and what a dancer."

"He is perfect for a first dance," Ruth said, "a gentleman who knows how to make a woman look good." It wasn't hard to agree to that. I lost my smile when I saw Peter Charming from across the room. His eyes were on mine and he was walking toward the table. I looked away quickly, pretending I didn't notice, as embarrassment rose to the surface. I was sure he recognized me. I turned away, trying to find a place to move off to and avoid the confrontation. I rotated right into a sharply dressed man who begged my forgiveness even though it was I who bumped him.

"William Douglass," the man introduced himself with a smile, "I understand you are Cindy." Word was traveling fast. William had a set of bushy sideburns that reminded me of some of our ex-presidents from way back. Everything was neat and clean, but I had a strong desire to take a razor to those sideburns.

"Yes," I said smiling. anything was better than facing Peter, "it's very nice to meet you."

"Do you think I might have this dance?" William asked. It was a question, but the way he worded it I don't think he expected a no. With Peter on his way, it was as good an escape as any.

"I would be delighted," I replied. He held out his arm and I wrapped mine through it. Escorted, I moved to the dance floor and away from the impending embarrassment.

The tune was a bit livelier than when I danced with George. William kept it sensible, but did teach me a few spinning moves that were fun once I got the hang of it. He didn't have half of George's dancing skill, but he made up for it by ignoring my mistakes and laughing with me while I learned.

"I haven't seen you around before," William mentioned, his eyes were sparked with interest.

"This is my first one of these dances," I said, "I must say, I am enjoying myself."

"A lot of people see these things as some kind of requirement," William continued, "it's refreshing to meet someone who is here to have fun."

"What about you, William?" I asked, trying to get the conversation off me before he delved into my false identity, "fun or duty?"

"I thought it was duty," William smiled, "now it seems to have turned into fun." He spun me around again as I digested his veiled compliment. I was feeling pretty good about myself and he was feeding my ego even more. I was having a really good time.

"Something tells me you always have a good time," I bantered back. His confidence and smile defied his pretense of showing up being a duty. We did a couple movements that brought our opposing hips together which we executed rather smoothly. I was proud of myself.

"Maybe you can test your theory," William smiled, "Allow me to take you out to dinner next week." I must have looked prettier than I thought. It was a tempting offer, but Cindy wouldn't exist after tonight. How do you explain something like a name change? Not to mention, I was basically a janitor and he was obviously used to the finer things in life.

"You move quickly, Sir," I joked, not able to find a way to say no nicely.

"Too much pressure for a first dance?" William asked with a big smile.

"A little," I shrugged and promptly stumbled on the next step. He steadied me with a kind chuckle.

"I'll retract it then," William said, "but know that if we find ourselves at another function like this, I will make the offer again." I could hear the humor in his voice. He had expected me to decline his first offer. I instantly felt better.

"Next time," I said, "I might be inclined to accept." That seemed to please William and we finished the dance with good feelings. I needed to take a break. Sweating in my gown didn't really appeal to me. I was about to head back to Ruth and Betty when I saw them talking with Peter.

"William, can you show me the ladies room?" I asked. At least I could stall for a few minutes and hope Peter would move on.

"This way," William said, once again offering me his arm. He escorted me out of the main room into a hall, its sole purpose was to house the bathrooms. I thanked him kindly for the dance and we went our separate ways though I suspected I would run into him again that night.

The bathroom was huge. Along one wall, ten marble sinks, each with an individual oval mirror trimmed in some kind of gold leaf pattern. There were two attendants constantly wiping up water and handing out cloth towels. Each stall was as large as my utility room, complete with hangers, hooks, and a dark wood bench. I wasn't sure the need of a bench when the toilet was right there.

After struggling for a few moments, I found it easier to just remove my gown and then relieve myself of the night's wine. A heated toilet seat graced my bottom which made me smile. Such opulence. Even the toilet paper felt luxurious.

While a washed my hands, one of the attendants came over and straightened my gown and brushed off some lint I had gathered from somewhere. I wasn't totally comfortable with the attention, but I couldn't take it out on her.

"So, you're Cindy, the one that has everyone talking." I recognized the voice immediately. It was Anastasia and she was right behind me. I started washing my hands a second time, giving me an excuse to not look up. Peter outside, my stepsister inside. I shouldn't have come.

"I'm not sure I know what you mean," I said quietly, trying to slightly deepen my voice. I was going to work a few layers of skin off my hands at this rate.

"New people always generate buzz." It was Drizella. Great, both stepsisters. I grabbed a towel and started drying my hands.

"It is my first ball," I admitted then an idea struck, "Ouch," I groaned and squinted my right eye and brought the towel toward it, "I think something flew in my eye." The attendant rushed over to give me a hand as I turned around, my eyes squinting and the towel covering half my face. "You'll have to excuse me, ladies, it seems I can't see," I added for effect.

"Oh, how terrible," Drizella said, "of course." They both exited the bathroom quickly, not wanting to get involved in my problems. I knew them too well. The attendant, a young women with dark hair, smiled with me when they left. She realized what I had done. I handed her the towel and looked back at the mirror. I hadn't messed up the makeup on my eyes, which was good since I had left my purse on the table with Ruth and Betty. I couldn't hide in the bathroom forever, so I left after thanking the attendant who had helped me.

When I entered the main ballroom, I saw that my sisters had cornered Peter off to the right. His desperate eyes saw me just as I turned to the left. For once, my sisters would do me a favor as I moved quickly around the outside of the room until I ended up with Ruth and Betty.

"Poor Peter," Ruth said, "he is being waylaid by the Tremaines." I looked back across the room and watched his fake smiles and nodding as my sisters did all the talking. I felt a little pained for him, but not enough to ruin myself by rescuing him. I already had enough close calls and started to think I should call it a night. It had been fun and I enjoyed the dancing. I had never put Peter in the calculations when I thought of coming here. He could easily wreck everything.

"Are they really that bad?' I asked. Ella already knew the answer, but Cindy wasn't supposed to know.

"Think of leeches," Betty replied, "then give them barbed hooks and inane chatter." I covered my mouth when I laughed.

"Really, Betty," Ruth scowled. It was a wonder these two stayed together for so many years. They were so different. I did start to notice that Ruth's eyes sparkled when she scolded Betty. Maybe, Betty was Ruth's alter ego, saying the things that Ruth always wanted to say but was too polite to engage the words.

"He was asking after you," Betty commented.

"Who?"

"Peter Charming," Ruth continued, "he came by when you were dancing with William. He thanked us for coming as a pretense but then turned the conversation to you." I waited for the bomb to drop. I was sure he recognized me from the flat tire and told them I had another name. Ruth misconstrued my apprehension and smiled at me, "You shouldn't wear such a pretty dress if you don't want attention."

"What did you tell him?" I asked, realizing he hadn't blown my cover.

"The little that we know," Betty said, "we've been pretty popular since you've joined our table. A lot of people are trying to figure out who you are. I, for one, prefer the mystery. I think it makes you more attractive."

I panicked when I saw Peter had broken away from my sisters. He may not have figured out who I was yet, but if I gave him a closer look he might put two and two together. He was heading toward our table seemly ignoring the rest of the ball.

"I think I'll mingle," I said and quickly turned away from Peter and headed in the opposite direction. I had no idea how to mingle with wealthy people. I didn't have the social experiences necessary to draw upon so I walked aimlessly between the tables smiling, hoping someone would save me. Luckily, It didn't take long.

"Hello, Cindy is it?" A man said. Artist type with his brown hair pulled into a short ponytail. He was rather handsome, but I sensed he knew it.

"Yes," I replied, "and you are?"

"Rayburn Funderland," he returned, holding out his hand which I gracefully shook.

"Pleased to meet you, Rayburn," I said cheerfully, thankful for his rescue, "It seems everyone knows my name and I know so few."

"The curse of being new," Rayburn said, "and beautiful." His eyes twinkled when he added the last part. He had no fear and, I was sure, a lot of practice praising women. Normally I would back away, but it was either Rayburn or Peter. Rayburn, I understood. The band began a slow song. "Shall we?" Rayburn asked, his open hand leading off to the dance floor. I wanted to say no just because he was so confident I would say yes. It was the Peter effect that made me ignore my intuition.

"I would be delighted," I lied and he led me to the floor. I saw Peter out of the corner of my eye, grinning as he slowed once he realized where I was headed. I turned away, pretending I hadn't seen. I knew for sure now, he was hunting me. I couldn't run all night. I would have to plan an exit. If only Peter hadn't stopped to help me with my tire.

Rayburn was not a gentleman. George and William had spoiled me into thinking wealth brought with it a certain class. Rayburn was classless. He pulled me tight to his body, I retreated as best I could and spent the next few measures raising his hand from my ass to my waist where it belonged. I began to regret not choosing the shame that Peter would thrust upon me.

"We move together well," Rayburn whispered in my ear. The words slithered with sexual innuendo. I pulled back farther and again corrected his hand. His smile held confidence in my submission. I had lost my smile.

"You expect too much," I said clearly. I grabbed his wrist before his hand could drop back down to my butt. His grip on my other hand tightened.

"The fight is kind of cute," Rayburn said, "I like tigresses." He spun me in a circle and somehow ate up the space I created between us.

"Enough," I said firmly, but *q*uietly. I didn't want to make a scene. I tried to break away from his grip but he tightened up and his confidence increased. I wasn't sure I could get away without making a scene.

"I think we both know where this is leading," Rayburn said, "why fight it. It'll be the most fun you ever had." I began to struggle and he just chuckled, tightening his grip and keeping me off balance with another spin. I got my knee ready. If you're going to make a scene, might as well make it a good one.

"No, Rayburn," I said clearly, knowing others would hear. Rayburn just chuckled and tightened his grip even more. He had been warned. It was the only warning I was going to give. I lined up my knee, aiming at his groin. It would ruin the dance, but I wasn't going to be treated like meat.

"I'm cutting in, Rayburn." Peter moved *q*uickly, grabbing Rayburn's wrist. Rayburn released my hand. The two exchanged a look that wiped the grin off Rayburn's face. Rayburn's other hand released my waist and I let go of his wrist.

"I don't believe the lady agreed to dance with you," Rayburn growled. I thought there might be a fight in the middle of the dance floor. I saw it in Peter's eyes. He wasn't going to let go of Rayburn until Rayburn backed down. Rayburn wasn't going to back down.

"Thank you for a wonderful dance," I said sweetly to Rayburn, loud enough for close ears to hear, "I apologize for forgetting I had promised this dance to Peter." I gave Rayburn an out. He visibly relaxed, his fake honor intact. It was better than a knee to the groin. Of course, now I had to face Peter and all that came with it.

"Of course, Cindy," Rayburn said calmly, "women sometimes forget their commitments in my presence." It was all I could do not to drive my knee forward. He smiled for the crowd and headed off the dance floor. To my surprise, Peter filled the void *q*uickly, hand to hand, hand to waist, respectable distance apart.

"You picked a bad way to avoid me," Peter said, his smile eating past the lies I was trying to form.

"Avoid you?" I said, trying to give myself time to think.

"It's my duty to greet all the guests and thank them for their kind donation," Peter smirked, "you have been most troublesome to try and thank." I was sure I was turning ten shades of red. To make matters worse, Peter was a terrible dancer. Stiff as a board.

"You're a terrible dancer," I said, my smile growing. Work on his weakness and maybe he will forget the avoidance. Instead of losing his moral high ground, he laughed. His eyes crinkled, his lips curled and revealed a set of pearly whites that grew my smile all the more.

"I saved you from the hound and still you try and keep your distance," He said, "I've checked my deodorant twice, made sure I didn't have something in my teeth and ate a few mints. You're going to give me a complex." I didn't see any recognition in his eyes. Of course, I was practically naked and he was a man. Maybe he only saw my breasts. I softened my grip on his hand that had been tighter than necessary.

"You call Rayburn the hound?" I asked, trying to keep the discussion off me. His eyes were on me, though. They were intelligent eyes mixed with a bit of a whimsical boy. They only saw Cindy. I had been hiding for nothing.

"I could have warned you," Peter said, his feet moving like they weighed 100 pounds each, "had you not been disappearing every time I approached." That's why he was grinning when I accepted Rayburn's offer to dance. He knew I had worked myself into a corner. He just walked up and rescued me - no need to chase me down anymore.

"I thought all you guys were good dancers," I joked. I didn't want to explain my running from him.

"That's stereotyping," Peter countered with humor. He felt no shame in his inability to dance. "I was reading when these guys were in dance class." His eyes were still drinking me in. They shifted across my face and always returned back to my eyes. I moved closer, cutting the respectable distance in half. I liked Peter looking even if he couldn't dance.

"Do you read a lot?" I asked.

"All the time," Peter answered, his smile shifted to sly, "Do you run from your hosts a lot?" He wasn't letting me change the subject. There was a lot of intelligence behind those eyes.

"Do you chase down your guests a lot?" I riposted. His laugh brought mine to the surface. His laughter made the bad dancing enjoyable. I was surprised when he answered.

"I usually avoid the guests," Peter said seriously, "there is something about you that piqued my interest. I am not sure what it is, but I am going to try and find out."

"I thought you said it was your duty," I pointed out.

"So was going to dance class." This time, I started the laughter.

"There's a wonderful walking path around the grounds," Peter said when we caught our breath, "Would you like to get some air? I assure you I am highly skilled at walking." I wanted nothing more at the moment. I was kind of wishing all the people would disappear so we make each other laugh louder. I was so happy that he didn't remember Ella. He didn't even know he already liked my breasts.

"I'm not sure my shoes are fit for walking," I said. My heels would most likely fail on a stone path. At $750, I wasn't sure I wanted to try. Maybe I could go barefoot.

"The Fountains is prepared for that," Peter said with a smile, "they stock loaner tennis shoes just for these occasions.." He paused for a moment, "I assure you they are cleaned well between each use." I would have worn them dirty. I nodded in agreement, trying to shrink my smile. It was hopeless. I was going for a walk with tall, dark and dreamy.

We swung by Ruth and Betty who smiled knowingly as I grabbed by hand purse. It would have been rude to make them watch it if they intended to move on. Peter took my hand and led me out the main door, past my stepmother and stepsisters. I could see the envy on their faces. They forced smiles to nod at Peter. His speed increased as we passed them. I could almost feel his trepidation of possibly confronting them again. The silly warmth of revenge washed over me in a wave. They would never know, but I did. It was more satisfying than I would ever admit out loud.

It took about ten minutes for The Fountains to outfit me in a pair of pink Converse All-Stars. My gown made changing shoes difficult and I considered traveling back to the bathroom to get it done. Peter discounted the idea and dropped to his knees. His hands were wonderfully tender as he removed my heels and replaced them with the All-Stars. I never had a man dress me before. It felt warmly intimate even if it was only shoes.

"How's that," Peter said, rising to his feet. I took a few steps, assuring myself that everything was set properly for a walk.

"Perfect," I smiled. He held out his hand again. I took it as we headed out the door.

The walk meandered through the grounds. It was composed of tightly compacted brick in a fishbone pattern that would have easily eaten my heels. What we could see of the foliage in the darkening light was immaculately cared for. There were small ground lights, strategically placed behind foliage, that cast diffused light across the path. Just enough light so you could stay on the trail, but not enough to detract from the privacy.

"So," Peter started as we lost sight of the main doors, "am I ever going to find out why you were avoiding me?" I could make out his smile. He was enjoying his teasing.

"I never admitted I was," I countered. His hand squeezed mine. Shamefully, I squeezed his back. Cindy was such a tease.

"That means no," Peter laughed. He wasn't going to let me deny it. He was going to let it slide. "I interrogated half the room and found out almost nothing about you," he admitted, "Who is Cindy Thompson?"

"A girl on a walk with a guy," I answered. I didn't want to make up any more lies. The thought that it was Cindy meeting Peter hurt a little. It could go no farther than tonight.

"Your mystery is beguiling," Peter said, "I suspect there are things you don't want me to know right now." He paused for a moment as my mind reeled at his intellect. He was analyzing me, dissecting only the facts and assembling a picture that wasn't far from the truth. "I will let you have your secrets," he turned his head to me and smiled, "not that I have much of choice."

"You seem to like the mystery," I analyzed him, "why would I give it up?"

"I do love puzzles," he admitted, "they are so much fun to solve." We walked for a few steps in silence, still hand in hand. "Let's try a differ..." A buzzing in his pocket interrupted what he was about to say. I disliked the buzzing. "I'm sorry," he stumbled, letting go of my hand. I began to hate the buzzing. "It's rude, I know, but there are problems at work." He fished his phone out of his pocket. "It will only take a second."

"Charming," Peter cursed into the phone.

"What do you mean you can't?" Pause.

"Well trace the destination. You know what was exposed." Pause

"Let me know what you find." Pause.

"No, I'm not coming in." Peter disconnected without saying good-bye. He shrugged his shoulders with an apologetic smile. "Sorry." This time, I held out my hand. He took it. Apology accepted.

"Sounds serious," I said, "if they want you to come in."

"Actually," Peter said, "I am normally working at this time. The world is a lot quieter at night, makes it easier to develop," he chuckled to himself, "my mother says I'm half vampire." I started at his admission. He was on the same clock as I was.

"What do you do for work?" I asked. I already knew it had something to do with computers.

"Ahh," Peter laughed, "a puzzle for you. Revenge is best served quickly before it gets cold." I pulled him closer, my laughter merging with his. It was only fair. We walked around a bend that circled an old oak tree. There were a couple of memorial benches surrounded by flowers off in the corner by the stone fence. It was pretty in the dark, I thought it must be phenomenal in the daylight.

"Favorite movie?" I asked. If we weren't going to talk about our real life, might as well move to entertainment.

"That depends on my mood," Peter said, "right now, it would be Forrest Gump."

"You liked all the historical entanglements?" I asked, trying to keep the conversation on him.

"History was only the flavor," Peter said, he shifted his hand to encompass more of mine, "the story is all about how the geek gets the girl."

"But she died," I said sadly, remembering holding in tears the first time saw the movie.

"All that doesn't matter," Peter continued, "everyone wanted Jenny, but who did she marry and whose child did she raise? Who did she finally admit she loved?" I had always thought she had settled on Forest out of desperation. I had never looked at it from Peter's angle.

"I always thought Jenny was using Forrest," I admitted.

"She just didn't know she loved him yet," Peter smiled. He had an incorruptible view of the movie. He saw love where I saw capitulation. I liked his view better.

"All this time I thought she was a bitch," I laughed.

"Nope," Peter insisted, "Forest was just smarter. It took time for Jenny to catch up." I pulled Peter closer. His view was so much softer than mine. I imagined his view on real life was softer as well. I lost some of my harshness at that moment. Good riddance.

We spent some time talking about the books we've read and places we've gone. We danced around topics that could give away our pasts. It was a game and Peter was a master. He wanted something for everything he gave. For me, it was becoming inwardly painful. It was no game that Peter liked Cindy. It was no game that Ella liked Peter. I had created an impossible situation. How was I to know I would meet someone like Peter. Cindy would die tonight. Where did that leave Ella?

My phone buzzed in my purse. I pulled it out, flashing its soft pink cover as I quickly turned it to silent and put it back. I wasn't going to interrupt what little time I had.

"Even your phone matches," Peter observed, as he once again offered his hand.

"Pink is my color tonight," I said, "I am consistent, if nothing else." We rounded a small fountain ringed with little cement ducks.

"I like consistency," Peter said softly, no smile. He meant he liked me. Cindy did something stupid. Something Ella wouldn't do. She leaned forward and tilted her head up. Peter responded. His lips were a curse. A beautifully soft, caring curse. He couldn't dance, but he knew how to kiss. His hand found the back of my neck, cradling it in safety as my world became the two of us. The edge of excitement took over my body, cascading from my lips to my toes. I wrapped my arms around him and pulled him closer. I wanted so much more of him. I didn't want to share him with Cindy anymore.

"That...that was unexpectedly wonderful," Peter stuttered in my arms.

"You expected it to be bad?" I joked.

"I expected to take the rest of the night to work myself up to it," Peter said, "I liked it better this way."

"So you assumed I would just let you kiss me," I teased.

"No," Peter laughed, "I assumed I would work up the courage to try." His bravery wasn't in question as his lips took mine again. My hands combing into his hair as we tried to see how close our bodies could get to each other. I could feel how much he desired me. He was delicious.

"We should get back inside," Peter said after we had kissed forever. His face was a permanent smile. I was sure it matched mine. We were really good at kissing. I wondered if we were good at other things. Things that didn't require clothes.

His phone buzzed again. I began to really hate the thing. He apologized profusely as he answered it. I smiled and nodded as if it didn't matter. Life must have been easier before the birth of the mobile phone.

"Charming," pause.

"Well get a warrant." pause.

"That senator, what's his name, on the armed services committee," pause.

"Yep, that's him. He'll expedite it," pause.

"Call me when you know more." Peter ended the call with another apology to me.

"Sounds serious,' I said as I returned my hand to his. He gave it a squeeze. I liked keeping the physical contact. It was a simple pleasure that seemed to affect my whole body.

"Someone is rattling my cage," Peter admitted, "it's time dependent or I would just turn off my phone. Sorry."

"You have senator's who do your bidding," I observed, "must be important."

"Actually, I do his," Peter laughed, "but if you find me more impressive the other way, I'll claim the power." We shared a smile as we continued our stroll back to the dance. Our hands swung together, our words easily finding things to agree on.

My mind was churning, trying to find a way to tell Peter about Ella. I didn't see a good way. Every way held shame and Peter's loss of faith. I couldn't handle him thinking less of me. I liked how Cindy looked in his eyes. I loved how he kissed Cindy.

I was about to remove my borrowed tennies when a cheer went up in the main hall. "The dancers must be here," Peter said. My confused look made him clarify. "Professionals. Come on," he said, holding out his hand. His excitement made me forget that I would be a few inches shorter without my heels. He led me quickly to a clear spot around the dance floor.

There were two couples, gymnasts by my calculations, throwing themselves around to a really wild Big Bad Voodoo Daddy song. The two girls spent almost as much time in the air as they did on the floor. Peter was enthralled, his hands clapping in rhythm with the crowd. I joined him as we traded looks, smiles, and a few hip bumps as the pros showed us all how poor of dancers we really were.

How they did it was a mystery. The four danced to two more wild songs, changing styles, but never tempo. I kept thinking one of the ladies would lose it and go flying into the crowd. It was an amazing feat of stamina as well as skill. The applause was deafening when the dancers finished the final dance. It was the first time I could tell they were breathing hard.

Without thinking, I put my fingers to my lips and whistled my appreciation. Heads turned, I flushed in embarrassment. The Fountains had never heard a whistle. On the other side, another whistle let loose. George, with a wicked smile, winked at me as he pulled his fingers from his lips. He felt no shame. I loved him like a brother at that moment. Protocol broke down as other whistles broke out and Peter wrapped his arm around me, laughing and pointing at George. I pulled Peter close, my shield against impropriety.

Peter's parents walked out to the center of the dance floor to congratulate the dancers. They made short statements, introducing the dancers and expounding on their exposition. Mrs. Charming then turned, looking directly at me, her smile was endearing. "It is no secret that my son spent his youth dodging lessons in the finer things of life," she paused as the audience laughed, "Tonight, he will pay the piper and please his mother by accepting a lesson from Mr. and Mrs. Longfellow." She indicated one of the pairs of dancers. I hid my smile as Peter vehemently shook his head, trying to wave off his mother with his hand. The crowd thought it a fine thing.

"I believe you have already selected your partner, Peter," Mrs. Charming said, waving us forward. Normally, I would shun the spotlight. This time, I relished it. At least I knew he was a worse dancer than myself. I found his fear was selfishly making me bolder. I took Peter's hand and, to a chorus of laughter and cheers, pulled a hesitant man to the center of the floor. Mrs. Charming seemed especially pleased.

"If you leave me out here..." Peter whispered as we came forward.

"I'll never leave you," I said quickly. My heart thumped as the words left my mouth. They were Ella's words. They held more meaning than a dance lesson. I saw Peter's face go from grim to a silly boy grin. I was no longer pulling, he was coming of his own accord. He had felt the double meaning as well. He liked how it sounded. I liked how it sounded.

"Introduction?" Mrs. Charming asked Peter, her face almost laughing at his attention to me.

"Of course," Peters said, returning to protocol, "Mother, this is

Cindy Thompson. Cindy this is my mother, Rebecca Charming." Rebecca held her hand daintily. I tried to duplicate as best I could.

"So pleased to meet you, Cindy," Rebecca said with more friendliness than I expected.

"Very nice to meet you, Mrs. Charming."

"Rebecca, please," Rebecca said, "I'm so happy you have convinced Peter to allow me to tease him." Her face was lit up. She was enjoying herself. I can only assume that Peter had been more difficult in the past.

"It will be fun," I said, looking up at the smiling Peter. His eyes were boring into me, ignoring the surroundings. I quickly looked back to his mother. Her eyes were traveling between Peter and I at great speed. She seemed to see something that pleased her. I felt like a pawn between mother and son. Luckily, Mrs. Longfellow stepped forward to end the awkward confrontation. Rebecca relieved me of my purse so I had my hands free.

"Cindy, Peter," Mrs. Longfellow started, "we are just going to do a basic swing step." Rebecca stepped back out of the way, her smile still glued on her face. "face each other. Peter, lightly grasp Cindy's right hand in your left..." The instructions continued. We both heard and adhered to the lesson, but none of it was reaching long-term memory. It was if they were spoken from a distance, miles away. Peter's eyes and mine were making love with each other. Our feet moved as instructed, our bodies shifted and arms moved, but the eyes remained.

"I think you have it," Mrs. Longfellow announced. There was brief applause and well-meaning jeers from those who knew Peter well. We didn't care. It was all so far away. The music started and we kept dancing as others joined us on the floor. I don't think Peter realized he was actually dancing competently. I wasn't going to break the spell to tell him. It was all so lovely. Almost perfect. I only wished Cindy would leave. Ella wanted Peter to herself.

When the music stopped, Peter leaned down and kissed me. Not as one would kiss a friend, but a lingering, don't-ever-leave-me kiss. It was in the middle of the dance floor and completely inappropriate. It was a lovely thing and all mine. I wanted Cindy to die.

"Would you like a drink?" Peter asked, ending the kiss before I was ready. People were staring so I assume the kiss went longer than protocol prescribed.

"Water," I answered, my smile letting him know I wanted more of his lips. To hell with protocol.

"Ruth and Betty deserve some attention," Peter said, "I'll meet you there." He followed with a kiss that was all too short. I let him go, holding his hand until the distance forced it away. I stepped off the floor in a euphoria, thinking only of Peter.

"Your purse, dear," Rebecca surprised me, coming up from behind.

"Thank you," I said as I took it. Rebecca's smile was on the edge of comfort. She wasn't trying to disguise it.

"Peter seems to think a lot of you," Rebecca observed. I stopped and turned toward her.

"And I him," I said truthfully.The thought of my false identity flashed back at me. I had to tell him. I couldn't leave and not tell him.

"I don't think I have ever seen him...smitten," Rebecca laughed once she got the word out. I was a little uncomfortable talking with Peter's mother about Peter. I hadn't known him long enough to be allowed that type of comfort level.

"I am sure he is just being kind," I said.

"No," Rebecca continued, "smitten is the correct word." I feared her smile might crack her face. She reached out laid her hand on my arm. "I am just surprised is all. No one has ever gotten him on a dance floor and you have done it twice in one night."

"Surely..." I stumbled with a response.

"Believe me, he is smitten," Rebecca said, her eyes glanced over me, "and I, for one, am not disappointed." She smiled then added, "you have a wonderful night, Cindy." I think she sensed my comfort level had been reached. She had the same intelligence in her eyes that Peter had.

"You too," I stammered as Rebecca turned to walk away. I was relieved when she left. I was under enough pressure. I had no idea how to tell Peter about Ella. How would I ever tell his mother? I was screwing things up just by being here.

"Have fun outside?" Betty joked as I moved to their table. Her eyes were bouncing with inference to salacious ideas.

"Betty!" Ruth warned. Her scowl was forced. She was holding back a smile.

"We just went for a walk," I said, trying to keep everything G-rated, "we had a wonderful talk. He's a nice guy." Betty smirked under Ruth's glare.

"Peter seems *q*uite taken with you," Ruth observed, "I don't think I have ever seen him on the dance floor before." I smiled because I couldn't help myself. To think, I might be his first real dance. I knew I wasn't his first kiss. He kissed too well to be a beginner.

"It was fun. Did you see that he was actually getting good near the end?" I asked, trying to stick to facts and get the conversation away from the relationship.

"Everyone saw," Betty replied, "I think he would have jumped off a bridge if you asked." This time, Ruth didn't admonish Betty. She watched me, trying to see my reaction. I couldn't fight it.

"I like him," I admitted. Betty laughed and Ruth's smile went warm. Cindy was digging a hole too deep for Ella to climb out of. I needed to just fess up to Peter and let the chips fall where they may.

"That's a good thing," Ruth said, "I would hate to see that man's heart crushed." I wondered if that is exactly what I was about to do. Ella, the heartbreaker. I pulled out my phone, more to create space between the ladies and myself. I needed to think. Work out the words necessary to convince Peter this all wasn't some malicious hoax. I was sure it would involve a lot of apologies and groveling.

I turned it back on and keyed in my impossibly long password. I smiled as I typed. So very appropriate, even if Peter was unaware. A flood of texts and unanswered phone calls were listed on the main screen. Only Raj had the number. I checked the latest text.

Dump the phone. They are tracing it.

There were more of the same, mixed with apologies about Raj missing something technical. I felt blood rush in strange directions and my heart rate increased. I hadn't thought I might be caught. I was essentially using my own money. There was no way my stepmother could have found out, not this early. Coupon Crave wouldn't care if everyone was paid. Who were they?

I was about to head to the bathroom, maybe throw the phone in the garbage. I turned into Peter, smiling with a two glasses of water in his hands. "Your water ma'am," he said, making sure our hands met as I took it from him.

"Thank you," I replied, trying to hide my nervousness.

"You're looking rather please yourself," Betty commented to Peter.

"And why not?" Peter returned, "I have danced with a beautiful woman and just had the most pleasant phone call." His arm wrapped around my waist. It felt so right there. I needed to dump the phone, but I placed it on the table instead. My arm found comfort around his waist.

"Unknown relative leave you a fortune?" Betty prompted. I could tell she liked to get the whole story.

"Better," Peter said, "someone has been hacking my firewalls. Someone really good. It was only a fluke we noticed. We had experimental code running in front of the ticket site for this event to test it out. The same code we are planning to deploy for the military." Peter sounded excited, "Whoever it is hardly left a trace. It's only because we were running exhaustive post-tests that we saw anything at all." My heart was beating so fast. I was hoping Peter couldn't feel it.

"Your happy that you were hacked?" Ruth asked.

"Nope," Peter smiled, "I am happy that I may soon know who." He looked around the room. "We couldn't trace the source, but the destination of the purchases was traced to a single phone." He was almost giddy. I was sure I was pale as a ghost. "That phone is here. A team is coming with a handheld sensor to find the phone."

"How exciting," Betty commented. She was thrilled. I felt bile rising.

"Ladies and gentlemen," the band announcer spoke. All heads turned toward him. "grab your special someone and prepare for the midnight dance."

"I..I have to get my heels," I said, trying to smile through it all. Peter looked a little concerned. I assumed I sounded off. "I'll just be a moment," I added backing away from the table. He nodded and continued the conversation with Betty and Ruth. I turned and moved quickly. I was near the exit when I realized I left the phone on the table. My heart was trying to climb out my throat. I ran some words through my mind, reasons for going back for the phone.

Two men rushed past me. Cheap suits and even cheaper cologne. One had some kind of device in his hand, the other following. I watched it unfold in slow motion. I backed away slowly, closer to the exit as I saw my imagined future dash itself against the rocks. The men kept moving closer to Peter, I prayed they would turn. My eyes began to fill when the lead man pointed at my phone.

I couldn't stop the tears. The look on Peter's face went from disbelief to horror. He turned toward me, his whole face a distorted misery. I ran as the band started. There would be no midnight dance for Cindy. No life for Ella. I should have never come.

I ran down the main steps in my now stolen All-Stars. The crime wave continued. I wasn't sure how I got to the bottom safely with my eyes flooded with tears. Jaq had seen me coming and sensed the urgency. The limo was already running with Gus holding the door open. I still couldn't stop the tears. I had destroyed Peter and any chance I had with him. His face, the disappointment, was etched in my mind. He would never look at me again with those lovely eyes.

Jaq pulled the limo out smartly and waited until we were on the main road before he spoke. "Are you alright, Ms. Thompson?" I tried to answer through the sobs. My throat wouldn't allow anything coherent out. I just nodded and buried my face in the seat. Everything had fallen apart. The dream that was Peter was now a nightmare. I heard the divider slide up. Jaq knew when someone needed privacy.

The tears were under control by the time I returned to Raj's house. Gus opened the door and peeked inside as I was taking a deep breath. I let it out slowly, closed my eyes and did it again. My heart was slowing. I was wondering if I could be lucky enough to have it stop.

"You're home Ms. Thompson," Gus said quietly. None of the flirtiness he displayed earlier was there. It sounded more like he wanted me out. Of course, Cindy had run her course. Only Ella was left.

"Thank you, Gus, " I said as I exited.

"I'm sorry you had a bad time, Ms. Thompson," Gus said as he closed the door. From flirty to pity. A perfect end of the night. I heard the front door open and Raj came out of the house. There was panic in his eyes. Perfect.

Raj handed Gus some bills, a tip. I hadn't thought of that. "Thank you," Raj said as he shooed Gus and Jaq on their way. I felt like I was a lawn ornament. I stood there as Raj said my goodbyes and protected me from more pity comments. Raj didn't acknowledge me until the limo pulled away.

"I am so sorry," Raj said, "I missed the logs. I should have washed the logs." He was shaking his head.

"Doesn't matter," I whispered, "my shitty life returns. I didn't belong there anyway." I turned and walked toward the house. Raj followed with concern on his face. I was selfish and didn't accept his apology. I knew it was my own doing, my choice, but for some reason, I wanted others to suffer with me.

"Oh no," Kiran said when she saw my face. She had waited up as well. The tears returned when she wrapped her arms around me. I let her hold me. I held her back. Someone felt my pain and I let that comfort me.

"What happened?" Kiran asked quietly, once the tea was steeping. She had sent Raj away knowing I needed to talk.

"I found him," I choked. More tears.

"Who?"

"Him," I cried. Kiran wisely held me again. It took a few minutes for my control to return. Kiran was silent as she added sugar to the tea. She handed me a glass and we sat on the stools in the kitchen.

"Who is he?" Kiran asked. She took a sip of her tea, never letting her eyes drift from my swollen ones.

"Peter," I sighed, "he was the one." Her eyebrows raised. I took my own sip.

"Not the same Peter. Not flat tire Peter?"

I nodded my head. I let my eyes drop. "He didn't remember me, but it was him." I looked up, "I kissed him. He kissed me back. For a moment, everything was perfect and then..." This time, I held back the tears. I think my eyes were empty. "It was his computer stuff that Raj hacked," My head dropped again, "he knows it was me. The look on his face... I wanted to die." Kiran's hand covered mine.

"What if you talk to him?" Kiran asked, "it's not like you meant to hurt anyone."

"You didn't see his face," I said. The kitchen floor tiles held my attention. "I lied to him all night. He kissed Cindy, but he hates Ella."

"Was it a good kiss?" Kiran smiled softly as she asked.

"More wonderful than I had ever known," I admitted, "I didn't want it to stop." I looked at Kiran and let the truth go, "Had we been somewhere private, I wouldn't have stopped." I shook my head, trying to not dwell on the impossible. "It's all ruined now. He'll never kiss me again. Not the girl who tricked him."

"Men don't always think with their minds," Kiran whispered, "maybe he liked the kiss as well. Maybe he'll overlook a few bumps in the road."

"Bumps? You mean prison," I said, "he was way to excited to catch the person who hacked him. He took it personally. No... Cindy is on his shit list and Ella can never show her face."

"I'm so sorry, Ella," Kiran said, "I never thought anything bad would come of this. We just wanted you to get out there. You're too sweet to be by yourself."

"You didn't leave anything?" Raj asked, coming in without me hearing, "no one knows who you are?" His voice was shaking a little. His words lacking confidence.

"The phone," I replied.

"They won't be able to break the encryption," Raj was thinking as he spoke, his eyes looking out the window, "at least not in a timely manner. Maybe years at the earliest." He paced over toward the refrigerator. "You used a long password, right?"

"Yes," I said. It was humorous when I typed it in, but now it hurt to think on it. Raj's concern was evident in his tone.

"Raj, this won't get back to her, right?" Kiran asked, "I mean, everyone got paid. No one was hurt. Certainly they won't pursue it."

"It was a Shark firewall," Raj answered. He was ringing his hands. "the same ones the military uses." His face held a little panic. "I didn't think they would ever find out."

"You mean they will look for her?" Kiran asked.

"Maybe...yes...I think they might," Raj admitted, "they will look for her and me." Kiran's hand covered her mouth as her eyes widened. They both shared worried looks at each other. If they found Raj, they would deport the family. Their worries far exceeded mine.

"I won't say a thing," I said *q*uickly, "If this falls apart, I'm in trouble whether or not they know about you. No one ever mentions this again."

"It was all my idea," Raj countered, "I can't let you do that."

"You can," I demanded, "and you will. I will not have your whole family be torn apart because I was pissed at my sisters. This will end with me." It felt better to stop feeling sorry for myself. Proclaiming self-sacrifice was better than crying. "I was complicit anyway."

"But..."

"Kiran, your family comes first," I interrupted. Kiran wrapped her arms around me. A mother knew what had to be done. A stubborn husband would have to swallow some pride. They had Aanya to think about.

"Thank you," Kiran whispered in my ear. If it came to prison, at least I would have an endless supply of those potato things.

"My shoes!" I shouted, "I left my shoes." I pushed the All-Stars out from under my dress. Ella bought the shoes.

~

*M*onday night I was back to my fate. Seven more years of emptying trash cans and mopping floors. The difference was that I had a vision of what life could be. Struggle as I might, the kisses I shared with Peter refused to leave my mind. I cleaned harder and it was still there. I created my own world, earbuds blasting music as I mopped. All I could think of was a lousy dancer who kissed like a prince. The cotillion was a wish that would never come true.

I moved to the next office. Agnus' garbage was always filled to overflowing. Scraps surrounding the can, no effort to tamp it down and save me the tedium of picking up after her. A little more well-disguised torture. Down on my knees, I scraped up some sticky gunk that adhered scraps of paper to the floor. I swallowed hard and tried to not break down again. I had promised myself I would let it go. No more fretting over what can't be changed. At least the police didn't seem to be knocking on my door.

I wiped the sweat off my forehead and stood once the floor was un-gunked. I switched my music to something slow and tender. I had to be nicer to myself if I was going to last seven years. I took a deep breath and mopped Agnus' office as if it was my own. I danced with the mop. Peter was about as good.

I pushed the bucket out the door with my foot and finished mopping by the door. Agnus wouldn't notice, but I felt a brief sense of completion as I closed the door on a clean office. At least I had small victories. I pushed my glasses back up my nose and brushed some hair, that broke loose from my ponytail, back behind my ear. I turned toward the next office. Rebecca Charming was standing there, two champagne pink Madam Winslet pumps in her hand.

"Cindy? Ella?," Rebecca asked, "what should I call you?" Her expression was blank. In her case, I believed that meant anger. The mop and bucket were both a shield and the most embarrassing things I had ever held.

"I...I'm sorry." It stumbled out as I removed my ear buds. Had I an hour to think of what to say, it would have come out the same. Rebbecca just stared at me. The mop handle shifted to cross in front of my body. It was a weaker shield than I thought. "Ella," I answered before I had to move my eyes from hers. The bucket was suddenly interesting as I tried to dam my tear ducts.

"Peter is livid," Rebecca said, "he doesn't get angry. He broods, pouts and goes silent, but never angry. Somehow, you have done what no one has done before. You have made him irrational." I could see her head dipping low, trying to find my eyes. Damn tears. "Was that your goal? To ruin him." I turned away, letting the mop handle drop from my hands to the floor. I tried to get my mouth to form words. I took a deep breath, louder than I intended.

"Ah," Rebecca said, "can't face what you've done. You're awfully weak for someone who plays so harshly with other people." A small bit of anger flared. My stupidity was clear. Never had my intent be to hurt anyone. I turned on her.

"I didn't mean for any of it to happen," I said, louder than I should have, "it was a stupid idea. I didn't know I would meet Peter. I didn't know I would..." I stopped myself, trying to let the unwarranted anger dissipate. Peter's mother stood before me with a half smile I didn't understand. "I'm sorry it turned out the way it did," I repeated, softer.

"So, you're not an actress hired to prove him a fool?" Rebecca asked. The thought that Peter might think the kiss a fake hit me harder than I would ever expect.

"Oh, God!" I said, covering my mouth. I no longer controlled my emotions. The entire night flashed by again. His face when he realized whose phone it was. I collapsed against the wall. He wasn't disappointed. He hated me. My ass found the floor, my hand covered my eyes.

"I thought not," Rebecca said warmer than I deserved. She sat down on the floor next to me. "Luckily, the men didn't recognize the heels. Dorothy Winslet has been a friend of mine for many years. Don't hold it against her. She thinks she was doing you a favor by giving me your name." Rebecca paused for a moment. "You have some time, but my son is very determined," she paused for a moment, "as is the military."

"I'm in trouble," I said, looking up. I was sure my face was a mess.

"Yes you are," Rebecca said, her hand compassionately covering my arm. "How do you feel about my son?" Her question was unexpected. My words caught, but I knew I couldn't lie.

"Hurting him...I would have rather died," I replied, "I couldn't stop it." I shook my head, "I was going to tell him, but it just kept accelerating. How do you stop an avalanche." I looked at compassionate eyes that I didn't expect. "I ran."

"That's not an answer."

"What do you want me to say?" I said, my eyes streaming, "I'm a damned janitor and he's a..a..businessman," I didn't know what he was. I just knew it was beyond my dreams.

"Again, you're not answering."

"He's everything," I yelled at her, "proof that I can fuck up anything." My uncontrolled blubbering got worse as my eyes found the floor again, "I fuck up everything," I repeated quietly to the tiles. Every mistake I ever made invaded my mind and overshadowed the few successes. At that moment, I was a complete failure.

"Well," Rebecca said, "that's closer to an answer." I turned to look at Rebecca. She was smiling, soft and forgiving, and sitting next to me on the floor. Next to a mop and bucket. This woman was the definition of high society, but she was down at my level.

"You don't hate me," I observed. Her soft laugh filled the empty hall. I was missing something.

"You had my son on the dance floor. Twice," Rebecca explained, "he wanted to be there with you. You have no idea what that means, do you?" I shook my head. "He always hated dancing. Felt it made him look like an idiot."

"He's not very good," I added. Then again, either was I. Comparing him to George and wasn't really fair.

"No. No he's not," Rebecca continued with a small chuckle, "but that didn't stop him. He would have spent the whole night there if you had asked." I must have looked dumbfounded. "I have never seen him so...so...alive." She struggled for the word.

"Alive?"

"Happy," Rebecca corrected, "he didn't care if he looked like an idiot." Her eyes sought out mine," he only cared that you were there with him."

"Now, I suppose, he wants me in prison."

"If you heard him rant," Rebecca smiled, "prison would be too lenient. I believe I left when he was discussing the finer points of burning at the stake."

"Why are you here then?" I asked. I should have asked why the police weren't here though I didn't want to give her any ideas.

"I want to see him dance again," Rebecca replied softly.

"Is that before or after he burns me at the stake?" Rebecca's laugh echoed down the empty hall. At least the tears stopped, but it was too hard to join the humor I barely understood.

"Will you meet with him, Ella?" Rebecca asked, then she quickly added, "before this mess catches up to you."

"He would meet with me?"

"No," Rebecca smiled, "but he could run into you." I felt my stomach churn at the idea. I couldn't look into his eyes and see hatred. I remembered the butterflies when I first entered the dance. An arranged meeting would be a hundred times worse.

"I couldn't...to trick him again," I said shaking my head, "I don't want...I can't do it again."

"Please, think about it," Rebecca said as she stood and brushed off her pants. She held out her hand. I took it and she helped me to my feet.

"It would only make matters worse," I stated clearly, "I'm not built to hurt people." Rebecca gave me her smile again. It was too confusing speaking to her about Peter. She had some vision in her mind about a reconciliation. I had hurt him too much for that. I hurt myself too much.

"You work nights," Rebecca stated, looking around the offices for the first time. She was looking to change the subject. I was going to let her.

"Until six," I added. She handed me my pink heels. They might look nice with this year's prison attire. "Thank you."

"Think about, dear," Rebecca said as she started retreating to the elevators. I lied by nodding my head. "Oh, I almost forgot. Peter somehow knew your first name and that you drive a beige Toyota." I was sure my face went bright red, "He said something about you setting him up good."

"Shit." It came out of my mouth before I could stop it. He had remembered the flat tire all along.

"You should really work on your language, dear," Rebecca said, as she turned to the elevators, "Both you and Peter sound so uncivilized these days."

~

"She was here?" Raj asked with panic in his voice.

"Yes," I said, "I think she saw Peter and I riding into the sunset together."

"If she could find you..." I nodded as Raj spoke. "I am so sorry Ella."

"It's my fault as well Raj." I shrugged my shoulders, "it's a first offense and all, I am hoping that it won't go far. I'm really hoping I don't have to face Peter again."

"I can't let you take the blame," Raj insisted, "It was my stupid idea, my ego that got you here."

"Nope," I said shaking my head, "If it was just you, maybe, but we have to think of Kiran and Aanya. Nobody is waiting for me to come home. They can't deport me. I'll probably get probation and have to stay away from computers." At least that was my hope.

I spent the last two hours of my shift deflecting Raj's apologies. We shifted a lot of the blame on Agnus since she was the reason it all started. It helped a little, but telling a judge that your stepmother is a bitch probably wouldn't help with reality.

I took stock of myself in those two hours. Raj and Kiran were my only good friends. My other friends had drifted away over the years. They slept nights and worked during the days. Our schedules prohibited anything meaningful. I was basically a janitor, stashed away to keep me out of my own business. I had let it happen. I'm not sure if there was anything I could have done, but I hadn't put up much of a fight. Agnus held the puppet strings and I never tried to cut them. I had a lawyer, young though he was, who said I was at her mercy. She was the executor until I was thirty-two and there was nothing I could do about it. I wondered if I had given in too *q*uickly. It mattered little now.

Peter was on my mind as I was riding the elevator down. For a brief moment at the cotillion, I felt our shared desire. I wondered if there was only one person on the planet for me. If so, I was in trouble since I just kicked my one and only in the nuts. I tried to get that last image of him out of my mind. That look I had thought was misery, was most likely the beginning of hatred. I really wasn't any good at hurting people. It hurt me more.

I exited the building, thankful that Agnus decided to not do one of her early morning inspections. I had to take the good where I could find it. I fumbled for my keys in my purse and accidentally ran into someone outside the door.

"Excuse..." Peter's eyes met mine. I started backing away as I saw the recognition in his eyes. The building stopped my retreat. I watched as his face went through a hundred emotions, some of them frightening. He tried to speak. I tried to speak. I had no words. Sorry was too feeble. His shoulders lost their strength.

"You left me," Peter finally said. It wasn't an accusation. There was a tremendous amount of sorrow in the statement. My damn eyes were welling up.

"Do you hate me?" I asked. I didn't know what to do with my arms. They were moving like they were lost. Peter looked away, then back again.

"I can't," Peter admitted, "you're too close."

"I never..." I stumbled over my words, "I didn't mean...I didn't want to leave you." He moved toward me, his eyes as cloudy as mine. I leaned into him, risking everything. His arms wrapped around me so carefully, I knew I risked nothing. I tilted my head upwards and the most wonderful lips met mine. This time, it was he who led the dance.

"My mother set me up," Peter said, his smile defying his tone. I pulled him closer, not wanting to let him go.

"I told her not too," I whispered. How wrong I was.

"I suspect you are to join me for breakfast instead of her," Peter said, pointing to the 24-hour diner next to my building. "She spoke with you?"

"Last night," I replied, "don't be mad at her." Our lips joined again. Soft, forgiving and so filled with desire. I could feel my heart speeding. No, Rebecca had little to fear of retaliation from her son.

"You work nights?"

"Vampire," I nodded. I loved his smile. It was if the hacking incident never happened. All of the problems of the world disappeared and it was just to the two of us necking in the street at six in the morning.

"Breakfast?" Peter offered, his hand caressing the small of my back. I was leaning into him, liking the way his body felt against mine.

"I would love breakfast," I replied. I didn't want to lose contact with Peter, but we couldn't stay on the street like love-starved teenagers. We were love starved adults after all. He took my hand, obviously desiring the contact as well. I walked as close to him as I could without tangling our feet.

"I hate it when I have to admit my mother is right," Peter said, "she has this I-told-you-so expression that gnaws at me." I bounced my shoulder into his as we walked. "Don't snap to judgment Peter, you have to hear her side Peter, now you're just being irrational Peter." Peter's imitation of his mother's voice was way off. It made it all the more comical.

"I like her."

"I love her," Peter said smiling, "It's just that I sometimes I feel ten years old when I'm with her." He stopped walking and turned to me. "She was right, though. I don't care about the hows and whys. I just want to be near you."

"Even if my stupidity lands me in prison?" Peter's hand moved to the side of my face. I leaned into it, loving the way it felt against my skin.

"Even if," Peter promised. The street once again was treated to two people who couldn't keep their hands and lips off each other. I felt my pulse quickening as I let my passion loose. Our kiss became deeper, tongues dancing to our heartbeats. I was no longer hungry for food.

"I want to be with you," I said. The meaning coming from deep inside. A place that had been quiet for far too long.

"I would love to skip breakfast with you," Peter whispered, his fingers playing with my hair. I smiled at his agreement, taking his hand in mine. "I'm parked a block over," he said, pointing to the south. I had no apprehension. I led him down the street as a comfortable joy warmed me. I knew practically nothing about Peter, but I felt I knew him better than anyone else in the world. We were in some sort of sync. We knew we wanted each other and there was no wall of proprietary blocking the way. The excitement in his eyes fueled mine. Everything was exactly as it should be. Perfect.

"I have a million questions," Peter said, "but only one seems important right now. I don't know whether to call you Cindy or Ella."

"Ella," I replied, "Cindy was just for the cotillion."

"Ella...Ella," Peter tried it out for size, "Hello, my name is Peter and this is my girlfriend Ella."

"Girlfriend?" I said smiling. I knew I was. The kisses told me so.

"Why yes," Peter joked, "but you need to give me some time to break it to Cindy." It was tough to kiss him while I was laughing, but I managed.

The ride to Peter's condo was no different than our walk around The Fountains. We laughed and spoke freely about unimportant things. In silent agreement, we both ignored the outstanding issues. That was talk for later.

I walked into Peter's apartment expecting a dark bachelor pad. Instead, the morning sun was filling the open floor plan through tinted windows. A vista of Lake Michigan to the east, thin curtains blocking out the Chicago skyline to the south. I had never been in a Lake Shore Drive condo, much less a corner unit with a spectacular view.

"It's beautiful," I said with a little awe in my voice. I moved toward the window. The twenty-second floor hid the grime of the city below. It didn't hurt that it was a clear day.

"It certainly is," Peter said. I turned. He had been staring at me when he said it. I loved the look in his eyes. The idea that he felt the same way that I did was intoxicating. What little hesitancy I had, fled at the sight of his smile. For once in my life, I had no fear. I reached up and began unbuttoning my blouse.

Peter looked off toward what might be the bedroom door, then back at me. He was going to say something when I reached the last button of my blouse, revealing a rather boring white work bra. I raised the blouse over my shoulders and let it drop to the floor. His mouth began to move again, his eyes glued to my chest, nothing came out. I reached behind my back, unhooking the bra and unceremoniously let it drop to the floor. 'This is me, the normal me, in the bright light, take me or leave me,' I thought boldly.

I NEVER FELT SEXIER IN MY LIFE

Peter's eyes took me in. I saw something click behind his eyes, triggering his smile loaded with desire. I had just left work, probably a mess, and I never felt sexier in my life. Peter moved toward me, lifting his shirt off over his head. On his trim waist, just above that pants line, there was an adorable small tattoo of a purple flower bloom. I tried to pretend not to notice, but a giggle escaped from my lips. Peter looked down at his flower, his smile deepening.

"Lost a bet," Peter said, "I have a sordid past." I reached down and ran my fingers along the purple ink. His stomach reacted in a ticklish manner. I could see the shadow of another reaction between his legs.

"Any other secret art?" I asked, my lips moving toward his.

"Nope."

"Damn," I said, just before my mouth found his. I pushed my breasts into his chest, enjoying his skin. Peter's hand ran up my waist to cup the side of my breast. Tingles ignited wherever his fingers traveled. Our tongue entwined as we explored. I could feel his heart beating as it fought to be louder than mine. Impatience got the better of me. I reached between us and began undoing his belt.

Peter's hand left my breast and moved to my pants. We separated slightly, trying to remain kissing as we raced to get the other out of their pants. Kissing turned to laughter as we fumbled to undress each other. Everything was backward and neither of us was particularly deft at the task. Neither of us was going to give up either. I was slightly disappointed when Peter claimed victory by sliding my pants down my hips.

Dropping to one knee, Peter lowered my pants toward my ankles. I lifted up my foot and he removed my shoe and sock. He repeated the process with my other foot. I stepped out of my pants and stood before him in only a conservative white panties. He reached up and sank his fingers in the elastic and slowly removed my last bit of clothing.

I had no idea why I wasn't running to hide. There was something about Peter that I trusted beyond good sense. I had never braved the light with any man before. With him, it felt like a requirement. A level of trust given. Trust that his eyes told me was well received.

Peter ran his hands up the back of my legs sending wonderful shivers through my body. His fingers teased along my backside as he leaned forward and kissed the top of my mound. His lips left wet trails has he kissed his way up my body, stalling on my breasts as he slowly stood.

"Absolutely beautiful," he whispered. I combed my fingers into his hair, pulling his lips to mine. I loved how his hands explored, sending pleasant waves across my skin. I have hidden nothing, me at my worst and he wanted more. I tried to get closer, climb into his skin. I no longer wanted to just touch. I wanted to join completely.

My hands moved quickly, finishing what they started with his pants. I felt animalistic, tugging anxiously, lowering his pants and briefs together. I paused when I felt his arousal. I was rather pleased my body had that quick of an effect on him. I turned him and pushed gently. His feet tangled in his pants and he fell back onto the couch. We laughed as I struggled to de-shoe and de-pants him.

Peter tried to rise when he was fully naked. I gently put my hand on his chest and held him down. Well, in truth, he let me. I slowly climbed up his body, my lips caressing what they found. His erection jerked when I gave it some attention. His desire. like mine, was wound tight and I heard him gasp. I rose higher, smiling at how excited he was. He looked so delicious as he reached out to help me up.

"You want to lead?" Peter asked. His smile told me he would be happy either way. I nodded as I dragged my breasts along his chest, our lips meeting again. I did want to lead. I had felt so out of control for so long, the idea of controlling things, however briefly, was exciting. I felt him shudder and knew he didn't mind at all.

I straddled Peter's waist, never breaking our kiss. He helped me, guiding my hips with his hands. I reached between us, grasping his manhood and lowered myself. Foreplay was for next time. Neither of us had the patience or the need. I separated from his lips and watched his eyes as we joined. We exhaled simultaneously as we became one. The glorious sensation of completion made my stomach curl and Peter moan. It was deeper than my past experiences. Meaning, I wasn't prepared for, emerged. I saw Peter's eyes water. I stopped when he was fully in me and stared in awe at how it felt.

"You're perfect," Peter said. He was so wrong.

"We're perfect," I corrected. Alone I was a mess.

"We," he whispered. Drawing our lips together again. Every movement became a new sensual experience. A hand down my side, my hand in his hair. I didn't matter how trivial, every touch ignited a new flame. I began to move my hips, desiring the wonderful internal friction that sent pleasure through us both. His hips joined mine though the leverage was all mine. I wanted it to last forever, but my body wanted more. A tingling began, his eyes, the way he looked through me, the heavenly feeling between my legs, traveling deeper than I thought possible.

"Let go," Peter said, sensing my need, "my love." His words, the sunrise over the water, the perfect us. My insides blossomed. Pleasure surged, following my bones to my extremities and I began to shake uncontrollably. Peter held me as his legs stiffened. His eyes found mine was we lost ourselves together. I collapsed into him, my muscles becoming happy rubber. I could feel him twitching inside of me, his breathing heavy with his release. We were perfect.

"My love," I whispered into Peter's ear. I kissed the lobe and felt his chest rise and fall in a chuckle.

"I meant it," Peter returned. I bit his ear with my lips and felt him tremble. I liked the reaction it generated.

"So did I," I whispered. Peter held me tighter. We stayed that way for a long while, enjoying the comfort of being as close as we could get. I learned how his heart beat in those minutes. Two quick beats followed by a pause. Slowly it degenerated to single steady beats. Each time it beat, I knew it was for me. It had to be. My heart was beating for him.

~

I remembered a bigger shower in high school, but it was built for entire PE classes. Peter's was the largest I had been in since then. It had a digital thermometer to set water temperature, a long bench along one side and many nozzles that shoot water in all directions.

"It came with the condo," Peter said as we stepped in. He set the temperature and pushed the on-button. It took a few seconds before the water began. "It doesn't start until the water is at the desired temperature."

"Such luxury," I complimented.

"You'll love this," Peter said, pushing a few more buttons. A large, overhead shower head began to gently sprinkle water. He took my hand and pulled me under the warm rain that seemed to be everywhere. It was a soft summer shower and we were naked in it. Kissing in the rain was a beautiful thing.

We spent a long time in the shower. Our after play more than made up for the lack of foreplay. It was if we had always known each other. I loved how he washed me in such a cherishing way. The way he would make me moan when his hands found my more intimate areas. The way I could make him squirm with my own fondling. The laughter that ensued from jokes only we could appreciate. It was by far, the most enjoyable shower I ever had.

Peter's phone rang while we were in bed. I was snuggled into him, enjoying the comfortable pillow he had become. He lifted the phone and gave a faux groan.

"Hello, mother," Peter said in a strained tone. He smiled at me so that I knew he was toying with her. I could hear bits of Rebecca's voice, but couldn't make out the words.

"I don't know what you thought you were trying to prove," Peter said firmly, "but it went horribly. A yelling match in the middle of the street. I tried to hold her for the authorities." There was a pause as Rebecca's voice chimed in. I could hear the desperation.

"No.. No, she scratched my face to get loose," Peter continued, "I'm sure it will scar." I couldn't take it anymore. I tried to grab the phone and Peter pulled it away. I scooted on top of him, my breasts in his face and used both hands to pin his arm and grab the phone. I was laughing so hard I could hardly speak when Peter finally gave in and let me have it.

"He's torturing you," I laughed into the phone. Peter tickled my side, making me drop the phone on his chest. He grabbed it *q*uickly and put it on speaker.

"You're on speaker, Mom."

"I gather things went well," Rebecca said. I could hear the glee in her voice. I am sure Peter only heard 'I told you so.'

"Very well," we replied in unison. More laughing.

"You don't know how pleased that makes me," Rebecca admitted, "you two belong with each other. I saw that from the beginning. I am sorry I used deceit, but you both seemed intent on screwing it up."

"That reminds me," Peter said, his face becoming serious, "I'm still trying to arrest you. I mean have you arrested."

"You haven't dealt with that?" Rebecca asked.

"We...were talking about...other things," I said. Peter and I shared a smile. I could swear he was blushing.

"Peter, where is your head?" Rebecca scolded. Peter immediately buried his head between my breasts. I tried not to laugh, but it leaked out anyway.

74

"Mom, we'll take it from here," Peter said, then softened,"and thank you." There was an apology buried in those words.

"You call me if he gives you any trouble, Ella." I could hear the humor in Rebecca's words.

"I will, Mrs. Charming," I answered. I was naked in her son's bed. Using her first name seemed wrong. It was some kind of high school impropriety flashback.

"It's Rebecca, Dear."

"Goodbye, Mother," Peter said. His hands were getting amorous again. Our wrestling for the phone must have set him off. He ended the call before Rebecca could say goodbye. I let him take me, and joyfully he did. As far as I could tell, dancing was his only weakness.

~

"So, tell me everything," Peter asked softly. My head was tucked into his shoulder, one leg over his torso and my hand was making sure his chest didn't have any imperfections. I couldn't remember feeling so good.

"In the beginning God created..." I teased.

"Smart ass," Peter laughed, "everything about how and why you hacked my firewall." I should have been prepared for the question. I was too busy being naked to think of much else. I lifted my head and looked at this eyes. There was nothing but trust in them. Lying would have to be saved for the authorities.

"I can't," I said, "I'm protecting someone." Peter's eyes widened. There was no admonishment, just a strong curiosity.

"Someone else hacked my systems?"

"As a favor to me," I said, then quickly added, "he's never done it before. We didn't think anyone would find out."

"He?" Shit, I let that slip.

"I'm in trouble either way," I paused for a moment, "a family I love very much will be destroyed if this goes past me." Peter's eyes were shifting back and forth between my left and right eye. I waited to see if my trust was well placed. He smiled and kissed me. There was a mountain of trust in that kiss. I hadn't gambled at all.

"Tell me what you can," Peter said. I did. Everything about my father's death. Agnus and the will. How I let my pride and envy of my stepsisters drive me to choose an illicit outlet. He listened, his hand played with my hair as I spoke. At times, I wondered if he was really listening or thinking of us instead. He was a computer guy, so I assumed multitasking was ingrained.

"Agnus is a bitch," Peter surmised. He had been listening. "You had no idea that it was my firewall your friend hacked?"

"Nope," I replied, "I was avoiding you at the dance because I thought you might recognize me from the flat tire. I thought it would be embarrassing." Peter laughed. I slapped his chest. Not hard, just enough so he knew my feelings were important.

"I recognized you immediately," Peter admitted, ignoring my slap, "that day in the rain was all I could think of. I was kicking myself for not asking for your number when it happened."

"Why didn't you tell me?"

"I was waiting for you," Peter replied, "I didn't feel right announcing that I already knew how beautiful your breasts were." that earned him a quick kiss, "for a while, I thought you were avoiding me because you remembered and thought me...well...not your cup of tea."

"Not true, my love," I said, stroking the side of his face. Peter was my cup of tea. Green tea. The kind that is not only tasted good but was good for you. He was good for me in so many ways. A few kisses later and I was satisfied he was as sure as I was.

"You get some rest," Peter said, untangling from my arms, "I'll get on the phone and see about undoing what I started." It was actually way past my normal bedtime. His too, I suspected. Visions of falling asleep in his arms were painfully thrust aside. After he leaned down for the last kiss, I watched his naked ass as he left the bedroom. It was a cute butt. I closed my eyes and thought of how the day had progressed. I learned that you can fall asleep smiling.

Not my alarm woke me. It was an annoying chirp that kept repeating at an ever increasing rate. A warm body reached across mine and slammed down on top of the clock. I felt Peter's naked form pull against me under the sheets.

"It's going to go off again in seven minutes," Peter whispered. His lips were so close to my ear it sent a shiver down my neck.

"Mmmm," I moaned as tucked my butt into him. Peter was a wonderful way to wake up. He wrapped his free arm around and pulled me in tight.

"The FBI is looking for you," Peter whispered. My eyes opened. I was awake. "The military thinks the breach was a test for a foreign intrusion into our nation's digital infrastructure."

"Ah..it was a charity dance," I stuttered. I felt physically safe in Peter's arms. Mentally, I was changing my name and running to Bora Bora.

"I know," Peter said, "I guess I was pretty angry when you left and I said things." I turned my head to see his eyes. He looked like a four-year-old who just broke his mother's favorite lamp. "I'm trying to undo it, but the wheels have been turning for a few days."

"What did you say?"

"I thought you deceived me," Peter confessed, "I didn't know you were...you. I was a little irrational."

"Peter, sweetie, what did you say?"

"Something to the effect of; only a foreign government would have the necessary resources to mount such an attack ." Peter shrugged his shoulders guiltily, "I used other words to describe you that I hope you ignore if they get repeated." I was in a world of trouble and all I could do is smile at my four-year-old who was trying to glue the lamp back together.

"Will you visit me in prison?" I joked.

"Ella, this isn't funny," Peter's guilt was hurting him. I rolled my body around, breasts to chest.

"Will you stand by me?" I asked.

"Of course."

"Then I don't care about anything else," I smiled, "I don't care about my inheritance, the FBI or my stepmother." Peter eyes turned loving, "I hear they have conjugal visits in prison," I teased. His lips were just as wonderful as earlier that morning. I looked at the clock and did some quick math. If I got going right then, I could make to work on time. I looked back at Peter.

"I'm going to be late," I decided.

"So am I," Peter said. We made love, interrupted briefly while Peter beat the snot out of the snooze alarm.

~

"You're late," Agnus said, her hands on her hips as I got out of the elevator. I smiled at her and ignored her comment. All I could think of was Peter. My body felt light as a feather and the thought of cleaning offices was not depressing. "No excuses?" Agnus stated as I passed by her. I was going to let that comment go, but I was too happy not to share. I turned, my smile growing opposite to her frown.

"I'm in love," I said and then I added something completely inappropriate, "mother." I made it sound like more like 'bitch.' I watched her face turn red. It was incredibly pleasant. Her mouth moved, but nothing came out. I had caught her by surprise. A preemptive sneak attack. I would pay for it later, but right now, I could still smell Peter on me and didn't care about later. I left her there, stunned, and started my night's work.

~

"You and Peter Charming?" Raj verified.

"He's wonderful," I said, my euphoria hadn't faded even after cleaning twenty offices. "is this how you feel with Kiran?" I smiled.

"That the rest of the world could fall into a bottomless pit and it doesn't matter?" Raj returned.

"Yes, that's it."

"Kiran makes me feel that way," Raj said, "Aanya brings us right back to caring that the world doesn't fall away." The thought of a family drifted into my mind. It was too soon to think of such things though the idea of sharing Peter with a son or daughter was not unpleasant.

78

"The FBI is looking for me and I don't even care," I said, letting my joy fill the room.

"The FBI!" Raj said as he turned quickly from his workstation, "That is the worst thing that could happen. I never wanted it go this far." His face was losing all its color.

"It doesn't matter, Raj. Peter will stand by me and that's all that matters." I had a humorous vision of Peter standing before me, swinging a sword to protect my honor. I had no idea where all the thoughts were coming from, but they were wonderful.

"FBI means prison," Raj continued, "I can't let you do that."

"You can and you will," I said firmly, "This whole mess was my choice and I got Peter out of it. There's no way you are going ruin it by getting your family deported."

"I don't feel good about this," Raj rambled on, "it is not right and honor says I step in."

"Your honor is for Kiran and Aanya," I said, "I will be fine. If anything does come of this, it is my first offense. I doubt it will amount to much." And Peter will stand by me. The FBI is looking for me and I could do nothing but smile. My phone vibrated. It was a text from Peter.

I would really love to skip breakfast again

me too

6?

pick me up?

hard to work - too happy - see you at 6

kisses

I just scheduled sex. I had never done that before. I had accepted dates that I figured would become sexual, but never a flat out naked appointment. I laughed at my phone. If it was anyone but Peter, I would have thought it slutish. With him, it was so damned perfect and felt absolutely appropriate. It was all too much fun. The rest of the world could fall into a bottomless pit for all I cared.

"Is that Peter?" Raj asked. He still seemed depressed about the FBI.

"Yes," I said, then added a white lie, "he wants to pick me up for breakfast this morning."

"Does he know about me?"

"Not you personally, but yes, he knows I don't have the knowledge to hack the firewalls," I replied.

"He must think me a coward," Raj said, his eyes finding the floor.

"No," I said softly, "he thinks I value your friendship enough to not destroy your family."

"I will not forgive myself if you end up in prison," Raj mumbled.

"You must," I said, "for Kiran and Aanya. If it was just you, I would have told the FBI long ago." Raj looked up and saw my smile. At least my joke lightened the mood. I changed the subject to trivial things. I knew Raj hadn't forgotten about the FBI, but at least he was willing to let it go for now.

I spent some time in the bathroom trying to clean up before Peter arrived. I felt rather pleased with myself and the way life was going. I thought my life wouldn't really begin until I was thirty-two with my freedom from Agnus. Now, that was merely another birthday. My life began the previous morning, when Peter was too close to hate me.

I undid my pony tail and ran a feeble comb through my hair. It took a while to break through the tangles, creating organized lines that looked softer. I suppressed a laugh knowing it would soon be a mess again. I touched up my mascara and brushed the lint off my clothes. I liked the smiling woman in the mirror. It had been a long time since she was my friend.

Agnus was waiting for me when I exited the bathroom, wearing a superior smile. That I could ignore. The men in suits next to her, I could not.

"You have surprised me," Agnus said, then she added, "daughter." It was laced with as much bitch as she could muster. "These gentlemen seem to think you have an alias. Now, I said, not my little Ella. Tell me it's not so." Her smile grew as she stepped off to the side. Out of everything that happened, her glee was the most irritating thing.

"Ella Tremaine, you're under arrest for wire fraud and espionage," the taller suit said. My eyes widened. "Please turn around and place your hands behind your back."

"I need to make a call," I said. An unexpected begging invaded my voice. I felt fear. Espionage. That was quite a bit more serious than I had expected.

"Sorry, ma'am," the shorter suit said, "the warrant is explicit. No communications or contact with any technology."

"I have rights," I demanded.

"National security trumps those rights," tall suit said. He moved toward me. I thought he intended to forcibly cuff me if I didn't comply. I turned and put my hands behind my back. I couldn't help it, my hands were shaking.

"I haven't seen a badge," I stammered. What rights did I have? Tall suit turned me around once my hands were secure.

"Agent Dawson, FBI," tall suit said as he held his badge so I could read it. I guess I had some rights.

"Agent Phillips, NSA," the shorter man said, holding up a different badge. My knees went weak. I was in more trouble than I knew.

"It was only a dance," I whimpered.

"This way, Ms. Tremaine," Dawson said. Agnus was covering her mouth. She was hiding a smile. I no longer cared about her little victory. I was concerned for my freedom.

"Agnus, I need a lawyer," I stated as Dawson took my arm and led me to the elevator. She was my purse. My finances were drained by a flat tire and shoes I only wore once.

"I'll see what I can do," Agnus said with a chuckle in her throat. I was sure she was going to hire someone straight out of school. The elevator opened and the agents and I stepped in. When I turned around, Raj was standing down the hall, his face ashen. I straightened up and tried to look strong. I subtly shook my head. Thankfully, he didn't move. At least his family would be unscathed.

Agent Dawson read me my rights on the way down. It was more frightening than I could have imagined. There was no innocent-until-proven-guilty in his tone. They placed me in the back of a blue sedan and, once I was buckled, pulled out into traffic.

"Where are you taking me?"

"FBI offices, Ms. Tremaine," Phillips said, turning in the passenger seat to look at me, "it would be in your best interest to cooperate, though you can choose to remain silent." He shook his head, "I would think that unwise for a person in your position."

"I went to a dance," I repeated, "it was stupid, but I'm not a spy or anything."

"We can recognize a trial run," Phillips continued, "you purposely compromised a military grade firewall and tried to ingratiate yourself with its creator." He shook his head again. "It is my understanding that you laid the seeds for you con*q*uest by flaunting yourself prior to the dance. A seemingly random encounter that defies coincidence."

"It was a flat tire," I begged, "I didn't plan anything."

"What was it that turned you?" Phillips continued, "tired of waiting for your inheritance." My eyes widened at his knowledge, "Yes, we have an extensive file on you. Impatient spoiled rich girl. As we speak, your home and car are being searched. It would better for you if you came clean and told us who you work for."

"No one," I insisted *q*uickly, "I was envious of my stepsisters. I'll admit that, but I would never do anything against America."

Phillips turned to Dawson and shared a smile. "They are all suddenly patriots when it's time to pay the piper." Dawson chuckled. I was in over my head.

"I want a lawyer," I begged, "you said I could have a lawyer present." At least that's what Dawson said when he read me my rights.

"Then they go all stubborn," Phillips chuckled. He turned back to me. "I dislike people like you. You trample all over your country then demand the same rights you work so hard to destroy." There was an unwavering hate in his eyes. My eyes began to well up. Handcuffed, I couldn't even wipe the shame away. Phillips rolled his eyes, "and then they try the crying thing."

Unbidden, my eyes began to drain down my cheeks. I needed Peter.

~

*W*aiting was the hardest part. I sat on a hard metal chair, handcuffed to a metal table that was bolted to the floor. The room was empty except for an empty chair on the other side of the table and two cameras mounted on the ceiling in opposite corners. Not even a clock to know how long I had been there. I only knew it had been hours.

I was strip searched when I arrived by two rough female agents who thought less of me than Phillips did. With rubber gloves, they probed to find secrets I didn't carry. The humiliation brought more tears. I tried desperately to remain strong, but each time I found my backbone, they crushed it again. I was hungry, thirsty and I really needed to pee. Instead, I sat on the rock hard chair and tried not to break down.

"Good afternoon, Ms. Tremaine," A woman said as she entered the room, "I am Agent Stratford with the FBI." She smiled and placed a thick folder on the table. Her dark brown hair was cropped short and she had an athletic build. Unlike the suits earlier, she was more casual in her brown slacks and tan blouse. Her badge was hanging off her belt.

"I have to use the bathroom," I said desperately. Surely, a woman would understand.

"We'll get to your needs after you answer a few questions," Stratford stated as she sat in the empty chair and opened the folder. On top of the papers was my pink phone in a plastic bag. The more I thought about it, the more I needed to pee.

"I am confused," Stratford continued as if my bladder wasn't her concern, "you have little money," I watched her removing papers from the folder, my bank statements among them, "yet you were able to finance a $5,000 a plate ball." She chuckled a little, "I thought my finances were bad until I got a look at yours." They hadn't traced the money back to Tremaine Marketing, Inc. Raj had hidden his tracks well. I could never tell them where the money came from.

"I really have to pee," I said.

"I really need an answer," Stratford said, leaning back in her chair. Her smile told me that she meant to hold me there until I complied. I remained silent and pushed my legs together to try and quell the urge.

"Whatever government you're working for will deny you even exist," Stratford continued, "your loyalty to them is now unfounded. We are the only ones who can help you now."

"Don't I get a lawyer?" I asked. Maybe a lawyer could get me the bathroom.

"In time," Stratford said, "but do you really want to give up your chance at leniency? Speak to us now and it will be taken into consideration at sentencing." They already had me convicted in their minds. "Who financed this operation? Who compromised the firewall?" she looked back down at the folder full of paper and waved her hand over it, "there is nothing here that even indicates you know how to turn a computer on. We know you are working for another organization." I crossed my legs and squeezed them tight.

"It was a dance," I pleaded, "I hacked the firewall myself. I just wanted to go to the dance." My bladder felt like it was going to burst. "Please let me go to the bathroom."

"Give me the password to the phone," Stratford said, holding the phone up. "They tell me the encryption is something new. Are you trying to tell me you created it as well?"

"I...I forgot the password," I stammered. I hated lying, but Raj's texts and voicemail were on the thing.

"Where did you get the money?" Stratford yelled, slamming the phone down. "Do you think we're stupid?" My eyes betrayed me again. I didn't want to break down in front of her, but I couldn't think quick enough to stall the fear. "Do you know what prison will be like? Traitors are dealt with harshly." I dropped my head down to my cuffed hands to wipe away the tears.

"I have to go to the bathroom," I cried.

"Who are you working for?" Stratford yelled louder, "You tell me what I need to know or you will rot as a slave to 300-pound dyke in prison." The floodgates opened and I lost control of my bladder. Stratford scooted back quickly as the puddle grew beneath the table. I no longer knew if I was crying for my freedom or the fact that she made me pee myself. I never felt so weak in my life.

The door opened and a man poked his head in. "Shit," the man said, "get her cleaned up fast." I lifted my head. "Get those damn cuffs off her."

"Give me ten more minutes," Stratford said, her smile was bordering on evil. I prayed he wouldn't give her ten more seconds.

"I doubt you have thirty seconds," the man warned, "her lawyers are here." Plural? Agnus sent more than one. A ray of hope.

"Keep them out!" Stratford argued.

"You do it," the man complained, "they're from the top firms in the city. I got the division head wanting to know why they haven't seen their client. I can't fight politics." Stratford looked at me with anger. I think she saw herself saving the free world. I was strengthened by the thought of lawyers and firms. I couldn't believe that Agnus pulled out all the stops. Maybe I misjudged her.

"It was just a dance," I said stronger. I liked that some sense of control had returned. "I'm going to need some clean clothes, or is that against the rules." I wiped the rest of my tears away. The fear in man's face gave me courage. I had lawyers.

"Uncuff her," a man in a very expensive black suit with a blue tie demanded. He looked at the floor and I saw his temples pulse. "Is this your idea of proper procedure?" he said, looking at the two agents. He had a touch of gray on his sideburns with perfectly groomed short black hair.

"Brendan Mcelroy of Finnegan, Roy, and Clausland," the man introduced himself to me, "I have been retained as part of your counsel team, Ms. Tremaine. That is, of course, if you agree." Stratford was moving with acuity, ignoring the mess on the floor in an attempt to get the cuffs off. I smiled as relief washed over me.

"Yes, please," I replied. I could have kissed him if I wasn't sitting in a pool of urine. Stratford released me from the cuffs and I resisted the urge to stand. Brendan recognized my hesitancy and took a step back.

"Please secure an unmonitored room so we may confer with our client," Brendan ordered. He had an authority about him that made you want to comply. "I expect her there shortly after she has had a chance to freshen up. I also expect a copy of the video of the inter-rogation," he added pointing to the cameras. Stratford's face lost its color. I felt better.

Stratford hustled to get me into the bathroom. There was no apology or contrition, but a definite shift in power had occurred. I was innocent until proven guilty again. It was the agent's bathroom, complete with lockers and showers. Stratford supplied me with a towel and some soap. After grunting out some instructions about not touching the lockers, she left to get me some dry clothes.

The shower was heavenly warm. I was human again. It took a few minutes before I was sure the last traces of the accident were gone. I succeeded in keeping my hair mostly dry which was surprising since I had an urge to douse myself and let the warm water shield me from the world.

Stratford returned with brand new, still in the package, FBI sweats. I would have to go commando, but clean and dry was better than wet and smelly. I dressed quickly and asked politely to be brought to my lawyers. Stratford complied without verbal acknowledgment. I could tell that the situation was killing her on the inside.

"I am sorry we did not get here sooner," Brendan said. I looked at the four faces of obviously successful lawyers. Three men and one woman dressed as if they had just stepped out of a catalog.

"I am so happy you came when you did," I said, "I'm just surprised my stepmother responded at all." There were a few confused looks.

"We have been retained by the Charmings," Brendan responded, "is there a problem with that." I think my smiled convinced them there wasn't. Screw Agnus. Peter loves me.

"Let's see about getting you out of here," Brendan said. Introductions were made and my interrogation discussed. I informed them that I did request to go to the bathroom multiple times and did request a lawyer. Dollar signs ignited in their eyes, but all I wanted was to get out of there. I didn't want to sue the FBI or anyone else for that matter. I especially didn't want a courtroom full of people see me pee myself.

There was a knock at the door. A female agent I didn't recognize entered with a folder and an uncomfortable expression. "The recording equipment didn't seem to be working during the interview," she said. I rolled my eyes. My attorneys saw red.

"You disallowed my client an attorney, chained her to a table and didn't allow her to use the bathroom for what...three, four hours?" Brendan seethed, "and now you tell us you have no record of it."

"I am not aware of any illegal or inhumane treatment, sir," the agent claimed, "I am only stating that the recording equipment was not working."

"I wonder if agent Stratford would like to be subpoenaed," Brendan added.

"National security allows us great leeway," the agent said.

"Not that great, and certainly not with American citizens on American soil," Brendan informed her, "If you wish Ms. Tremaine to not pursue the issues involved with the interview, I suggest you move quickly on a bond hearing. I am sure there are judges that will recognize Ms. Tremaine has no priors and isn't a flight risk." My lawyers all glared at the agent. There was no fear in their eyes, but I saw plenty in the agent. I folded my hands across my chest and added my confident stare as well.

It was four hours later before I found myself exiting FBI headquarters. About twenty years earlier than Agent Stratford would have preferred. The judge found the espionage linkage weak but agreed that the wire fraud charge was relevant. A $10,000 bail was paid by Brendan on behalf of the Charmings. I had to agree to stay off all computers and not leave the city without informing the FBI.

I would have hated the building itself if it wasn't for what I saw slumped in an uncomfortable chair in the foyer as I was leaving. A tired, frustrated and oh so beautiful Peter. HIs eyes brightened and a smile emerged as he saw me approaching. His arms and lips were just as I remembered.

"Why are you in FBI sweats?" Peter asked.

"Can we get out here first?"

"Yes...Yes, we can," Peter said enthusiastically. My hand in his, he led me out of my mini nightmare.

~

"So, they think you're a spy?" Peter asked. He was scrambling eggs while I was laying bacon across a pan. I hadn't realized how hungry I was until he mentioned food. I liked that idea of cooking with him. It was wonderfully domestic and a little charming that he thought of my needs.

"You can't imagine how happy I was to see the lawyers," I said, leaning over to kiss his cheek. I liked making him smile. "a few more minutes in that room with that woman, and I would have claimed to have shot Kennedy." I didn't think we could be any closer. Our shoulders kept rubbing against each other was we worked. We weren't even taking the trouble to make it look unintentional.

"Raj wants to confess," Peter said. I sucked in my breath.

"How do you know about Raj?"

"He found me on the street looking for you," Peter admitted, "I guess he knew we were supposed to meet this morning. He told me what happened and pretty much told me everything else."

"Oh, Peter," I begged, "you can't let him confess. They will deport his family and things won't go well for them in India. They are the best friends I have and I don't want to lose them."

"Deport him?" Peter smiled, "I want to hire him. He's brilliant and thinks way out of the box. The way he tricked my firewall into thinking the packet streams were authorized was ingenious. He sees holes where the rest of us see solid walls."

"You like him too," I summarized.

"Yes," Peter said, his eyes looking up as he thought, "I think I do."

"Good," I agreed, "his wife and daughter don't need to be brought into this. I am in trouble either way."

"I think my ranting made this worse," Peter said as he moved to the stove and poured the eggs into a pan.

"I should have never run out of the dance," I confessed. Peter saw me coming with the bacon and opened the oven door. No need for words, we were in cooking sync. I placed the bacon the middle rack and Peter closed the door.

"Yay, I took that badly," Peter admitted.

"But you rescued me today," I said. I put my hand over his and we stirred the eggs together with a wooden spoon. Highly inefficient, but so nice.

"I wish I could have found you sooner. I would have liked to spare you the interrogation," Peter said as his lips moved closer to mine. I ran my hand up his arm and behind his neck and pulled him closer. I wanted to let the eggs burn and let the intimacy continue. Every moment of our joined lips increased his passion. I heard the spoon fall free as he wrapped me in his arms.

"We are going to starve to death at this rate," Peter whispered into my mouth. I could feel his lips curving against mine. Starvation wouldn't be so bad, but the loss of stamina might slow us down. I pulled myself away. Not far away - still touching. I didn't want to lose the closeness.

"Food first," I said, struggling to lessen my smile. I told my body to put the tingle that was growing on hold. I saw a shiver run down Peter's spine. He was feeling what I was. There was more in sync than cooking.

"Are you going to work tonight," Peter asked.

"Without sleep," I said, shaking me head no, "I have some time off I can use." Peter's smile grew and he stirred the eggs more vigorously.

"I was thinking of taking the night off as well," Peter said. His eyes weren't looking at me, almost if he were afraid of his salacious thoughts.

"Are you planning to take advantage of an exhausted woman?" I teased.

"Well, now that your resistance is down, I thought I would lull you into a false sense of security with a backrub."

"Mmmm."

"Then...once your muscles become lazy and useless, I figured I would lead the first dance," Peter smiled as he stirred. The eggs were beginning to clump. "A slow dance to start. Something that requires very little movement on your part. I was planning on having my way with you." He smiled, "I have never seduced an international spy before."

"You intend to learn all my secrets?" The tingle wasn't listening to my brain anymore. I knew I should eat something, but the thought of food was becoming less important.

"Everyone of them," Peter teased, "hopefully, even ones you don't know about." The idea of naked exploration blossomed in my mind. It should have scared me. With Peter, it sounded so wonderful. My trust was his for the taking.

"Those eggs done yet?" I asked too quickly.

"Almost," Peter replied, "what about the bacon?" I had forgotten all about it. We scooted our feet back and I pulled the oven door down and peeked inside. The four pieces were sizzling well as the smell of bacon filled the room. They were still on the rubbery side of done.

"Oven mitts?" I asked. Peter pointed to a drawer where I found two fat red mittens. I pulled the pan out and flipped the bacon. I replaced the pan in the oven while Peter was moving the eggs to plates.

"Bacon has a few more minutes," I complained.

"Ahh, the smell of bacon and a beautiful woman," Peter quipped, "I do believe I have found heaven." I had to laugh. I tried not to, but he seemed so proud of his silly humor. How could a beautiful woman not laugh?

~

*P*eter was true to his word. The massage was wonderfully slow and turned my muscles into wet noodles. He leaned down every once in awhile to tease my ears with his lips, whispering tender things to make sure I was awake. His fingers were firm, yet gentle as they glided around my back. Sometimes he would find a knot and spent extra care to rub it out always followed by a loving kiss. I could barely form words and mostly moaned my encouragement.

I rolled over and tried to rise to thank him properly when it was over. He pushed my lazy body back to the bed. It wasn't over. He lightly kissed my lips then trailed off to the side of my neck. Soft wet kisses trailed down my neck, climbed my breasts and concentrated on my nipples. His tongue tickled, mixing a chuckle into my moans. His kisses continued down my tummy. I closed my eyes as he slowly made his way between my legs.

There are certain pleasures in life that defy description. The senses mash the feelings, sights and sounds together into a ball of lovely luxury that defies recall. Peter found all my secrets. Had I been a spy, I would have betrayed all. His sweet tongue teased little strings of bliss tied to my core. My hips rose off the bed when the pleasure could no longer be contained. My entire body stiffened as pure joy invaded every crevice of my being.

I was half laughing, half crying when reality slowly crawled back.

Little bursts of pleasure exploded, fighting the return of normalcy. Then, as if a switch was thrown, pleasure became a ticklish torture. Laughing I tried to squirm away from Peter's tongue. I could hear his soft laugh as he continued the torment.

"Stop," I cried, laughing so hard the word barely came out. Peter did. His face rose with a grin that was both proud and happy. I reached down and pulled him up my quivering body. "Such a lovely man," I complimented. If this was life with Peter, I wanted more.

I reached between us when we kissed. His excitement was strong. I spread my legs and guided him into me. I exhaled as my parts found their perfect match. Peter's smile faded to a dreamy expression that said more than any words ever could.

"I'm yours," Peter whispered.

"And I'm yours," I repeated as my eyes watered. He moved slowly like he intended it to last forever. I desired it to last a lifetime. We cemented the 'us' in that coupling. Sex was no longer just sex.

~

"Can you call my mother?" Peter asked. We were laying in bed enjoying each other in the peaceful afterglow of our sharing. I reached over and wiped away a drop of sweat that threatened Peter's eye. We must have burnt off a ton of calories.

"Your mother?" I returned. I wondered if my hair looked as wild as his right now. It was incredible cute the way it exploded off his head in wrong directions. It was even better knowing I was the cause of its calamity.

"I promised I would call as soon as you were released," Peter admitted, "she'll rip me a new one if I call her now." I smiled.

"You would prefer she yell at me?"

"In truth, yes," Peter smiled back. He reached forward and tucked an errant strand of my hair behind my ear. "but she won't yell at you."

"Are you afraid of your own mother?"

"Terrified," Peter laughed, "it's that grating tone of disappointment she can put into her words. She mixes it with a blend of I-told-you-so. It can be very emasculating."

"She loves you dearly," I said.

"And that's what makes it so effective." Peter pulled me closer. He cared little that I was as sweaty as he.

"For you, I will make the call," I feigned capitulation. That earned me some loving kisses. I would have gotten them anyways, but it is always sweeter when you earn them.

Peter disappeared into the bathroom when I rang Rebecca. Her tone changed immediately when she realized I was on Peter's phone. She listened intently as I retold my arrest saga. I left out the peeing part figuring she didn't need to know a weakling was dating her son.

"So it was a horrible day," Rebecca summarized. I had already forgotten the emotions prior to seeing Peter in the lobby of the FBI building. I smiled thinking of Peter saving me and discovering all my secrets. He was mine.

"Actually," I said slowly, trying to find the right words for a mother, "it was...Peter turned it into one the best days of my life." There. Might as well own up to the truth. There was silence on the other line. I said too much. "Rebecca..." There was a tone that indicated another call on the line. It wasn't my phone, but I found the ignore button quickly enough. 'Gen Rickers,' whoever that was, would just have to wait.

"Do you love him?" Rebecca asked. It was asked quietly, almost as if she were afraid to ask. I was now afraid to answer.

"Yes," I answered with the same lack of enthusiasm.

"That is the most wonderful thing I've heard in a long time," Rebecca stuttered. She was crying. So many tears today and somehow my eyes found more.

"He is kind of wonderful," I slobbered out.

"I've been waiting for someone to figure that out," Rebecca slurred. The conversation deteriorated into words half spoken, but totally understood. If anyone would have been listening, they would have thought us mentally challenged. We ended the call with a promise to talk later, over lunch perhaps.

I wiped my eyes for the umpteenth time and promptly pushed the wrong button on Peter's phone. Instead of turning it dark, I initiated the voicemail from the call I ignored. The VCR controls were in a different position from my phone and they took me a moment to locate. My heart fell and I never pushed stop as the words began to resonate.

Charming, this is Rickers. FBI surveillance has informed me that you have taken an interest in Ella Tremaine. That is a breach of our security agreement and we are within our rights to void your contract with armed services. Cease all contact with Ms.Tremaine and contact my office immediately. We may yet preserve the contract and prevent a lot of headaches on both sides.

The voice was authoritative. 'Gen' was most likely 'General.' I had ruined myself, risked Raj's family and now I was destroying Peter. I was a curse. I put the phone down with shaking hands. Quietly, I started to dress.

"Going somewhere?" Peter asked. I turned to tell him I had to leave. His eyes wouldn't let me. He was too close. I stopped putting my shoes on. All I could offer was weak tears. Peter rushed over and folded me in his arms. I pointed at the phone.

"What did my mother say?" Peter demanded. I shook my head.

"It's the voicemail," I said weakly. I watched his face go ashen as he listened. He slammed the phone down when the message was done. He stood and walked across the room and stood near the door. I could hear him taking deep breaths. When he turned, his face was red and I saw anger in his eyes.

"Those assholes are following you," He said in a deep voice, "I'll not have you spied on." His hand slammed on the dresser for emphasis. Spied upon. Did he not hear the same message I did?

"I'm wrecking your business," I said, "I can't do that to you."

"Fuck the business," Peter shouted. This was irrational Peter. The shock of his outburst scared me and I jerked away involuntarily. Peter's eyes changed and he visibly calmed at my reaction. He slowly moved forward and knelt before the bed I was sitting on. "Fuck the business," he repeated quietly, "I don't want it if it means losing you."

"I can't ruin you," I said. He took my hand in his.

"Ruin me?" Peter smiled, "the only way you could do that is to leave me." He kissed the back of my hand softly. "I'm not in this for a minute, an hour, or a day. I want you forever. To hell with the rest of the world."

"The rest of the world could fall into a bottomless pit and it doesn't matter," I whispered back. How I loved his lips. Forgiveness, love and passion seeped from his lips to mine. A hurricane could have swept through and I wouldn't have known.

"What did my mother say?" Peter asked. With all the problems we were facing, it was my conversation with his mother he was worried about.

"She wants to have lunch with me soon," I said, unable to describe the conversation.

"See, she won't yell at you," Peter said with happiness. I think I was just promoted to mother-buffer.

"What are we going to do?" I asked, not wanting to break the spell, but desperately hoping he had a plan.

"Well... we aren't going to hide," Peter said, "we'll face up to what was done and hopefully the truth will override the speculation."

"But your business."

"You are my business," Peter said, picking up his phone. He hit a few buttons and put it to his ear. He had a sly smile on his face.

"You're not doing something stupid?" I asked. He nodded yes, but the way his hand stroked the side of my face I could only smile.

"Evening General." There was a pause while Peter listened.

"Well that's going to be a problem." another pause.

"It looks like you'll need to go out for another procurement." Peter's smile grew and he winked at me.

"Sorry General, I love the lady." Now I was smiling. Peter's eyebrows gave a little bounce. "by the way, I have a line on how the firewall was breached. I'll probably have the only product that can thwart that type of attack. But, rules are rules. Have fun with the new procurement." Peter was almost giddy when he disconnected.

"Raj told you how," I said.

"Not all of it," Peter admitted, "but Rickers doesn't know that." I had to laugh. No sleep, rollercoaster emotions all day, made the laughter a bit more than it should have been. Peter took in stride and joined. Truly, it was us against the world.

THE WEEKS THAT FOLLOWED WERE WONDERFULLY STRANGE

The weeks that followed were wonderfully strange. Agnus had put me on indefinite suspension from work. An unpaid vacation of sorts. There were clauses in the employee handbook that applied to personnel that did not present a good moral character. She made sure I understood that my job depended upon the results of the criminal case against me. I would have flat out *q*uit, but the suspension seemed to cause Agnus more work. It was petty but pleasing. I no longer desired to wait seven more years.

The FBI had a constant tail on me. They were so sure I was working for a foreign government, I couldn't even get my mail without a photo being taken. Peter and I learned to recognize them. They always traveled in twos. I suspected that was necessary so they could keep each other awake. My life wasn't exactly 007 *q*uality. Being put on my detail was probably a punishment.

Peter and I started to go out more. We figured a life in bed would warp us in the long run. We found interesting places to eat. The more obscure the better, just to tease our followers. Peter had fun sending out plates of au dourness to our shadows. In time, we waved and they waved back. We invented names for them as we began to recognize them by face. I wondered how many real criminals were running loose because of the wasted resources.

Rebecca invited me to a luncheon. I thought she intended a one on one but was surprised when I saw two other women sitting at the table. Rebecca had chosen a fancy tea room, The Green Leaf. It was obviously designed to please female senses. There were ten women to every male and most of those males looked uncomfortable.

As I approached the table, I was met by two smiles I recognized. Ruth and Betty were sipping tea. Ruth treating the cup as if it was fragile and Betty like she was drinking from a mug.

"Hello Cindy," Betty said loudly. The teasing in her tone was not lost on me. Ruth scowled at her and smiled at me as she patted the seat next to her.

"Hello, Ruth, Betty," I said as I sat down between Ruth and Rebecca, "thank you for inviting me, Rebecca." I was little nervous knowing I owed these two an apology. "I'm sorry about the dance," I started.

"I'm not," Betty interrupted,"it was the most exciting party we went to all year." Ruth actually laughed. I think it was more for my benefit than Betty's.

"I've brought them both up to date," Rebecca said. "I thought it might be nice to have some friends in case you end up at another of those functions." She said 'in case' but she meant 'when.' It would be one of the requirements for being with Peter. Not a bad one either.

"So, are they following you now, Ella?" Betty asked leaning forward and dropping her voice so the other tables couldn't hear. Her interest was real. She liked the cloak and dagger stuff. Ruth didn't admonish her, so I suspected she was interested as well.

"Tom and Jerry are parked right outside," I said, "at least that's what Peter and I have named them. One is short and the other is a bean pole."

"I've never met an FBI agent," Betty continued.

"And were not starting now," Ruth injected. Betty liked to stir the pot.

"What kind of car are they driving?" Betty asked. Ruth rolled her eyes. Rebecca covered her smile with her hand.

"Black SUV. A Cherokee I think, " I answered. Betty rose and walked over to one of the front windows, ignoring the full table of customers she had to maneuver around. "What is she planning?" I asked Ruth.

"Heaven only knows," Ruth said, "she never grew up." Her lips curled, "one of the reasons I love her so." We watched as Betty spotted the car and then promptly left the tea room.

"My, she is in a mood," Rebecca commented.

"So...you and Peter," Ruth said, ignoring her partner's departure, "Rebecca was telling me that you two fancy each other." Ruth had a way of turning back the clock 100 years. Rebecca became extra attentive.

"He is my one," I replied to Ruth, "I am his," I directed to Rebecca. All kinds of happiness appeared on Rebecca's face. She reached for my hand and grasped it. Visions of what it would have been like growing up with my true mother appeared in my mind. The part of my life that was always missing became more pronounced, and yet less empty.

"I told you it was real," Rebecca said to Ruth, "I saw it in Peter's eyes at the cotillion. Have you ever seen him on the dance floor before?" She turned back to me, "you have his heart. That means you have mine as well."

"I don't know what to say," I admitted. My smile forcing it's way to the surface.

"Peter has needed someone for a long time," Ruth said, "Somehow, he lost track of what was important and put everything into his business. Too nice of a boy to marry a corporation."

"I'm afraid our relationship is damaging his business, " I added, "the military thinks I am a security risk." Rebecca patted my hand.

"Happiness first, work second," Rebecca said, then a sly smile formed, "and how do you feel about children." I felt my face flush. I hadn't gotten that far in my thought process. I always envisioned one or two. Two if at least one was like Aanya.

"We haven't gotten that far," I said, knowing that was a future conversation I needed to have with Peter.

"I'm not holding you to a decision," Rebecca said, "Just asking if you see yourself as a mother." I nodded yes, my face on fire. "Grandchildren!" Rebecca said a little too loud. She acted as if I was pregnant.

"I haven't talked with Peter about that," I whispered, "we haven't talked about the future past my trial."

"It's not leaving this table, dear," Rebecca assured me, "I'm just trying to imagine Peter as a father. It would change him...for the better."

"He would be a good one, " I smiled.

"The best," Ruth agreed and then her expression changed, "She didn't." We followed her eyes to the front door. Betty was leading Tom and Jerry toward our table. Rebecca chuckled at Ruth's surprised expression.

"May I present agents William Henderson and Frank Dolchee," Betty introduced first the short, then the tall agent.

"Ms. Tremaine," William said with a nod followed by Franks nod. Betty introduced Ruth and Rebecca and then asked the waiter to bring two more chairs and place sets to the table.

"I assured them that we would talk scandalously so they could take notes, " Betty said.

"I'm sorry you got stuck following me around," I said.

"It's our job, Ms. Tremaine," Frank said in an apologetic tone, "as we told Betty, we've become convinced it's a waste of time." Betty looked so proud of herself. Ruth was trying to decide to smile or scowl. Rebecca was truly amused.

"Ella, please," I said, "I hope I haven't made it too difficult."

"No Ma'am," William said, then his voice dropped to a whisper, "and that Calamari you and Mr. Charming sent out last night was delicious. Never thought I would like squid." I laughed. At least the entire FBI wasn't out to get me.

"Isn't this against the rules?" Rebecca asked.

"We're paying for our own lunch," Frank said, "so it is more of a violation of the flavor of the rules. Technically, we're still conducting surveillance." Ruth gave up and chuckled.

Betty spent lunch coaxing out FBI stories from Frank and William. It turns out the job is mostly boring with small bits of excitement mixed in. William had only pulled his gun out of its holster once. Frank once tasered a suspect but never unholstered his weapon. Most of their work was white collar crime, limited to people who would surrender to a badge. They had first thought I would be an exciting case, but that wore off quickly. My life wasn't as exciting as they had hoped.

After that lunch, I stopped driving through yellow lights. I was afraid my shadows would lose me or cause an accident trying to make the light. I had no desire to make their life more difficult than it was. Peter, on the other hand, thought the yellow lights were fun.

My court date was approaching quickly. The government had it on the fast track and I instructed my lawyers, against their advice, to not delay. I saw no need in delaying. I wanted it all to end as quickly as possible. I had a new life to build.

Peter was off at meetings, I assumed trying to repair the business I had damaged. I promised him a home cooked meal and I had decided to go gourmet. I was exiting an upscale fishery with a couple of fresh sablefish steaks. I heard my name called just as I approached my car. I turned and found Rayburn violating my comfort zone. It was then that I realized he had called me Cindy.

"Long time, girl," Rayburn said in his over confident tone.

"Hello, Raymond," I said. Mistake. Never acknowledge an idiot.

"I knew you would remember me," Rayburn said, his hand closing around my elbow with way too much familiarity.

"I wish I had time to talk," I lied, "I have to get this fish into the fridge before it spoils. It's good to see you again though." I maneuvered my elbow out of his grasp. I tried to open the car door, but he was too close. "Excuse me," I smiled.

"Maybe you should let the fish spoil," Rayburn said, his smile growing, "let me take you out to eat. We'll hit a club. If I remember, you owe me a dance." He moved closer. The strong scent of alcohol was on his breath.

"Please Rayburn," I said, trying to keep it light, "I need to get home. I promised Peter dinner." I figured that the mention of Peter would end the discussion. I was wrong.

"That stick in the mud," Rayburn continued, "he doesn't know how to treat women." He moved closer, pushing me against my car. I held the wrapped fish between us. A horribly flimsy shield. "I'll make you queen for the night. Rock your world."

"No!" I said loudly. I pushed him back. He was stronger than he looked and barely moved in inch. He laughed as if it were a game. His eyes were tinged in a drunken red.

"No always means yes," Rayburn chuckled.

"No means no," A deep voice said. Franks large hand closed on Rayburn's shoulder and pulled him away. William immediately put himself between Rayburn and me.

"Who the fuck are you two," Rayburn demanded. It looked like he was considering a fight.

"Agents Henderson and Dolchee," William said with authority, flashing his badge and exposing his side arm, "FBI." I smiled at my heroes.

"May I suggest a cab, Sir," Frank said, pulling Rayburn farther away from me. I heard Rayburn mumble something back as he allowed Frank to escort him down the street. I let out the breath I was holding.

"Thank you," I said to William.

"Finally, some excitement," William laughed. Frank joined a moment later with a proud smile.

"Mr. Funderland has decided to call it a day and head home," Frank said, "I hope he didn't ruin yours."

"He tried," I said, "but not with America's finest on duty. I don't know how I can thank you."

"It was kind of nice stopping a crime before it was committed," Frank said, "maybe you could stir up some more trouble to give us something else to do."

"I'll see what I can do," I laughed. Frank and William smiled, said goodbye and headed to their car. I watched them go, thankful that they were there. I wasn't sure how I would have handled a drunk

Rayburn if they weren't. I smiled to myself. Frank and William slid from the acquaintance to the friend category. I held back a chuckle as I realized I liked them following me.

"That bastard," Peter said when I told him about Rayburn.

"He was drunk," I calmed him, "I don't think it would have gone too far. Besides, I think Frank and William scared him pretty good."

"Tom and Jerry still downstairs?" Peter asked.

"They're on until 7:00, I think." Peter smiled and grabbed his phone. I laughed as he ordered the two a large pizza and drinks. I had no idea how many rules we were breaking, but friends took care of friends. Damn the rules.

~

My trial was a week away. I had almost fully moved in with Peter and his parents now considered me family. His father, Daniel, was a workaholic, but took plenty of time out to make sure I was welcome. He, like his wife, had little concern how I had met Peter. Peter was happy and that's all that seemed to matter. Which was good, since that is all that mattered to me.

I went home to gather more of my clothes. I have been moving them piecemeal into Peter's condo. He had given me an entire closet and half the dresser drawers. There was no ring, no ceremony, no license, but we were married in the heart. We started and ended each day with a kiss and shared the bathroom like we had been together our whole lives. More importantly, we could make each other laugh. We didn't even need words anymore. Something would strike my eyes as funny and a quick look at Peter would set him off as well. A wonderful connection I never wanted to see go away.

Agnus, unfortunately, was home. Her smile told me she would attempt to ruin my day. I tried to ignore it and moved quickly to my room, packing another box of clothes away.

"There are some discrepancies in Tremaine Marketings books," Agnus sang gleefully, "money is missing that is awfully close that the amounts the FBI was inquiring about." It felt as if a needle entered my heart. I continued packing while she leaned against the door frame obviously wanting to see my reaction. I did my best not to give her one.

"Embezzling is an awful, awful crime," Agnus continued, "I tried to make it clear to them that my daughter wouldn't have anything to do with that." There was a chuckle in her voice. I continued packing, praying she hadn't connected Raj to me.

"I told them that type of crime would get you fired," Agnus added, "and as no longer an employee of Tremaine Marketing, you would lose all rights to inherit the firm." I turned my head to her and cringed at her smile. "Those rights would fall to me as your father's next heir." I couldn't control my tongue.

"Bitch!" The company was my last tie to my father. It was his legacy and my duty to see that it remained strong. Why he ever put Agnus between me and that legacy was still lost on me.

"I'll take that as a guilty plea," Agnus laughed. Damn my mouth. She would delve deeper. If she uncovered Raj's complicity everything would unravel. I sped up my packing. I had to preempt Agnus. It would cost a large chunk of my inheritance, but I had Peter. He was worth more than a hundred companies. Sorry dad, I hope Agnus was worth it.

The weight of the defeat hit hard when I exited the house under Agnus' gleeful stare. I had wasted many years struggling to maintain my temper. Working impossible hours trying to outlast the bitch. It had been a waste. I tried to think of Peter and all I had gained. I needed his arms to quell the pain. He was in meetings again, so I wouldn't seem him until much later. The tears came while I waited at a red light. I had failed my father. It was his fault, but I failed nonetheless.

I pulled over into a big box store parking lot. Leaning my head on the steering wheel, I tried to slow my heart and stem the tears. I had cried too much over all that had happened. This was just something I had to let go of. The golddigger would be out of my life. I should be happy with that consolation prize. I was startled by a soft knock on my window. William was there, his face full of concern. I had forgotten my tail.

"I'm sorry, William," I said, after wiping my eyes. Frank was on the other side of the car, looking for some kind of threat I suspect, "I forgot you guys were there."

"You're not supposed to know," William chuckled. At least his humor made me feel better. I stepped out of the car when Frank came around.

"I just had some bad news is all," I said, talking to them like we were friends, "I screwed up a lot of things when I went to that dance."

"You seem happy enough with Mr. Charming," Frank injected.

"Yes, I do have him and wouldn't trade it for anything," I smiled, "It's just some of the costs are higher than I wished. I think I just lost my father's business."

"How's that?" William asked. I explained to them what I could, leaving Raj out of it. The will, embezzling my own money, and the probable cost of being so foolish.

"Agnus sounds like a Bitch," William commented.

"That's what I called her. Probably not a good thing to say given the circumstances." Frank laughed at my words. At least sharing my pain made me feel a little better. Sometimes you just need to put a voice to it and let some of it burn off. I laughed with him.

"Are you going to be all right?" Frank asked.

"I think so," I replied, "this is the second time I'm grateful to you guys." I surprised Frank by giving him a hug. I followed with William who hugged me back. I am sure I just violated a whole bunch of FBI rules. They could just tack it onto my sentence. At least the guys were smiling when they headed to their car and I was done with my self-admonishment. No point in second guessing if I can't have a do-over.

I called Brendan as soon as I got home. I hated leaving my lawyers in the dark, but I also didn't want them exposed to ethical dilemmas. I informed him where the money for the cotillion ticket, limo and hair-dresser came from. He seemed to take it in stride, asking some probing questions to clarify issues. He was most interested in the dollar amounts and the provisions of the trust my father had saddled me with. I clarified what I could and he promised me everything would be alright. I was surprised when I found out that I wouldn't be taking the stand. "Some rights are best exercised," Brendan insisted. The Charmings trusted him, so did I.

Peter and I had been slowly switching our internal clocks. Since I didn't have my night work, he began working during the day and spent evenings with me like non-vampires. His abundance of meetings made me feel guilty. I was sure I had greatly wounded his business and healing it was taking an enormous amount of time. He assured me I hadn't done anything he couldn't handle. Every night, he would erase my doubts with love. I always found them again when he left the next morning.

The night before my trial was especially tense. I had spent the day feeling I had lost control of my life. Rebecca had called to say that she and Daniel would be in court for support. I was glad of the diversion her call gave me. Too much time to think is not good for the condemned. Peter had cleared his afternoon so he could spend it with me. He sensed my apprehension when he left that morning. I had to practically shove him out the door. I knew he had an important meeting first thing. I placated myself by playing a house-wife. I cleaned and made a salad for lunch. I hated being a housewife.

I was busy cutting carrots when I felt a kiss on the back of my neck. Peter had snuck in and was rather pleased with his stealth. I turned into him and all the bad things in the world drained away. In each other's arms, we were unstoppable.

"Whatever happens tomorrow, know that I love you," I whispered once my lips had tasted him.

"And I you, no matter what happens tomorrow, or the next day, or the one after that," Peter added.

"So, I am screwed next week," I joked. We could always turn silly words into laughter. Peter lifted me off the floor with a deep hug, then reached past me to grab a piece of carrot.

"You were screwed the moment I met you," Peter said, throwing the carrot in his mouth, "now you're stuck with me." I kissed him, not caring that he was munching on the carrot. He reached for another piece and I slapped his hand playfully.

"Wait," I said, "let me put some in the salad." He laughed, backed away and held up the piece I thought I had stopped him from taking. "Salad," I demanded, pointing at the bowl full of salad. His eyebrows bounced and tossed the carrot into his mouth. Men! I dropped the knife on the counter and tackled him.

Peter let me win the brief wrestling match. I liked being on top, in control. Weeks of bowing to things out of my control and now I had the man I loved beneath me. He reached up slowly, some attempt to bring me closer. I took his wrist and pushed it back to his side. I lowered my head, my smile meeting his, and gave him my love. I felt his resistance fade, muscles relaxing. I broke the kiss and began unbuttoning his shirt.

"I am yours," Peter smiled. I tried not to laugh at the small speck of carrot in his teeth. I kissed the carrot away while I went to work on his buttons. Peter sensed my desire and allowed me to control our love. My lips found his secrets as he had found mine. It was the first time he had given up everything. We had shared often, but this time it was me giving pleasure and expecting nothing in return except tacit obedience. For a short while, I was the most powerful person in the room. Peter had given me his strength and I needed it more than he knew.

"I need to come home early more often," Peter whispered. I could feel his heart slowing as I lay on his chest.

"I don't want to be just a housewife," I said. I wanted Peter, but I also wanted something of my own. It was as good a time as any to clear things up, now that I had some strength back. I could feel Peter holding back a chuckle. I looked up, thinking he found my statement funny.

"You don't need my permission," Peter said, "though...if I disagree...does that mean I have a chance of getting tackled again?" The little boy whimsy in his eyes made me laugh. I slapped his shoulder and he feigned pain making me laugh harder.

"I just wanted you to know. I'm not sure how you see our future."

"I want you," Peter said, rolling me to my side, "I can hire a maid."

"I don't want to disappoint you. I have no idea what you're expecting and..."

"You," Peter repeated, his hand lovingly caressing my neck, "I am expecting you and no one else. I have the same worries, but every time I kiss you, they fade away. So I figured, I just need to keep kissing you." I loved when he was like this. Playful and meaningful at the same time. He was correct, kissing solved a lot of issues.

~

$\mathcal{W}$alking into the courtroom was surreal. I had seen it on TV and been on a few tours in grade school. The one time I had been selected for jury duty, I was never called to serve. As a defendant, it was an imposing room. I walked in with my lawyers, hopefully presenting an imposing sight myself. I refused to look meek. If they were going to take me down, then it would be with a straight back and a proud face. Enough with the self-pity. I would take my lumps, solve the problem and continue the next chapter of my life. The chapter entitled 'Peter.'

I was surprised to see Jaq and Gus seated in one of the rows. The FBI must have been busy tracking down all my transgressions. Gus waved with a flirty look in his eyes. Jaq smiled. I felt bad for them being dragged to my trial. The thought that their pay might be retracted as stolen funds sent a chill through me. That would have to be rectified. Another debt.

My fears were confirmed when I saw Daphne and Beatrice in another row. I tried to give them an apologetic expression. It probably came off as stupid mixed with insanity. They didn't shy away and gave me friendly smiles.

Rebecca and Daniel were all smiles. They had an aura of confidence I didn't share. Ruth and Betty sat next to them. Ruth with a polite nod and Betty with a thumbs up.

Right behind what I suspected was the prosecutor was Agnus. She was smiling ear to ear. It was the most unfriendly thing I had ever seen. I had a brief unhealthy desire to claw it off her face. Thankfully, I buried the thought with the idea that this might be the last time I ever see her. She would get what she wanted and I would have Peter and a new life.

My lawyers and I sat at a large wooden table that mirrored the prosecutor's table on the other side of the room. I took a deep breath and straightened in my chair. Brendan conferred quietly with Mary, another of my counsel, and she passed down a set of papers. Brendan looked at them a moment then pushed them down the table to me.

"We took the liberty of handling your taxes this year," Brendan whispered, "if you could sign these, it will help in your defense." I looked down at the stack a papers in front of me. I usually only had a couple of sheets when I did my taxes. This was at least twenty pages of IRS forms. There were two sign-here stickers poking out the right side. Brendan smiled and I felt his confidence. I shrugged my shoulders and signed. Mary stood, gathered the document and headed out to make copies. At least my taxes were done. One headache not to worry about.

We stood when the judge arrived. Judge Manfred was black-gowned with a round face and gray beard that reminded me of a well trimmed Santa Claus. He didn't smile like Santa when the charges were read. In fact, it looked like humor was foreign to him. I sat back down and listened to a slew of perfunctory statements on both sides. The trial began in earnest with the first witness.

The first witness was Peter. I cringed when his name was called. I should have expected it since it was his team that first recognized the breach. He smiled to me as he walked from behind me. I hadn't seen him walk in. I lost track of him when my lawyers briefed me on what to expect.

Peter took the witness stand. He looked adorable. I scrunched my eyes, trying to separate the naked Peter from the one in the chair. I couldn't, so I smiled at him. I received a loving smile in return. The prosecutor was staring at me with an expression that didn't contain any love. I guess I was compromising his witness. Peter winked at me and then became serious, stating his name and promising to tell the truth.

"On the night of..." The prosecutor began, describing the events that were undisputed fact before he hit on a question. "did you identify a breach of the Shark firewall?"

"Yes," Peter said and didn't elaborate. I knew he wouldn't lie, but he had no intention of helping the man. I liked Peter in his suit. When he wasn't smiling at me, he was the picture of authority and strength. His power weakened greatly when he smiled. He became approachable. I looked over to the jury. I had a flash of jealousy when I saw the eyes of the four women jurors. They were fixed on Peter. My Peter. I had to look away. They were supposed to be looking at him. I straightened my back and returned my mind to the proceedings.

"How did you identify the incursion?" The prosecutor's question was followed by a long list of technical procedures that would have bored Bill Gates. I could see the jurors eyes glaze over as Peter used acronyms and long-winded techno jargon with abandon. Twice the prosecutor tried to interrupt, but Peter wasn't having it. By the time he was done, we all realized that he was highly skilled and we had no idea how he identified the incursion.

"How would you categorize this assault?" the prosecutor asked.

"I'm not sure I understand the question," Peter responded. He was so cute when he played dumb. Somehow he could change his eyes from intense to innocent in a heartbeat.

"Amateur, skilled, highly skilled?" the prosecutor clarified.

"It was the most sophisticated attack I have ever seen," Peter said. He was looking near the prosecutor's table when he said it, almost as if he was answering the question for someone else. I turned my head and glanced toward the table. There was an older man in a blue air force uniform with a star on the color. General Rickers, I assumed.

"In your opinion, would the development of this attack take the resources of a government to design and execute?" The question was followed by a series of objections that were overruled by the judge who followed up with instructions to the jury that Peter's response would be an opinion of an expert and not necessarily fact.

"No." Peter's answer took the prosecutor by surprise. He looked down at this notes, then back at his table where his assistant shrugged his shoulder.

"We have depositions that state you have claimed that only a foreign government had the capability to develop such an attack."

"Yes," Peter said calmly, "I know longer feel that is the case. I was rather...upset when I made those assumptions."

"So, you want this court to believe that an individual has developed, in your words, the most sophisticated attack you have ever seen?"

"As his honor has stated, it is only my opinion," Peter said. Again, he was speaking to Rickers. The prosecutor walked back to his desk and conferred with his assistant for a moment. Rickers leaned into the conversation. Then a third joined, Agent Stratford. I felt my bladder contract. The judge called the prosecutor back to the questioning after a moment.

"What is your relationship with the defendant?" Peter considered the question then looked directly at me.

"I intend to ask her to be my wife when this is over." I heard Rebecca audibly gasp at Peter's response. My heart nearly burst.

"Yes," I answered the unasked question. I wasn't thinking about where I was when it came out. All I saw was Peter looking at me. All I saw was love. The pounding of the gavel and the commotion of the courtroom was lost on us. The rest of the world could fall into a bottomless pit for all I cared.

"Order!" The judge yelled again. This time, I heard the gavel but ignored it. I smiled at my love and nearly melted when he smiled back. It took awhile to bring the courtroom under control as Peter and I continued to absorb each other with our eyes.

"Mr. Charming!" the prosecutor said for the second time. Peter turned away from me and looked questionably at the prosecutor. I couldn't hide my smile and didn't really care who saw it.

"Has your testimony been comprised by your relationship with the defendant?"

"Comprised? No," Peter responded, "though I am sure it has been tainted. Have you ever been in love?" The court broke out in laughter. More gavel pounding and the judge looking less and less like Santa all the time.

"Mr. Charming," the judge instructed, "you are here to answer questions, not ask them."

"Yes, your honor."

"Could your assessment of the capability of the attacker of your firewall be tainted by your relationship with the defendant?"

"Absolutely not," Peter said, "My firewall, and, therefore, the armed force's networks, are completely exposed to the talents of a single individual." General Rickers stood quickly and leaned down to the assistant prosecutor who immediately waved the prosecutor over. The judge rolled his eyes and slammed his gavel down.

"This court does not have tolerance for interference, even by the military," the judge decreed.

"Your honor, may I approach the bench?" the prosecutor asked.

BRENDAN JOINED THE PROSECUTOR AT THE BENCH

"Lead counsel only." Brendan joined the prosecutor at the bench. There was a bunch of whisperings that seemed more spirited than it should be. I looked over at Peter. Our eyes met and I mouthed 'yes' again. His smile was so wonderful. I didn't need him on his knee. I just needed him.

"There will be a thirty-minute recess while counsel confers in chambers," the judge announced with a tone that sounded less than pleased. Lead counsel and the judge headed through a door behind the bench. The jury was led out by the sergeant at arms.

A soft hand found my shoulder. I turned to see Rebecca, happy tears in her eyes, leaning over the waist high divider.

"Welcome to the family," Rebecca said. I rose and we hugged. I promised myself I wouldn't break down again. I failed.

"Sorry," Peter said from behind me, "I didn't want to commit perjury." I was in his arms before his words were finished.

"Yes," I said again.

"I haven't asked yet."

"Yes," I repeated. I was sure there were rules about the defendant kissing the witness, but there was no one to tell me what they were. More importantly, there was no one stopping me. Whatever happened, Peter was in my arms. Nothing else mattered. I barely heard the clerk call General Rickers into chambers.

"I was planning something more romantic," Peter whispered, "I hope you aren't disappointed."

"I only need you," I whispered back, "we make our own romance."

"Peter Charming!" the clerk called. Peter smiled at me as if he knew the summons was coming.

"They will call you next," Peter told me, "I am throwing a hail mary. Do you trust me?"

"Until I die," I answered. Peter's smile grew as he separated from me and headed to chambers.

I waited for ten minutes. None of the other lawyers could guess what was going on. It was rare when nonlawyers were called into chambers.

"Ella Tremaine." I followed the clerk into the chambers.

"She needs to be under oath," the prosecutor said as I enter the room.

"Cut the crap, Larkin," the judge said, "we are way past formality now." He looked at me and waited for the door to close. "We have reached a point where national security tramples on civil proceedings. I have been informed that you know of an individual who has the capability to compromise the Shark firewall," the judge looked toward General Rickers, "and therefore, the nation's security networks." I looked at Peter and he gave me a small nod. Raj's family was wrapped in the answer I was about to give. I almost lied, but Peter asked for trust.

"Yes," I said as I prayed inside. The judge nodded and then looked at Rickers.

"Given immunity, would this individual be willing to work for Mr. Charming?" Rickers asked.

"Yes," I answered, "and he would only require one thing." My hands were shaking.

"What would that be?" Rickers asked. My next statement was a blind leap of faith. The request would practically paint a target on Raj. I looked at Peter. He smiled and nodded.

"More than anything, he and his family want to be citizens of the United States," I replied. My heart was beating so hard, I was surprised no one else heard it.

"Is he that good?" Rickers asked Peter.

"Ingenious. He thinks way out of the box," Peter replied.

"A foreigner?" Rickers stated more than asked, "I wish I could be certain of his intentions." I closed my eyes, took a deep breath, and leaped.

"The phone from that night has messages from him," I said quietly, hoping I hadn't just signed Raj's family's deportation order, "you can hear it in his voice and read it in his words. He had no intention of attacking America. He and his family love it as much as you and I."

"Where's the phone?" Ricker's asked.

"We were going to submit it as evidence," Larkin answered, "It's on the table, but it's encrypted and NSA hasn't been able to break into it yet."

"I know the password," I admitted. There, I just hung Raj out completely. I was about to hand the prosecution everything.

"Can I see the phone?" Rickers asked. He looked at me and I saw some compassion in his eyes. He was beginning to see what it was costing me. Maybe this was just a dance.

Larkin looked desperately at the judge. He didn't want to give up a piece of physical evidence, especially when I just stated I knew the password.

"Produce the phone," the judge ruled. I could see he didn't like the interference nor the extra time this was taking. Larkin left and shortly returned with the phone in a plastic bag. The judge nodded as Rickers removed the phone from the plastic.

"Password?" Rickers asked. My face went red.

"I can type it in," I said, moving forward.

"No," Larkin jumped in, "if this isn't what you say, I don't want the phone tampered with."

"The password, Ms. Tremaine," the judge said, agreeing with Larkin. I looked at the five men in the room and thought I would die.

"Can I whisper it?" I begged Rickers. The curious looks I got made it all worse. Rickers looked to the judge.

"Yes," the judge said. I was blushing horrible when I leaned toward Rickers' ear. I couldn't believe I had to do this. I should have chosen a different password.

"Peter likes my breasts," I whispered so only Rickers would hear it, "no spaces." Rickers eyes shot to Peter and he struggled to keep the corner of his lips down. "It was from before," I defended the password, "the flat tire, before I knew Peter was Peter Charming." Rickers lips were straining as he typed in the code. The phone let him in and he looked back at me. He knew then, before he even read the texts, it was only a dance.

We watched as Rickers scrolled through the texts. He fired off one of the voicemails and held it to his ear. The humor in his eyes grew as he listened to another. Raj confessing to missing the logs and begging my forgiveness, praying that his stupidity didn't get me in trouble.

"You say the NSA couldn't break this man's encryption?" Rickers asked Larkin. Larkin shook his head no. Rickers smiled at me.

"It really was just a dance," Rickers stated. I nodded my head. "This phone and its encryption are also considered a national security issue." Rickers told the judge. The judge nodded.

"So, you'll get him and his family citizenship?" I asked desperately.

"Done," Rickers told me, "Charming will handle the logistics. Nothing of this leaves this room." He directed the last statement to the prosecutor.

"The wire fraud still exists," Larkin said. The judge looked at me.

"Legally, that is correct," the judge said to me, "if it is determined you are a participant of the fraud, you will not be able to bring up the aforementioned individual. You will stand alone." He looked at the prosecutor, "you will have to refrain from any mention of a third party."

"I agree," I said with a smile. Raj was out of it and his family was safe. Espionage was off the table.

"You don't have a choice," the judge said. I saw his lips curl for the briefest moment. Maybe he did have a little Santa in him.

I left the chamber floating on a cloud. Though I wasn't wearing a ring, I was engaged to the only person in the world who I truly loved, Raj and his family were safe, and I was only on trial for wire fraud. What a wonderful turn of events.

The trial began again with the judge instructing the court to ignore all references to the Shark firewall and the skill level of the person or persons who comprised the network or networks. I watched the jurors eyes glaze over again. Peter was once again seated in the witness chair and the prosecutor continued his *q*uestioning.

"Were you responsible for the children's hospital charity cotillion website?"

"Yes."

"Were your systems the target of fraudulent activity prior to the cotillion?"

"No." Peter held a straight face. The prosecutor's face was starting to look a little flush.

"No one compromised your system?" the prosecutor asked.

"I believe someone did find what you would call a backdoor into to the network." Peter clarified.

"So, fraud was perpetrated," the prosecutor said exasperatedly.

"No."

"Either they broke in or they didn't, Which is it Mr. Charming?"

"Someone definitely entered the network in an unexpected way," Peter answered with a straight face.

"You do not consider that fraud?"

"No. No data was taken, altered or deleted. A ticket was inserted into the database and the charity received the prescribed payment for that ticket." Peter let a small chuckle, "I'm not sure why they just didn't use the standard web interface. The results would have been the same." he paused for a moment then added, "I saw no fraud, just an unorthodox transaction."

"What was the price of that ticket?"

"$5,000."

"No more questions," the prosecutor spat as he returned to his table. A hushed conference between his assistant and the Agent Stratford.

"Cross-exam?" the judge asked.

"No *q*uestions at this time," Brendan announced. Peter was excused. We shared a smile as he moved to a seat directly behind me. I liked having him close.

A representative for Coupon Crave was called next. He was unaware of any unauthorized intrusions to his company's network. He was most adamant that everyone in the courtroom knew that they take enormous care of their customers data. I had to smile at Raj's skill.

Ja*q* and Beatrice were called in turn. They were both adamant that they had received full payment from Coupon Crave and controlled no networks. They were both asked the price of their services to me. I smelled a trap in the dollar amounts. I conferred *q*uietly with Brendan who just nodded and said it will be alright.

Agnus was called to the stand next. She didn't even try to hide her pleased smile.

"You heard the previous testimony of the purchases made and received by Ella Tremaine?" the prosecutor asked.

"Yes I did," Agnus answered. She looked at me as she answered. She was enjoying this.

"Are those dollar amounts familiar?" the prosecutor prodded.

"Yes, they are," Agnus announced, "they are the exact amounts missing from a company account." The prosecutor walked over to his table and grabbed a set of papers.

"Here is the independently audited transaction log for the account mentioned. I would like to submit it as exhibit A." There were no objections, which surprised me, and it was placed in evidence.

"Did you authorize a disbursement of those amounts?"

"No, I did not."

"Did any other authorized person disburse those amounts?"

"No," Agnus replied. Her grin was growing.

"What do you think happened to those funds?" the prosecutor

asked. Brendan stopped one of my other lawyers from objecting. He seemed comfortable with the line of *q*uestioning. I wasn't.

"I think it was stolen by Ella Tremaine," Agnus said. The words came from her mouth like music. Her happiness was apparent to everyone in the room. She was rattling my nerves.

"No more *q*uestions."

"Cross-exam?" the judge asked. Brendan rose confidently and moved toward Agnus.

"Mrs. Tremaine, what is your relationship to Ella Tremaine?"

"I am her stepmother."

"What is your legal relationship with Ella Tremaine?"

"I am the executor of her father's will," Agnus said confidently, "the trustee of the assets until Ella is 32."

"What assets would those be?"

"Tremaine Marketing, Inc, a few bank accounts, a house and some stock holdings," Agnus said, her confidence wavering. Brendan nodded.

"Did Ella Tremaine mention the cotillion prior to the event?"

"I'm not sure?" Agnus lied.

"We could call your daughters to the stand to help your memory," Brendan said.

"Oh yes, I do remember having a discussion pertaining to the event."

"Did Ella Tremaine express interest in going to the cotillion?"

"I'm not sure I remember," Agnus lied again. At least her smile had disappeared. I liked nervous Agnus.

"Again, would your daughter's memory be more complete?"

"Yes, now I remember. She did express interest." I think I saw sweat on her forehead.

"What was your answer to that re*q*uest?"

"I...I believe I didn't think it prudent," Agnus stuttered.

"Who from Tremaine Marketing did go to the cotillion?"

"If memory serves, Anastasia and Drizella, and myself, " Agnus said slowly.

"Who are they?"

"Sales representatives for Tremaine Marketing."

"What is their relationship to Ella Tremaine?"

"Stepsisters," Agnus said after an uncomfortable pause.

"So, to summarize, you disallowed Ella to use her own company's money to attend the cotillion because you thought it not prudent." Brendan paused for a moment, rubbing his chin as if he was trying to understand, "but you thought it prudent to use Ella's company money to send your daughters to the same cotillion."

"It was a business decision," Agnus justified, "my daughters were representing the firm."

"You sent two sales representatives instead of an owner?"

"Ella doesn't own Tremaine Marketing until she is 32," Angus countered.

"No, I believe the law would disagree with you. You are the trustee, not the temporary owner. You have a fiduciary responsibility to represent Ella Tremaine as if she was 32."

"She can't just take money," Agnus argued.

"The amount is immaterial to the total worth of the company. More of a mistaken withdraw than a theft. She has declared it on her taxes as dispersed earnings." Brendan walked over to our table and grabbed a copy of the tax form I had just signed. "A minor disbursement from her own company declared legally to the IRS. I do believe the error lies with your fiduciary responsibility, not with such a small disbursement she is entitled to anyway." Agnus was visibly perturbed.

"I would like to note that my own compensation had to be paid by a third party," Brendan continued, "since Ella Tremaine's trustee refused to release funds for Ella's defense."

"I am failing to see a crime here," the judge said, "I am beginning to see a breach of trust that precipitated the events. Larkin is there any evidence that the money in question was not ultimately Ella Tremaine's? Are there any victims beside Ella Tremaine."

The prosecutor was in a conference with Agent Stratford and his assistant.

"Larkin?" the judge repeated himself.

"There may be," the prosecutor stated, "the funds in question resided in a US bank. Depending upon how those funds were accessed, it could very well represent a crime." The judge rolled his eyes.

"Agnus Tremaine, you are excused," the judge said, "I would recommend you find legal counsel of your own. I doubt your decisions as executor will stand up to legal scrutiny."

"There will be a two-hour recess," the judge continued, "after which the prosecution will have to convince me there is a reason to continue this trial." The gavel came down and the judge left *q*uickly.

I turned to Peter and found him gone. Rebecca shrugged her shoulders and pointed at the door. I walked out to the hall and didn't seem him. I couldn't believe he left me. He just sort of asked me to marry him and he disappears. I wanted my sort-of fiancee.

Peter came up the stairs, a smile across his face. I jumped into his arms and tasted his wonderful lips.

"Where did you go?" I asked.

"Picking up some leverage," Peter answered cryptically.

"I already said yes. What do you need leverage for?" I joked.

"Not for you. For her," Peter said, pointing at agent Stratford. He split away from me and went directly to Stratford and directed her to the side, away from others. He pulled out his phone and showed her something that made her face lose its color. They had a brief heated conversation that never rose above a whisper though the faces said they were yelling. After a moment, Peter came back smiling.

"Looks like it will end now," Peter said. I wrapped him in my arms.

"And why is that?"

"Someone, protected by immunity, happened to locate some security camera footage on FBI servers that was not supposed to exist," Peter said.

"Oh god," I said, "Raj didn't see it, did he?" Peter pulled me close.

"He loves you," Peter soothed, "not as much as me, but enough to forget."

"You saw it?"

"Yes."

"It's embarrassing," I admitted shyly. Peter's hand caressed the side of my face, his eyes caressing my soul.

"Nothing is embarrassing between us," Peter said before he kissed me. It was still embarrassing, but I could ignore it.

Peter's parents took us out to lunch. Rebecca scolded Peter for announcing a pending proposal without the proper romantic setup, especially a ring. I assured her, I was more than willing to wait. I started that morning believing there was a good chance I would have to spend some time in prison. Now, it was looking like I might get away with a slap on the wrist and gain a husband to boot.

Daniel rolled his eyes as Rebecca and I started preliminary talk on wedding arrangements. I had no desire for Agnus to participate, so that left me with only one woman to lean on. I knew Peter would just nod his head and say yes to everything, Rebecca on the other hand, had the style and the desire to make it wonderful. I didn't want a big wedding, but I did want it wonderful.

"What do you think about a garden wedding, Peter?" Rebecca asked. I had already agreed that it sounded wonderful.

"That sounds like a good idea," Peter said, nodding his head. True to form. He turned back to the discussion he was having with his father.

"What about using The Fountains, Peter? Somewhere along the walking trail." Rebecca pushed. I smiled, expecting acquiescence followed by a nod. He seemed deeply entrenched into the conversation with his father.

"Yes," Peter agreed, turning to his mother, "but it has to be by that small fountain. The one with the little cement ducks." He returned to his father.

"But there are better spots on the grounds," Rebecca countered, "like the corner with willow trees or the tiered flower beds." Peter turned to me.

"'I believe we shared our first kiss by the ducks," Peter said. I smiled at the look in his eyes. There was all the romance I needed right there.

"By the ducks," I agreed.

"Oh," Rebecca said, her smile mirroring ours, "then it must be by the ducks." Daniel chuckled at his wife's quick change of heart.

"Why don't you wait until it's official, Rebecca," Daniel said, "the girl doesn't even have her ring yet." That comment was followed by a brief discussion on the idiocy of men. I half-heartedly sided with Rebecca. Peter, of course, was the exception to the rule.

~

*J*udge Manfred looked less than pleased at the prosecutor. Agent Stratford and Larkin were in a heated discussion. Another man in a suit, next to Stratford, seemed to be supporting her argument.

"You have had sufficient time, counselor," the judge growled, "I do not appreciate you wasting the court's time as well." Larkin turned, his face poorly masking his anger.

"At this time, your honor," Larkin's words seemed to struggle out of his mouth, "we lack sufficient evidence to proceed with prosecution." Both Stratford and the man next to her sat down, staring straight ahead. Agnus, sitting behind them, looked pale. I was feeling much better.

"I would like to make a motion to dismiss," Brendan said quickly as he stood. My legs felt all jittery as the excitement began to creep up my spine.

"Does the prosecution take issue with that?" the Judge asked.

"No your honor," Larkin said quietly.

"Case dismissed!" the judge announced and slammed his gavel down. A smile appeared on his face as he looked at me. I smiled back at Santa. "I am a Justice of the Peace," he continued, looking at me, "if you are ever in need." He winked and headed off to his chambers.

Peter wrapped me in his arms before I could turn around. The world disappeared as we kissed. I had to force him away so I could thank my lawyers. Each getting a hug and my gratitude. Peter followed with handshakes and his gratitude. I was free.

Rebecca and Daniel joined us in the hall outside of the courtroom. More hugging and shared joy. I saw William and Frank coming toward me, smiles on their faces.

"Peter, this is William and Frank," I said, "our Tom and Jerry." Frank laughed as Peter shook his hand and then moved to William.

"Helping Ella with Rayburn," Peter said, shaking his head, "I owe you guys for that."

"Forget it," William returned, "it broke up an otherwise dull day."

I mouthed 'I'll tell you later' to Rebecca who looked fairly confused over the conversation.

"So, you two are getting married?" Frank asked, his finger moving between Peter and I.

"Yes," I replied happily, pulling Peter next to me, "It kind of made this all worthwhile." I saw Frank look past me. I followed his eyes and saw Agnus leaving the courtroom. Frank traded a look with William and nodded his head toward Agnus. William moved quickly.

"We have an early wedding present for you," Frank smiled and quickly followed William. They approached Agnus with badges out.

"Agnus Tremaine," William announced loudly, "you're under arrest for fraud and conspiracy to commit the same." I covered my mouth as Agnus made a move to run away. In heels, she was no match for Frank.

"What's going on?" Peter asked me.

"I have no idea," I admitted. Agnus was handcuffed, her mouth spilling vulgarities at Frank and William. I had never heard her completely lose it before. She was never the image of purity, but now she sounded like a drunken street walker. Frank sat her down on a bench and began reading her her rights. She was shaking her head, demanding to be let go. William just smiled and walked back over to us.

"White collar crime is our beat," William said proudly.

"What just happened?" I asked.

"After what you told us about Agnus, Frank did a little investigating," William reported, pointing at Frank, "we are quite familiar with her lawyer." William put air quotes around the word 'lawyer.' "A little bit of questioning, some deal making and he sang like a bird."

"What did she do?" Peter asked.

"Why, altered your father's will to suit her needs," William said, looking at me. My father didn't screw me. That bitch did.

"Oh, my!" Rebecca said. Peter pulled me close, allowing me to

borrow his strength. Wonderful thoughts of my father not intention-
ally leaving me to that woman began to be replaced by an anger. The
things I began to think were awful and the handcuffs on Agnus made
them seem doable. I looked up at Peter and he squeezed me in his
arms. The anger dissipated and a smile formed. I took Peter by the
hand and marched over to Agnus. Frank, thinking the worst, stepped
in front of Agnus to protect his prisoner. I smiled at him and he
relaxed.

"Thank you, Agnus," I said sweetly, as if I was talking to someone I
cared about, "without you, I would have never found Peter." I watched
her fume on the bench, looking everywhere but at me.

"Whiney bitch," Angus whispered to the wall.

"By the way," I said clearly, "you're fired." It was my company now
and I didn't have to wait seven more years.

"I don't think we should invite her to the wedding," Peter said. I
laughed.

"Frank, I hope you and William will come," I added.

"We wouldn't miss it," Frank replied, "you think you'll have more of
that calamari there?" Peter laughed.

≈

The wedding was a beautiful thing. Rebecca had pulled out
all the stops. Everyone I loved was there, including three
new US citizens. Kiran was my maid of honor and Aanya beside her.
George stood for Peter, which had surprised me. I didn't know they
were such good friends, though the idea of seeing George in the future
pleased me. He had such a wonderful happiness about him. Raj stood
in for my father and walked me down the aisle, or a walking path in
our case. Judge Manfred was true to his word and presided happily.

Rebecca cried throughout the whole ceremony. I, for once, did not.
I knew what I wanted and it was called Peter. There was nothing
standing in the way anymore. When I said 'I do' it was clear and I
made sure everyone heard it. Peter didn't stop smiling through the
whole proceeding, almost as if he had a secret. I found it delightfully
charming.

The Fountains was decked out for the reception. Food was in abundance, including a tray filled with calamari. Daniel contributed by locating the FBI logo and affixing to the side of the tray. The smiles it brought to Frank and William was worth Rebecca's scorn for having something out of place.

"So, I understand Tremaine Marketing was officially transferred to you yesterday," George mentioned as we gathered at the head table. I took Peter's hand in mine. I really liked being married.

Walking into the special board meeting, yesterday, seemed like a dream. The board members congratulating me, then looking shocked when I began to list the changes that were to occur. I shifted funds to the east coast where sales had been dropping off, enacted bonus adjustments that reflect actual profit gains, not status quo, and informed them of the need to replace Raj. They expected a girl and found a strong woman instead. It was exhilarating.

"Signed and sealed," I replied, "exactly how my dad wanted it." I looked at Peter, "he really would have liked you." Peter leaned in for a kiss. One of many that day. I saw George jerk suddenly and sit up straighter.

"Ahem...how will you balance work with a family?" George asked. It sounded foreign coming out of his mouth. Rebecca was sitting next to him, looking away with feigned indifference. I smiled knowing that George was Rebecca's patsy. It was Peter who answered.

"We've decided against children," Peter said as serious as possible, "they cry too much and there aren't enough qualified babysitters." I kicked him under the table for teasing his mother.

"I could babysit," Rebecca said in a panic before she realized that Peter was teasing her. The idea of a grandchild was plastered all over her face. I rose and walked over while Peter laughed.

"We think two is a good number," I whispered in Rebecca's ear. Peter and I had already had the conversation.

"Oh!" Rebecca said, her smile spanning the room. It was for her ears only and she kept it there. I sat back down, sharing a few more smiles with my mother in-law. She was now as happy as I was. Peter gave me another kiss, which I returned more passionately than I should in public.

After dinner, the band started warming up. Rebecca had mentioned that she wanted to see Peter dance again, and for once, he would be required. I didn't care that he lacked agility and grace. It would be our first dance as a married couple. His awkwardness would probably make it our last dance together, which was something I could live with. At least I would have tonight.

Peter rose when they called us out. He took my hand confidently with a smile and led me to the floor. I knew how difficult that was for him. That he went willing, spoke well of his love. I followed him, mirroring his smile. Preparing to compensate for his lack of skill. I suspected I would have to lead.

"I have a confession to make," Peter whispered, once we were on the floor.

"Yes?"

"Those meetings I have had to attend lately weren't really meetings," Peter sighed, "I have been secretly seeing a lot of George lately and we've gotten pretty close." Stupid thoughts ran through my head as Peter took my lead hand in his and placed his other on around my waist.

"What?" I asked, trying to understand. I tried to shake off the stupid thoughts. Peter smiled.

"He's taught me to dance, my love," Peter said, humor and love in his eyes. The music started and he stepped off, leading me with a grace I didn't know he possessed. He danced like a prince.

DIRTY EROTICA SHORT STORIES

EXPLICIT SHORT STORIES FOR ADULTS
INCLUDING FORBIDDEN FILTHY TALKS

I WAS SWEATING AGAIN

I was sweating again. I closed my eyes and tried to calm my thudding heart. I saw her there, in my mind. The light brown hair cropped short and barely covering her ears. I remembered every detail, how her hazel eyes crinkled when she smiled, the way the left side of her lips curled more than her right when she laughed. The look on her face when we made love, her soft, sensitive neck. I could still see the few freckles that lay speckled across the bridge of her nose. All of that was still mine, but I knew it wouldn't last. Holding on to her image for two weeks had been a miracle. I just had one last promise to keep.

I was jostled by the nervous girl sitting next to me. She was littered with piercings proclaiming her to be a courageous rebel; her jitters spoke of the same fear I felt. They had packed us in like sardines on little plastic chairs that looked like they belonged in some school lunch room. Most of us would leave disappointed and I prayed I was one them. I had only promised to show up -- I hadn't promised to succeed.

Most of the contestants were younger than I. I closed my eyes again, to shut out their youthful anxiety. I took a few deep breaths, and brought the image of Amber back into my mind. It was still so easy to see her. I knew my memory, such a weak tool, would begin to fail. I had pictures, but they weren't the flowing 3-D I could call up in my psyche. Still so beautiful and perfect.

I heard the door open and hoped it wasn't for me. "Sandy Riggers?" I opened my eyes as the smartly-dressed woman wearing a headset called out the name. A bouncing blonde three rows away jumped up excitedly. I was just as excited for her. I had been here for over half a day and knew the auditions had to be coming to a close. It was a long shot to be chosen and I had never won a lottery. I had my bad luck going in my favor. I closed my eyes again and spent more time with the memory of Amber, my wife.

"Ken Fischer?" The lady had returned, and blessedly called out a name which was not mine. I didn't open my eyes this time as Ken gave a quick cheer, and I heard him head quickly to the door. I wished it would end. I was hoping he was the last, but no one dismissed us. I tried to breathe slowly. My pulse was still racing and I needed it to slow down. One way or another, this little bit of personal hell would be over soon. It was getting too late for it to continue much longer.

"Last one," the woman called, when she returned fifteen minutes later. I could feel the emotions shift as one in the room. The silence was deafening. I closed my eyes again and saw Amber's smile. Her face shifted slowly to a look I knew all too well. The mischievous one, the expression that lovingly told me I had no choice in the matter. My heart plummeted to my stomach and I knew the next words before they were spoken. "David Thaxton?" The groans were loud as hopes were dashed, mine included. My hands were shaking as I opened my eyes, armed only with a promise. I stood slowly, trying to stall as fear mixed with my sorrow.

"God, you're lucky, man!" the pin-cushioned girl said as I stood. I looked at her, sweat forming on my brow. I was about to say something; maybe offer her my place. The promise kept me from that escape. I just shook my head and headed toward the door I wished was miles away.

The woman with the headset led me down the hall. She was babbling *q*uickly, in an indifferent manner, about what I was to expect. I stopped listening after she told me I was to stand on a small red X on the stage. I was met, just off the stage, by a young man who fitted me with a wireless mic. He warned me not to touch my chest while I was out there. A man in a green shirt came up and wiped my brow and *q*uickly put some kind of powder on my face. He warned me the lights would be bright, and I should just look at the judges. I closed my eyes again and saw Amber smiling. It didn't slow my heart, but I didn't feel so alone.

I heard my name reverberate in the auditorium. It quieted the low drone of the audience I hadn't realized was so close. I stood there, my legs unwilling to move. Someone pushed me and I half stumbled toward that little red X. The lights were blinding; I could only make out the first twenty rows behind the four judges' seats. A weak, cordial applause welcomed me to hell. I stopped on the X and turned toward the judges. I could feel the blood driving painfully through my veins.

"Welcome, David," a man I recognized, the fourth judge on the right said. He had a wild frock of black, curly hair running down his shoulders and back. He wore sunglasses and an overly confident expression. I knew I should know his name, but I never watched these stupid talent shows. I found myself jealous of his sunglasses. I nodded to his greeting, not yet trusting my voice.

"Do you think you have what it takes to win?" the judge asked. He looked a little perturbed that I hadn't really acknowledged him yet. At least he asked an easy *q*uestion.

"No," I answered truthfully. I didn't expound on my answer which seemed to bother him all the more.

"Then what are you doing here?" he asked exasperatedly. I had a feeling procedures would change at the next tryouts. Another easy *q*uestion. The answer was more difficult to get out.

"I promised my wife," I responded. I remembered when I made the promise and the pain hit hard again. I had to take a long blink.

"So, your wife thinks you can win?" the man asked with a bit of whimsy. The thought that he would even pretend to know Amber's wishes infuriated me. I know there was anger in my voice when I answered. It felt better than the fear.

"I don't pretend to know why," I answered thickly, "I promised her and I am going to keep that promise." The audience gasped a little and the judges looked surprised at my venom. There was a pause while Mr. Sunglasses considered my response.

"What do you plan to sing for us, Promise Keeper?" the judge asked sarcastically. This elicited a small chuckle from the audience. I really didn't like this guy making fun of my promise to my wife.

"Amber," I answered. The judges looked at each other strangely.

"The reggae song?" Mr. Sunglasses asked incredulously. I kicked myself for not looking up the name before. Of course there was already a song called 'Amber'. I really didn't want to answer any more questions.

"No. I wrote it myself," I replied. There was surprise and a bit of laughter at that response. I was gritting my teeth wishing this would just end.

"Well this should at least be entertaining," Mr. Sunglasses said with a superior smile, "go ahead and keep your promise." He made it sound so amusing. The audience was laughing openly at this point. I rallied around my rising anger, trying to hold the fear at bay. I had to close my eyes to make the faces disappear. I had never sung in public. Only for my wife. I saw Amber there, smiling and proud. I could always sing to her.

I wrote the words to fit to 'Greensleeves.' I had to borrow others' music since I couldn't read, much less write, music. The tune was almost as pretty as Amber, and fit our love as well as possible. I heard the music start in my mind and I slowly sang to her about how we met and how our hearts merged. I sang of her beauty, comparing it poorly to a sunrise. I sang of her smile, of our dreams and mostly of our love. Amber's face changed, and I saw her concern as I got to the end. I sang about my loss and of her death. I couldn't help the tears or the crack in my voice. My promise kept, I dropped my head and listened to the silence.

I raised my head and stared into the blinding lights. I think they were waiting for more. The applause started slowly and my anger flared quickly. The death of my wife was not a celebration. I raised my hand in front of my face, trying to shut out the din and the lights. The idiots went on, but my promise was kept. I headed off the stage at fast clip, my pain as sharp as when I last held Amber. The song had fully renewed the misery.

I heard the judges shouting at me. 'Fuck them,' I thought. The producer lady, the one with the headphones, wisely moved out of my way as I exited. The man behind her wasn't so smart.

"You signed a contract," he informed me as he attempted to block my way. I was glad of it -- more anger to replace the pain. I tossed the microphone at him and I grabbed him by the collar.

"Sue me!" I shouted and threw him into a pole. He slipped and fell to the ground and quickly squirmed away. It took a couple of turns down the halls before I found an exit. The crisp open air hit me in a wave. I breathed it in deeply as I headed down the alley, darkness already cloaking the city. I had left my jacket, but the coolness wrapped my pain well. I heard a door open behind me. I ran to the street and disappeared into the city.

I was at the bridge when my phone rang. I didn't recognize the number so I hit ignore. I walked along the walkway, looking at the silently-lowing river. Cars passed, their occupants oblivious to the death of my wife. The whole world was oblivious. My phone rang again -- another number I didn't recognize. I ignored it as well and stopped at the apex of the bridge.

I closed my eyes as I leaned on the rail. I could see Amber again, so cheerful. I would begin to forget soon. I can't see my parents' faces any more. I didn't want to lose Amber again. I knew it was grief, but that was all I had of her. I never wanted the grief to end. My phone rang again and I didn't even look. I pulled it out of my pocket and dropped it into the river.

It was joyous to let it go. I laughed at the thought of it, throwing away the world and all its useless machinations. My watch followed and I wrapped myself in a cloak of my memories. I pulled my wallet out and looked at it closely. It was my connection to the world. My driver license, credit cards and the employee badge I should have turned in when I had quit. I opened the billfold and saw an old lottery ticket and a couple hundred dollars. None of it had meaning. I had kept my promise and everything else was moot. I threw the wallet farther. My keys were heavier, they went the farthest.

I walked to the east end of the bridge, where the river lapped up next to the rocks far below. I was no longer cold, or cared if I was. I climbed over the railing and aligned myself with the rocks the water was kissing below. I closed my eyes and there was Amber again, in all her perfection. Every freckle, every dimple, her arms outstretched and inviting. I didn't jump, I just leaned into her arms. I saw the most precious expression, the same one I would see as we made love. I folded into her as I fell away from the world. I had kept my promise.

<<<<<>>>>

It was damn cold. My entire body was shaking and I could feel my back spasm with each shudder. I tried to lift my head, and pain shoot down my spine. I lay back down and tried to open my eyes. There was light, but not oppressive light. Slowly, my focus returned, and I glanced unknowingly at my surroundings. The light was coming through an assembly of cardboard and wood surrounding me. One side looked to be a pallet that had a series of flattened cardboard boxes woven through its slats.

I had a torn green blanket over me. I tried lifting my shaking hands, but more pain shot across my back. The blanket smelled foul, like the inside of a wet sneaker. I raised my head enough to see the white stains, obviously bird waste, speckling the blanket. I choked at the thought and tried again to move. The pain was too much so I collapsed on the hard surface making my bed. I was lying, slightly inclined, on cardboard sheets. I suspected there was unyielding cement beneath them.

My shaking was getting worse. I was soaked from head to toe, and the water was foul. Maybe it was I who smelled so bad. The bridge drifted back into my mind. The events leading up to it and then, Amber. Grief flooded back as the uncontrollable shaking continued. I couldn't even fall off a bridge properly. It would be slow, but I was going to freeze to death. I could feel my fingers going numb and my lips weren't moving right. I closed my eyes, they say it is just like falling asleep. Amber was there, in my mind. Something was missing and I couldn't figure out what it was. My memory wasn't perfect. I knew it was her, but something was off. It didn't look *q*uite right and I struggled, shaking, to bring back the perfect image and things got worse. I was losing her. I hated myself.

Footsteps, walking through loose gravel, echoed into my cardboard tomb. I opened my eyes, and turned my head toward the sound. The steps left the gravel and became *q*uieter as they hit a harder surface. I realized this must be the person who unsaved me.

A small section of the cardboard cocoon was pulled away to reveal a cloudy, dismal day. I could make out some large concrete supports and the brownish iron underlying a portion of the bridge. An old black man, his hair graying on both his face and head, grinned at me. His teeth would furnish a dentist with months of work.

"You're up," he said with eyes brighter than his weather-beaten face. "They call me Houser. I pulled you out the water." He tossed a bundle into the tiny shanty and it landed on my chest.

"Should have left me," I chattered, not realizing talking would be difficult.

"This side's mine," Houser stated firmly, "you want to die, go to the other side." He used his head to gesture along the bridge to the other bank. "Them's dry clothes. They ain't the finest," he smiled again, "but they's dry. Got them from the shelter so they's clean." He crawled into the hovel and reclosed the opening. He didn't smell any better than I did. I tried to sit up and a sharp pain put me back down.

"Just roll me back into the water," I groaned. Houser laughed. It was a halting laugh that didn't speak well of his mental state.

"You missed most of the rocks, but found a few. Houser chuckled. "Bet you're real sore about now." That's all I needed, some homeless guy laughing at me about my failed suicide. I took a few deep breaths and cried out as my muscles protested. I forced myself to sit up. The dirty blanket fell forward onto my lap and my upper body felt even colder. I sat shivering, trying not to move much. My lower back would have preferred I lie back down.

"Give me your shirt," Houser demanded. I took a couple of deep breaths, trying to give my back time to get used to the new position. It wasn't fast enough for Houser. "The shirt or you leave. You have to go somewhere else to die," he said, while holding out his dirty hand. I was in no condition to leave and I guess he had a right to demand I didn't die in his home, as crappy as it was. I tried to unbutton my shirt with my shaking hands. The mixture of the cold, and the shooting pains as I moved my arms made it very slow going. I couldn't feel much in the tip of my fingers which made it difficult to shove the button back through the wet hole. Houser started laughing again. "Maybe you don't miss the rocks next time." He barely got it out before resuming his inappropriate laughter.

"My fingers are too cold," I stuttered between shakes.

"I'll do it, but don't get no ideas," Houser stated as he, and his stink, moved forward. I tried to give him my 'are you out of your friggin mind' look. I don't think I fully managed it. He deftly undid the buttons and quickly scooted back again. It was agonizing pulling the wet shirt off my shoulders. I must have really bruised my back. The air hit my wet skin sharply, and my shuddering increased. Houser quickly took the wet shirt and handed me a dry one he had liberated from the pile in my lap. It was only an old t-shirt, but it was dry. Pulling it on was another slow, agonizing process. Houser handed me a worn flannel shirt that buttoned down the front.

"Layers, I learned that my first year," Houser spouted proudly. There was more pain putting my arms in the arm holes. The shirt smelled clean. I truth, it didn't smell at all and that was clean from where I was sitting. I was able to get the shirt buttoned myself, much to Houser's relief, who seemed overly concerned about his virtue. The dry clothes started warming my chest quickly. The shivering didn't stop, but the severity receded, and I had more control over it.

"Now the pants," Houser said, and quickly stepped outside, "let me know when you're done." I smirked, my lips working a bit better, at his worries. Even if I was gay, Houser wasn't my type. I laughed inwardly at that thought. He was old and homeless and had all the right in the world to be from the kooky side of the street.

It took a long time to switch my pants. My lower back must have taken quite a hit and the muscles were screaming. I more or less scooted out of the pants since I was unable to fully bend my legs. Houser had brought a pair of cotton exercise shorts and some old stained cargo pants. I replaced my boxers with the exercise shorts, almost screaming to get them over my feet. The cargo pants were even more difficult. I looked around and noticed for the first time that my shoes were missing. They were probably the same place my socks were.

"Houser, where are my shoes?" I asked as I rolled over onto my hands and knees. I wasn't sure I could stand up without passing out. I certainly couldn't stand up in the hovel.

"I put them on the vents," Houser answered, "they's be dry soon." I crawled to the exit and poked my head out into the gray day. I was housed under the bridge, right where the supports met the land. My shaking had stopped. It wasn't terribly cold now that I had dry clothes. Houser looked down at me. "There's socks in there too," he said, pointing into the hut. I crawled back and painfully donned a pair of dry black socks.

"What's your name, jumper?" Houser asked with a bit a sarcasm. I decided it was best he didn't know. I didn't plan on staying, and I didn't really trust him.

"Frank," I answered. It was the first name to come to me. I subconsciously felt for my phone and remembered it was at the bottom of the river, along with my wallet. I really wasn't planning to need them anymore.

"Why'd you do it?" Houser asked. I looked up at him and saw the glint in his eye. I could see he wasn't really concerned about me. He was more interested in the story. I guess I was what passed for entertainment under a bridge. "You bankrupt, kill someone?" he continued. He gave me the best lie, the one that said I was not worth anything.

"Bankrupt," I lied. Houser laughed his crazy laugh.

"I'm always bankrupt," Houser said, "don't need no money so I don't care if I don't have any. It's you idiots that put worry in it." I chuckled at that. He was right in his own way.

"You're a wise man, Houser," I praised, His face lit up like a Christmas tree. I have no idea why I found that pleasing. He's an old man who lives under a bridge. Why would I care if he was happy? Nevertheless, his dental disaster of a smile made me feel good. I tried to stand and decided against it when my back fought against it with pain.

"Lie flat," Houser instructed, "you might be stuck here a day or two. I will take care of you and then you owe me....that's how it works." I slowly rolled over on to my back and slowly straightened my legs. I smiled at him.

"What will I owe you?" I asked. I was thinking in terms of dollars.

"I don't know yet!" Houser snapped, "you share what you get or do me solid. Nothing more than what you get. I'll ask when I see it. Can't live without helping each other out here." He was talking at me like I was an idiot. It was a simple barter system, favor for favor.

"Sounds more than fair, "I responded lightly, "you just let me know. I will owe you good when I get out of here." Houser smiled again, and nodded his head. He really enjoyed the idea of being owed. I would have to find a way of paying him back. I was impressed how simple his life was. Right now, I envied him.

"It's almost four," Houser said absently, "kitchen will open soon. Sadie said I could bring you back something 'til you feel better. She won't do it for long so you got to get better."

"Sadie?" I asked.

"She runs the kitchen," Houser said incredulously, "don't you know anything? You're lucky I found you." He was shaking his head as he headed off beyond the bridge supports. He acted like the whole world knew about the kitchen.

I lay on the cardboard mattress feeling physically better than when I woke. I closed my eyes and saw my flawed vision of Amber. "I miss you baby," I whispered. The vision didn't improve. I had already lost perfection and I knew it would only fade more over time. My grief returned and I wished Houser hadn't left. I needed his simplicity, as strange as it was.

Houser returned as the sun began to set. I wasn't sure how much time had passed because my watch was on the bottom of the river. It was kind of nice not caring what time it was. I have spent my whole life watching a clock. All that happened was time ran out for Amber and me. Now time could just suck itself.

"I got you some fried chicken and a cup of jello," Houser said as he handed me a chicken balled up in a napkin and a paper cup filled with red jello. Strangely, it seemed like a feast. I hadn't realized how hungry I was until I smelled the cold chicken. There was a leg and half a breast that had been cut with a knife.

"Got to eat out here," Houser pointed to the cement. "Don't want critters inside." More homeless wisdom. I crawled out and sat up slowly. I was starting to figure out how to move with the least amount of pain. The lower left side of my back felt like it had been hit with a sledge hammer. If I kept myself tucked a little to the left, I could withstand more movement.

"Thanks, Houser," I said sincerely, "I owe you." Houser smiled and nodded. I was getting the hang of this favor thing. Just acknowledge the debt and pay it back in kind in the future. If only the rest of life were that simple. I dug into the chicken and it disappeared quickly. It was actually pretty good as fried chicken goes. Even cold, the seasonings partied with my tongue in a snappy way. I was kind of wishing there was more. I emptied the cup full of red jello cubes into my mouth and enjoyed the brief sweetness. I stuffed the napkin into the cup and looked around for a waste can or something. Houser laughed and grabbed the cup out of my hand, walked down to the river and threw it in. Pollution was obviously not part of his ethos.

It was four days until I could stand and walk properly. Houser said I had one hell of bruise on my back. I guess I was lucky, or unlucky depending upon your point of view. I was certainly happy I didn't have to crawl down to the river to relieve myself anymore.

Houser and I became good friends. I liked him better than anyone else I knew. I liked his philosophy. There was no way I was going back to my old life, not without Amber in it. Jumping off a bridge didn't appeal to me any more either. I was losing weight, something I always wanted to do. I couldn't care less what time it was and there was absolutely no stress. My home, job, car and old friends would do nothing, but remind me of what I had lost. A week ago, I would have never guessed I could live without all my stuff. Now, I couldn't care less how full my DVR was or whether I had checked my email. I was dropping out and going off the grid.

Houser was a brilliant teacher. He had been on the streets for over twenty years. He dropped out when he lost his factory job. He couldn't find another even close to what he had been earning, so he hit the streets. For him, it worked. He really didn't care how the world turned and had no desire for the finer things in life. I wasn't sure how long I could hack it, but, after four days under a bridge, I was feeling pretty free. I didn't have any obligations to clutter my time. Grief would visit, but never stay long. There was nothing under the bridge to remind me of Amber except my own thoughts.

"I guess you could make it to the kitchen today," Houser said, "it's almost four so we better get started if we want more than scraps." I looked at him strangely. His time-telling skills were gnawing at me. He wore no watch, but he always had a good sense of the time. Even when it was cloudy.

"How do you always know what time it is?" I asked with a smile. Houser was always proud of his secret knowledge of the streets. It's one of the reasons why he liked me. I always made a point of drawing it into the open so he could show off.

"Traffic," Houser answered, pointing to the bridge, "I can hear rush hour starting." He was beaming and I gave him a small bow in praise, which caused a little pain. I had ignored the traffic, but he was right. You could almost count the tires crossing the breaks in the pavement. In his own way, Houser was a genius.

I followed Houser into the streets for the first time in four days. I am sure I looked a mess. I hadn't shaved or even combed my hair in all that time. I received a few disgusted looks from suited professionals, but most people just ignored us. I felt invisible and found it exhilarating. I am sure my smell wasn't invisible, but Houser didn't seem to be offended.

The kitchen was in a rundown district. It looked like it had been some kind of factory at one time. It was a three story brown bricked building with large windows, mostly boarded. There was a large sign above a double set of doors that said 'City Kitchen.' One of the doors was propped open, but a line had already begun to form just before the two steps that led to the doors. There was no indication why we couldn't just go inside.

"Can't go in until 'Sugar Magnolia,'" Houser said as we got in line behind an old woman. "Maggie, this here is Frank." Maggie turned, her face was wrinkled like elephant skin. She smiled, nodded and turned to face the line again. I said 'Hi,' but I don't think she heard it. She was humming to herself and it wasn't offensive, almost like she could carry a tune.

"'Sugar Magnolia?'" I asked.

"You'll see," Houser smiled. I waited with everyone else as the line got longer. I let Houser have his fun. I learned in four days not to get anxious about anything. Patience was a way of life on the streets. It was the cost of the freedom.

Houser seemed to know most of the people in line. A week ago, I would have never thought of them as people at all. It's strange how jumping off a bridge could change your perspective. Not all of the people looked like they hadn't showered for a week or more, and I was surprised at the number of kids in line. There was one mother trying to reign in three young boys who seemed very comfortable with the whole process.

The civility in the line was the most surprising aspect. No one seemed to mind the wait and there wasn't any attempt cut in or form a new line. I was expecting more of a herd mentality instead of the practiced order being displayed. It went against everything Houser stood for.

"It's so...orderly," I said. I almost gave it a *q*uestioning tone.

"Sadie don't put up with no shit," Houser replied. Maggie stopped humming and turned around.

"You cause trouble, you don't eat," Maggie said accusingly. She raised her finger and pointed at me with a scowl. I smiled at her, trying to prove I was a good person and deserved to eat. She turned back around and continued her humming. Sadie must be a beast of a woman to invoke such discipline in everyone. I imagined her at three hundred pounds swinging a rolling pin with deadly force. I didn't intend to cause any trouble, so I wasn't too worried.

I heard an electric pop followed by a hiss of speakers firing up.

"Four o'clock, here we go," Houser said patting me on the back. The line started moving forward just before the music started. The song 'Sugar Magnolia' wafted through the open door. I realized that was the tune Maggie had been humming the whole time. Everyone moved forward calmly; there was no pushing or arguing. I have seen ruder people entering high-priced theatrical productions. Maybe Sadie packed an Uzi.

The line moved forward slowly, but steadily. I patiently waited my turn to head into the door. I smelled chili as I neared the door and my stomach growled. I was hungrier than I thought. I know I hadn't eaten well in the last four days, but it really didn't bother me until that wonderful smell hit my nostrils. Inside the door, the line continued down a short hall and took a turn to the right. The music was more pronounced inside and Maggie was bouncing to the beat. Maybe she was a deadhead from way back.

I turned the corner just as the song ended. The din of plastic trays and plates replaced the music. There was a stainless steel cafeteria line ahead, manned by people who looked like they would fit comfortably in the line. The first station was being handled by a large woman wearing a white apron over mismatched pants and shirt. Her hair, black with streaks of gray, was pulled back and covered in a white scarf. She was filling bowls with chili and handing them over the sneeze guard with a smile that was missing a few teeth. I assumed she was Sadie. She was definitely imposing enough.

"I haven't seen you before," a female voice to my right said as I entered the dining room. The room held a good twenty long tables with metal tubed plastic folding chairs. My eyes followed the voice to a woman dressed in a flowing red flowery skirt. Her dusty brown hair was long down her back, held in place by the same white scarf the chili lady was wearing.

"No, I guess I'm new," I replied, a little lost for words. I wasn't expecting to be greeted. The woman's eyes crinkled when she smiled. She was petite, at least a hand shorter than I. Her cream-colored blouse was practical, but sharply ironed. She stood with both hands clasped behind her back. She looked completely out of place, for one thing, she had all her teeth.

"Sadie, this is Frank," Houser chimed in from behind me, "he's the one I told you about." Sadie didn't look anything like I expected. She was maybe in her mid thirties and not physically imposing at all.

"Welcome, Frank," Sadie said, and used her hand to direct me toward the cafeteria line. A small gap in the line was created when she greeted me and I think she was intent on seeing it closed. Something about her manner made me hustle to fill the gap. "You owe me five days, Houser," Sadie called as we moved toward the chili.

"Five days?" I asked Houser for clarification.

"Yeah, I gots to work the line," Houser said, nodding to the buffet line, "if you eat a lot, you owes days to Sadie." He smiled as he picked up a tray off the stack. "It ain't bad work, it's just she makes you clean up, you know, before you touch the food and stuff." Houser obviously cherished his grime. He wasn't quite as free as he claimed.

"Cheese?" the large chili lady asked.

"Sure," I answered and she dropped a tong full of shredded cheddar on top of my plastic bowl of chili. She made an effort to smile as she handed me the bowl. I found myself smiling back and saying 'thank you.' I moved to the next station, and a tall gangly guy with the same apron and scarf handed me a small bowl of fresh broccoli and carrots in some kind of oily sauce. He also smiled and warranted a 'thank you.' The whole process was extremely civil and the service was pleasant. I looked back at Sadie as she greeted everyone entering. You have to admire someone who can organize the unorganized.

"Brownies!" Houser said excitedly. I saw his eyes light up and he exposed all his bad teeth. An older woman was serving them at the end of the line. Same apron, same scarf and the same smile. With our trays loaded, Houser and I found a seat at one of the tables.

"Does Sadie run this all by herself?" I asked as we began to dig in.

"Yep, it's her kitchen," Houser answered with a mouth full of chili. I saw him eying my brownie. He wasn't trying to be overly obvious, but he wasn't hiding it either. I smiled and moved my brownie to his tray.

"I owe you," I said. Houser nodded his head as he stuffed another spoonful of chili into his mouth. I had a feeling I wouldn't be getting dessert for a while. It didn't really bother me, anyone who could help me forget was worth his weight in dessert.

We ate in the relatively quiet atmosphere of the cafeteria. There was talking, but it was all subdued and very cordial. Not what I expected at all. Houser informed me Sadie wouldn't allow raucous behavior in her cafeteria. I looked back at Sadie and wondered how she could possibly stop a ruckus if it started. Everyone just seemed to accept her iron rule here.

I was watching Houser enjoy his brownies at the end of the meal. Enjoying was an understatement. He was in ecstasy. He savored every bite, and his eyes glossed over. His joys were simple and this was one of his favorites.

"So, what are you doing here, Frank?" Sadie had sat down next to us without me noticing. I jumped a bit in surprise. I figured I would stick with the lie I started with.

"Financial problems," I answered. I wondered if I smelled as bad as Houser. If so, Sadie didn't seem to mind. She just looked at my face as if trying to figure out something. Her dark eyes seemed to penetrate past my lie and I sensed she didn't believe me.

"You're not buying Houser's freedom of the streets crap are you?" Sadie smiled sweetly at Houser as she said it. Houser was still lost in his second brownie and seemed oblivious to the teasing insult. For some reason I didn't feel like lying to her again. There was something about how she presented herself that just made it feel wrong.

"Right now, yes," I answered honestly, "it's kind of refreshing." Houser was nodding as he relished another mouthful of the brownie. He was more aware of the conversation than I gave him credit for. Sadie rolled her eyes and gave me an expression just short of disgust. I suddenly wanted to take my answer back and try again.

"You owe Houser?" Sadie asked, nodding toward the brownie monster.

"Yes," I answered quizzically.

"Then you take his five days," Sadie said as she rose, "I'll see if I can change your mind. Be here tomorrow morning at nine; don't be late." Sadie headed off before I could respond. I was shocked by the authority she just assumed she had. Houser smiled with a mouth full of brownie.

"We're even," Houser said, obviously pleased with the turn of events. I looked after Sadie, her skirt swinging from side to side as she headed toward the serving line. She walked with authority that no one seemed to *q*uestion. She inspected the line, and was pointing out things while workers hustled to make everything right. Not what I expected at all.

It was a chilling morning, doubly so since I had to leave the hovel before the sun was above the buildings. I made it to the Kitchen well before nine or at least Houser said I would be early. I was stamping my feet on the steps, and hugging myself when I heard the door begin to open.

"You're going to have to collect better clothes if you want to make this your lifestyle," Sadie said, while waving me in. "You're early," she commented.

"Don't have a watch," I responded as I stepped into the warmth. It was the first time I had needed a watch since I threw it in the river. She locked the door behind me and started walking to the dining area expecting me to follow. I followed like a dog.

"The door to the right," Sadie instructed while pointing to the far wall, "leads to a shower room. There's a wash basin to wash your clothes and a dryer. Clean up, and we'll get started in about an hour." She turned, and headed back toward what I expected was the real kitchen area. She left no room for dissent.

"What if I say no?" I asked. Might as well find out how this all works. I wasn't used to feeling like someone's slave. Sadie turned around and looked at me with a calm glare.

"If you're not clean, you can't touch the food," Sadie stated firmly, "if you can't help, we won't like each other." Her hands found her hips and she stared at me. I almost came back with a smart-ass remark, but couldn't find the courage. She was very imposing for such a petite woman.

"Clean it is," I said cheerfully. I really didn't want Sadie's ire. I had a strange feeling it would be a costly thing to behold. Sadie just turned and continued on her previous path.

The shower room was large. I guessed the building must have needed it in its prior life. It was set up like one you might find in an old dormitory. A row of sinks, a hall of toilets and a large, open shower room with five shower heads. In the sink portion, there was a utility basin with an old dryer next to it. I followed Sadie's instructions.

I stripped down and threw my clothes in the basin. There was detergent above the faucet which I used to scrub the clothes. The water turned a nasty shade of tan as I washed. I guess five days in the same clothes does that. I rinsed the clothes as best I could and went to toss them in the dryer. The dryer held a towel that I guess was meant for me. I exchanged the towel for my clean, but wet, clothes and put the dryer on a one hour cycle.

Above one of the regular sinks was a set of hotel toiletries sitting on the metal tray below the mirror. The tray held a cheap plastic-wrapped toothbrush and comb, along with a small bar of soap, a tiny toothpaste tube and a mini shampoo. I didn't recognized myself in the mirror. My reddish-brown hair, which hadn't been combed in five days, was matted, and it stuck out in strange directions. I was sporting the beginnings of a sparse beard, and I was shocked to see some of it coming in gray. I had never had gray hair before. My face was basically filthy with streaks of oily dirt where I had wiped it with my dirty hands. I had aged ten years in five days. Amber would have been pissed.

I grabbed the soap and shampoo and headed to the shower. I scrubbed myself thoroughly and then repeated the process a couple more times. I closed my eyes with my head under the warm rain and tried to see Amber again. She was there, missing the perfection I could once see. I hated losing that perfection, but it wasn't ripping me apart as before. I knew I wouldn't be jumping off any more bridges. I also knew I wouldn't be returning to my old life. The mirror convinced me Houser didn't have the answers either. I owed him five days, so that's how long I had to figure out things. At least Sadie had my day planned for me. I really didn't want to think any more.

I dried off, combed my hair and brushed my teeth. I felt slightly more normal. I lost a little portion of the freedom Houser had tried to instill. It was replaced with a desire to do something. I just wish I knew what that something was. I looked at my scraggly baby beard and wished I had a razor. I didn't like the gray hairs -- Amber would have hated them. I remembered trying not to shave on Sundays. It was just a lazy thing, to make Sunday a do-nothing day. Amber nixed it almost immediately. I remember her sitting me in a chair, then straddling me and shaving me herself. We made love like teenagers that day, me promising never to not shave and her promising to shave me personally if I reneged. The memory brought a mixture of tremendous love and horrible sadness. A potent mix that always caused tears. I wished I had a razor.

I spent another twenty minutes with my memories while I waited for the clothes to dry. I washed out my towel and exchanged it with my clothes in the dryer. I set the dial for thirty minutes on the dryer and fired it up. I walked out a clean man.

"A bit better," Sadie commented as I entered the dining hall. She was obviously waiting for me to emerge. "Let me see the hands," she ordered. I held out my hands with a small roll of my eyes. She ignored my eyes and looked closely at both sides of my hands with special attention to the nails.

"Take the chairs off the tables," Sadie ordered. I assumed she had accepted the cleanliness of my hands since she didn't make me rewash them. "Tuck them under, equidistant apart. Don't move the tables, they are exactly where they belong. Meet me in the backroom when you're done." She headed off with a purpose. I looked at the legs of the tables and the north sets of legs were lined up perfectly on a tile line. The northeast leg of each table was on a tile corner. Sadie may be a little OCD. I lowered the chairs and tucked them under and scooted them to make sure they were equally spaced. I walked around when I was done and adjusted a few, so the chairs lined up with the tables in the same rows. I rechecked each table to make sure it hadn't moved. Then I went into the backroom. I had no idea how Sadie got me to be so anal about tables and chairs.

I walked into the backroom, one of the cleanest kitchens I have ever seen. All the stainless steel sparkled and everything seemed to have a place. There were no utensils or pots and pans lying out. Even the tiled floor looked spotless. Sadie was sitting on a stool, working with a set of papers. She looked up as I walked in and pointed to an apron and scarf that had been laid out on the counter. I donned both.

"That's the hand wash station," Sadie said, as she pointed at a small sink along the wall. "Push the lever with your leg and wash your hands. Before you touch any food or anything that will touch food, you wash your hands. Paper towels are in the dispenser next to it." She went back to her papers, making notes on one of them.

I WAS A LITTLE SURPRISED TO NOT SEE ANYONE ELSE WORKING

I was a little surprised to not see anyone else working. I moved over to the sink and washed my hands. It seemed a little over-the-top since I had just gotten out of the shower. I guess I touched some chairs, but I assumed they were strictly sanitized like the rest of the place. I was drying my hands with the paper towels when Sadie looked up again.

"There are Roma tomatoes in the walk-in," Sadie said and pointed to the large steel door, "they are on the left side, second shelf. Bring out two boxes and set them on the floor by the prep sink." She indicated the large sink with the high curved faucet. She then went back to her papers. I started to walk toward the walk-in and decided my silent obedience was a bit much.

"By the way, good morning, Sadie," I said with a tiny bit of smart-ass. I kept moving toward the walk-in so she couldn't find fault. Sadie surprised me by looking up briefly with a smile.

"Good morning, Frank," Sadie replied and returned to her work. I guess authoritative regimes could be cordial. I found it pleasing to make the great leader smile -- my little bit of rebellion for the morning.

I hauled the two boxes of tomatoes out to the sink. They were a bit heavier than I had thought so it took two trips.

"Open the boxes, then, wash your hands again." Sadie didn't look up from her work this time. I sighed as I opened the boxes and washed my hands again. Sadie rose from her work and washed her hands as well. "We never allow our skin to touch the food," she instructed as she dried her hands, "We always use latex gloves; I'm guessing you will want the large ones." She pulled a pair of small, disposable latex gloves from a rack mounted on the wall next to the sink. I grabbed a pair of large.

"It's taco night and you're prepping the tomatoes." Sadie's motions were practiced as she blindly grabbed a metal colander from the wire shelf above our heads. "Both boxes need to be prepared. Rinse, core, slice then chop. These will be used for taco toppings." She handed me the colander, "Load it up and hold it under the water to rinse them." She walked off to grab some more tools for the job as I began rinsing the first batch of tomatoes.

Sadie returned with a cutting board and a pair of small clawed spoons. She deftly maneuvered, with her feet, a wheeled garbage can over toward the sink. "Touch the garbage can and you need a new set gloves," she warned. She retrieved a wet tomato from the colander and showed me how to take out the small hard core at the top with the clawed spoon. The core went into the can and the tomato onto the cutting board. We started coring the tomatoes together. She wasn't afraid to get her hands dirty.

"I have seen your face before," Sadie said absently as she quickly cored another tomato.

"I don't see how."

"No, I've seen it." I remembered her greeting everyone at the door last night. She was good with names. "'Frank' doesn't jog my memory. Perhaps you have another name." Her smile was slight, but I did see the small curve. I cored another tomato, conscious she was doing two for every one of mine.

"I like the name Frank right now," I said truthfully, while

respecting her deduction, "yesterday was the first time I have ever seen you, so I am sure you must be thinking of someone else." I couldn't see how our paths had crossed in the past. My mind was drawing a blank.

"It will come to me," Sadie said, "I never forget a face." I needed to change the subject. Amber didn't know Frank. It was easier to try and forget as Frank.

"I thought there would be other workers."

"Not until one," Sadie replied, "I only need one for prep." I felt like I was in a coring competition. Every time I moved to catch up to her pace, she would accelerate. Finally, I surrendered and slowed to a reasonable pace. "Nice try." Sadie was wearing a smirk as she slowed to a pace just a bit faster than mine. She obviously liked to win.

"So how did you end up here?" I asked Sadie. I was truly interested in how a model of efficiency could find herself running a free soup kitchen.

"Long story. Maybe I will tell you sometime." Sadie paused, then smiled and said, with emphasis, "Frank." 'Touché,' I thought. She was willing to trade stories, but not give hers up for free. I just smiled back. Sadie had a quick mind. Amber would have liked her.

"How do you fund this place?" I changed the subject to something more comfortable.

"Donations. Lots and lots of donations." Sadie lost her smile as she continued to core her way through the pile of tomatoes. The answer seemed to exhaust her.

"501(c)(3)?" It came out of my mouth before I could stop myself. It was habit. Sadie stopped coring and looked up at me.

"Do you understand financial statements?" Sadie had already surmised a lot. I wanted to feign ignorance, but I had asked the question too confidently.

"Yes."

"Will you look at my books?" Sadie's question sounded almost pleading. I sensed her confidence didn't extend into accounting. So much for totally ignoring my old life.

"I can do that." I didn't want to sound too confident about my abilities. Sometimes people hand you a horrible mess and expect you to create facts from thin air.

"Okay, tomorrow, same time. I'll get someone else to prep." Sadie's mood changed. She started coring with enthusiasm. I thought I might have just bitten off more than I could chew.

I learned a lot about mass food preparation. Sadie changed from authoritative to patiently instructive. Maybe her books were more than a mess. I was being buttered up for tomorrow. Strangely, I found the labor fun and relaxing. It was fairly easy, different and repetitive. Nothing you had to think too deeply about. Each task had an endgame, a place where I could identify that it was done and enjoy that sense of completion. I needed the mindless labor, and today I was good at it.

At 1:00 four other homeless workers showed up. Each had worked for Sadie before, and confidently went to work after reading a chart on the wall. Trudy, the large women who was serving chili yesterday, didn't read the chart. Sadie instructed her verbally as a matter of course. I suspected Trudy couldn't read. Sadie just took it in stride and ignored the limitation. In fact, she put Trudy in charge of teaching me how to brown the beef. Trudy smiled and waved me over to the grill.

Trudy redundantly educated me about washing my hands and using latex gloves, which I took in stride. She showed me the controls for the hood and emphasized the exhaust fan had to be on when the grill was on. I had lessons regarding grill controls and clean up. It was fifteen minutes before Trudy thought we were ready to get the meat from the cooler. Her personality was a lot like Sadie's, only leaning more toward the compassionate side.

Trudy's hands moved quickly, chopping beef and searing it on the grill. I watched her hand maneuver the large metal spatula with practiced agility. She handed it off to me and I proved my lack of coordination quite handily. Trudy found it entertaining and amusingly grabbed my hand every once in a while to steer it toward beef that might otherwise burn. My college degree was useless compared to her experience. It was refreshing to be taught something new and to have a teacher so enthralled with the experience.

We transferred the first batch of meat to a large metal pot and sent it off to someone else for sauce and seasoning prep.

"You single?" Trudy asked. There was a twinkle in her eye and I couldn't help blushing. The *q*uestion came out of nowhere. I mumbled, trying to come up with an answer that wouldn't scar the rapport we had. I could think of nothing that would not come out insulting. I whispered some truth for both our sakes.

"My wife just passed away." It was quiet enough to remain private. Trudy nodded slowly and leaned into me compassionately.

"I'm sorry," Trudy whispered back. I wasn't sure if she was sorry about my wife or the fact she flirted.

"Thanks."

"We have three more pots to fill," Trudy said, returning to the job at hand. I think she saw my need for manual labor. When I returned with more meat, there were two spatulas at the grill. We worked in tandem with the next three batches. She didn't flirt any more, but we bonded over the searing meat. She started humming 'Amazing Grace' as we cooked. I joined in after a few moments. Trudy smiled at me and I realized she was humming for Amber. I was touched that she understood, although she had never met my wife.

I turned to hand off the second pot of cooked meat to the next station. I caught Sadie staring at me. She clumsily went back to her paperwork. I wondered if she had heard my confession. I hoped she hadn't. I only told Trudy to spare her feelings, and mine.

If you do prep, you get to eat first. It was a wonderful rule that my growling stomach appreciated immensely. I had been smelling food all day, and had had nothing but water. I was getting used to eating only once a day, but it's tougher when watching it being prepared. There was no cheating or snacking in Sadie's kitchen. I even had to wait for 'Sugar Magnolia.'

Luckily, Houser was near the front of the line. I waited until he sat down before I started eating. It wasn't so much manners as it was a show of friendship. I liked him liking me without the need for my past. I loved feeding off his lazy enthusiasm for life. It was refreshing. Houser lamented about the desert. He hated jello day and passed on his wiggly lemon chunk to me. I like jello. The mix of coolness and sweetness always seemed to please my tongue. Amber used to make triple-layered jello concoctions for me, mixing flavors that should never go together. She never found a combination I wouldn't eat.

"Good evening, Houser." Sadie had snuck up on us in the middle of our desert discussion. Houser nodded with mouth full of food. She leaned down and whispered in his ear. He nodded again. Sadie placed a plastic wrapped brownie on Houser's tray. Houser smiled, showing all his awful teeth.

"I gots to get you warmer clothes," Houser said, never taking his eyes off the brownie. I snapped my eyes up, looking after Sadie. She was moving off, back to the front of the line. Her flowered skirt, greenish this time, swaying confidently back and forth. The books must be in really bad shape.

Houser showed me the shelter where I could get some warmer clothes. It wasn't exactly stylish, but I was now wearing an old brown jacket that looked like it might have been used by someone in construction, and a pair of military boots. The laces in the boots were brown and looked strange against the black leather. It was better than the old loafers I had been walking around in. I really looked the part now. Everything mismatched, but functional.

The next morning started the same as the first in all but one respect. Sadie was smiling when she opened the door. The books must be an absolute disaster. I took a shower, which I now appreciated greatly, and met Kevin . Kevin was a shy younger man who was to replace me on prep. We shared the dryer. Not unexpectedly, there were two of everything waiting for use. Two towels, two toothbrushes and two shampoos and soaps. Sadie never prepared more than necessary. Exactly what was needed and nothing more, but it was always exactly what was needed.

Sadie took me into a small office connected to the kitchen. It looked as clean and organized as the rest of the building. There were three four-drawer black file cabinets labeled by year, plus a small desk with an old computer and small printer. A stack of folders, each labeled with a month and year, were piled next to the keyboard.

"These are this year's receipts." Sadie pointed to the stack of folders, "I hope you are familiar with the accounting system." She logged into a small business system I was quite familiar with. I nodded my head. So far so good. "Can you make sure it is all correct. Nothing can be wrong." I looked at her worried expression. All of this seemed too neat and orderly to be worrisome. "You just want me to audit the books?" I asked, the surprise evident in my tone.

"Please, it's important." Sadie left before I sat down. She never even doubted I would do it, but I did note she used the word 'please.'

I made myself familiar with Sadie's chart of accounts and printed off a balance sheet as of the first of the year. With that starting point, I began matching receipts to journal entries. Her record keeping was meticulous. I had very little trouble reconstructing what she had done. There were no journal entries without supporting documentation and each receipt corresponded to an entry. I was impressed. It is rare to find such perfect record keeping. I ended with printing a current balance sheet and income statement. Everything was perfect to the penny. It had only taken me four hours to complete.

"What's the verdict?" Sadie asked as I walked into the kitchen with my notes. She seemed apprehensive and I couldn't understand where it was coming from. There was no way she could think her books were bad.

"All good," I responded confidently, "you expensed some things as repairs that I probably would have capitalized, but you did it consistently. There is nothing wrong that I could find. In fact, they are very accurate and well done." Sadie visibly let out the breath she had been holding.

"Do you think you could look at the three previous years?" It began to make sense.

"You're getting audited," I stated. Only the IRS could make someone like Sadie squirm. She waved me back into the office.

"Yes," Sadie answered once we were alone. She pulled an envelope from a drawer and handed me the letter inside. The IRS was auditing her last three tax returns and wanted to examine her supporting documentation. There was a paragraph about providing necessary documentary support to maintain her charitable status. The letter seemed to be worded a bit differently than a standard audit letter. The amount of money involved usually didn't generate IRS flags and certainly didn't warrant an audit this deep.

"This seems a bit heavy-handed," I offered when I handed back the letter.

"Will you look at the last three years?"

"Hell yes," I answered, with some fight in my words. I never did like it when the IRS picked on the innocent. Frankly, Sadie was doing the world a favor. I had only known her for three days and I could tell the city needed her. "It will take a few days and I'll need the tax returns."

"Each year has its own drawer." Sadie hastily pointed toward the file cabinets, "The first folder contains the tax returns." "It will be alright," I said, trying to calm her nervousness. "They can only go after fraud. I've seen nothing coming close to that. If your tax returns reflect your financials, this will be nothing but an annoyance." Sadie looked slightly more relieved and even gave me half a smile.

"Thanks." Sadie left the office for a moment then poked her head back in. "What the hell are you doing here?" I guess my skills didn't make sense with my homelessness.

"Nothing criminal, I assure you," I said in all honesty. Of course, if I was a criminal, I would have said the same thing. Sadie seemed to size me up and accept me at my word. Either that, or I was the only one convenient to trust. I was busy putting this year's files into their proper drawer as she returned to work.

Kevin and I were in the front of the line when 'Sugar Magnolia' came over the speakers. It seems auditors gain the same rights and privileges as prep cooks. It was polish sausage night and Trudy winked at me and gave me a slightly larger portion. I winked back in a friendly way and waited for Houser again.

Houser was happy as ever. It was white cake night which was half way to a brownie for him. I think he measured his happiness in grams of sugar. I, on the other hand, prefer a more mellow desert. I moved my cake to his tray.

"I owe you," Houser said with a mouth full of half-chewed polish sausage. I wished I could live day to day like he could. He seemed to have no concerns beyond the present. I envied the freedom he had built in his own mind. My mind was still lost in the past. My precious Amber was gone and I was forgetting her face. I could imagine her touch and her voice. It was her face that was fading. The rest would follow. My mind was too weak to hold on.

"You owe me nothing but good company," I said. Houser laughed and told me about the boat he saw get caught among the pilings under the bridge earlier. It took the better part of the day and two more boats to get it free. To him, it was quality TV. I laughed when he told me how one guy was trying to rig a pull line while straddling both boats. They invariably pulled apart and sent the guy into the river. To Houser, the incident was as good as white cake. For me, a moment not lost in the past.

"Good evening, Houser." Sadie had snuck up on us again. "Why don't you show Frank how get a warm bed tonight."

"Sadie, a man lives where he wants," Houser stated firmly. It was funny watching him consolidate behind his beliefs. I was strangely flattered. Sadie rolled her eyes, reached into the pocket of her blue flowered skirt and placed a plastic-wrapped brownie on his tray. Houser smiled and I stared dumbfounded at Sadie. "But a man ought to know all the options," Houser retracted quickly.

"Thank you, Houser." Sadie never really looked at me. She just headed back to monitor the line.

"You're the best thing I ever pulled out of the river," Houser said slowly as he unwrapped his precious brownie.

"Did you tell Sadie how you found me?"

"That's for you to say." Houser took a small bite of the brownie, obviously trying to make it last. "Sometimes it's best not to say -- leave it in the past." That I had to agree with.

I slept in a lumpy, but warm, bed that night with many other homeless guests. The shelter had rules, which I followed, and I was up, showered and out by 8:00 as directed. The rules were what kept Houser away. "If I want to sleep the day away, I will." His words, not mine.

Sadie was happy to see me the next morning. Maybe I was more reliable than the average homeless person. It was nice to start out the day with her smile.

"You ever going to shave off that fuzz?" Sadie asked. I could see her eyes on my chin. The mirror told me it added a few years to my looks, but I was getting used to it. Amber would have hated it. Strangely, that's why I finally decided not to shave it. It reminded me she was gone, and I didn't want to forget. I was worse off without her and my scraggly beard was proof.

"Someday," I answered with a smile.

"It makes you look old." Sadie turned and started walking toward the kitchen. I followed, liking my beard a little less.

I went to work on last year's financials. It took me all day to audit the financials and reconcile everything to the tax return. I questioned Sadie about a single donation entry marked Charity Ball. She produced a paper ledger with the handwritten names of all the donors and the amounts they gave. The Kitchen put on the ball every February. It was the biggest fundraiser of the year. I tallied the donations and they mirrored the entry. It was a pretty successful event, generating a little over $35,000 in donations.

"I notice you don't take a salary." It struck me as odd. She spent seven days a week here and there was no disbursements to her name. In fact, there was no payroll at all.

"I don't need the money," Sadie said nonchalantly.

"Independently wealthy?" I was grinning.

"I don't know, Frank." Sadie emphasized my phoney name. "Am I?" We were still in the trade story for story mode. I wasn't willing to give up mine and she was stubbornly holding on to hers as leverage.

"I'll just make up a story then," I said, tongue-in-cheek.

"Make it a good one." Sadie laughed and returned to her work. I liked her laugh. She didn't laugh enough. Neither did I.

I found only one entry without supporting documentation. It was for fifteen dollars and was expensed as window cleaning. Hardly material, but I followed up anyway. Sadie had given a young boy the money to clean the windows. He obviously didn't have a business that could generate a receipt. He was homeless with his mother and just wanted to help. Sadie allowed it and paid him out of petty cash. I assured Sadie it wasn't going to be a problem.

I now knew the words to 'Sugar Magnolia' by heart. I really

wanted to ask Sadie why she played that song every day. I knew it would cost me my past so I just sat with Houser and tried to quell my interest. It was jello night so Houser passed me his. He didn't say I owed him and didn't draw attention to it in any way. We were like a married couple. We knew what each other liked and just simply traded food. Amber and I used to raid each other's salads at restaurants. I would go for her onions and she for my olives. We would do it in the middle of a conversation, without breaking thought. It was a simple thing and I was fond of the memory.

"You have any family?" I asked. I wondered why I never asked the question before. I was so busy hiding my past, I never thought about his. He simply nodded and went on eating. I could tell he really didn't want to go into it. There was no eye contact, and his gritty smile wasn't evident. I dropped the subject and knew we would be better friends because of it.

I spent the next day on the two-years-back books. There was absolutely nothing wrong with them. I couldn't even find simple addition errors. Sadie was as stringent with her accounting as she was with her kitchen. I pulled the IRS letter out of the desk again and reread it. It used harsher language than I had seen in past audits. Something of the Kitchen's size was usually handled by mail. Here they were demanding an on-site audit with veiled threats hidden inside their demands. The two tax returns I reviewed didn't seem to warrant any kind of review. Nothing in them should have raised any flags. The letter was certainly not indicative of a random audit.

"This audit doesn't feel right," I said as Sadie came in to check my progress. "It almost seems hostile." She hesitated before she responded. Then she sat down.

"I think it is an attack, but I can't be sure." Sadie sighed softly, looking at the letter I placed on the desk. "The city tried to rezone this block for a developer. It would have forced me out so I fought it and won. I don't know how they could have done that." She pointed to the letter. "But I think it might be part of the same thing." She looked up at me. "The IRS doesn't do things like that, do they?"

"No, but people do." My anger was brewing again. Someone was the friend of an IRS field agent. It was the only way the letter made sense. Dismantling Sadie's enterprise would silence her opposition. It was a roundabout, but effective way. I simply wasn't going to allow it to happen.

"We'll just make sure they fail." There was determination in my mind and I wanted Sadie to hear it in my voice. I was surprised when she blushed at my words.

"Thank you, Frank. That makes me feel a lot better." Sadie stumbled the response out with an awkward smile. She hesitantly rose and exited the room. It almost seemed like she wanted to say more, but thought better of it. She was flustered and I wondered what I had said that caused it.

Sadie surprised me the next morning with a cup of coffee and a doughnut. I had never seen her serve any food before four. I had never even seen her eat. I stared at it in shock when she placed in on the desk. She blushed again and left quickly. I didn't even have time to get a 'thank you' out. It was completely unlike her.

I spent the morning, warmed by coffee, traversing the first year the IRS was interested in. They were as immaculate as the other two. I was determined to leave no stone unturned, so I went through the Charity Ball ledger as I had the other two years.

I was absently totaling the donations when my eyes were attracted to the name column. A sense of familiarity pulled my eyes. 'Amber and David Thaxton' was handwritten next to a donation of fifty dollars. My eyes welled up as I ran my fingers across the names. Amber was always giving small sums to one organization or another. My name must have come from the check. The irony of it all hit hard. I felt tears running down my cheeks and I squeezed my eyes to get them to stop. They didn't, so I let it go. I saw her perfectly again, my mind had rebuilt the image. With it, the pain came slamming back. I buckled under the pressure and the floodgates opened. God, I loved that woman.

Sadie picked that time to check on my progress. Fooling no one, I turned away and quickly wiped my eyes. I stumbled out of the office mentioning the need to use the restroom. The tears kept coming as I hurried past Kevin who was busy peeling potatoes. I spent fifteen minutes, sitting on the toilet, slowing my heart. I rinsed my face, trying to dull the redness around my eyes.

Sadie was sitting at the desk when I returned. "Close the door," she said, and motioned me to the seat on the other side.

"My husband died nine years ago." Sadie was looking directly at me. "The kitchen was Richard's creation, the only thing he had done right, he told me. I promised him I would keep it running. I don't think he envisioned me running it personally, but here I am." She looked down at the desk. "The whole world thinks you're dead." My mind was reeling. She made sense now, her running this place fit. Her telling me about it meant she knew something of me.

"Most of the world doesn't know I exist," I countered. I wasn't sure if I wanted to be angry. I just didn't want more memories. I was having trouble not remembering on my own.

"I'm pretty good with faces, it was your beard and name that through me off." Sadie tapped the ledger with Amber's and my names. "You just looked the same way I felt when Richard died, David." I excused myself again. Having Sadie know was just as bad as seeing Amber's name in the ledger. I was dousing my face in cold water when I began to wonder how she knew my face. She wasn't guessing, she knew. I don't remember ever meeting her prior to a few days ago. Maybe she knew Amber, that would explain the donation. I settled my emotions and returned for the second time.

"You knew Amber?" I asked, choking on her name.

"Close the door," Sadie responded while shaking her head no. "I know of her. The whole world knows her." I sat down confused. "I'm sorry, seeing the name in the ledger must have hurt." I closed my eyes and nodded. I really didn't want to start crying again. I wasn't confident my voice wouldn't crack.

"You can hide here for as long as you need," Sadie offered.

"The police looking for me or something?" I asked with *q*uite a bit of confusion.

"Not any more. They think you're dead." I shook my head, trying to wrap my thoughts around what Sadie was saying. Amber's image kept flashing in my mind. I had an estranged sister, it would have taken her twenty years to report me missing. I had *q*uit my job, they wouldn't have cared enough to check up on me. I guess maybe a friend, but I hadn't been gone long enough for them to worry enough to call the police.

"Why would they think that?"

"You don't know?" Sadie seemed surprised.

"Know what?" Sadie went to work on the computer as I looked on. A few moments later she turned the monitor towards me. My picture was on the screen under the headline, 'Promise Keeper Believed Dead.' The banner across the top was the daily paper's logo. It was a picture of me, on stage, with my hand held out before me.

"Your song 'Amber' went viral." Sadie said softly.

"It was just a prelim. It wasn't supposed to be broadcast," I said as I leaned into the computer screen to read the article text. The text mentioned finding my wallet in the east river. The fact that it contained money, indicated I wasn't robbed. Their assumptions were correct, the end result was not.

"How did your wallet end up in the river?" Sadie asked softly. I could see the concern in her eyes.

"Houser fished me out of the river," I answered. I wasn't ready to say the truth out loud and probably never would. I skipped over it and then added a weak justification, "It wasn't a good time for me."

"And now?"

"Time to think," I answered, "I just need time to think." Sadie looked like she might have misunderstood so I added, "No more bridges in my future." She smiled.

"Take all the time you need, Frank." I smiled at her use of 'Frank.'

"I'll figure things out as soon as we get through this IRS audit," I said as I continued perusing the article. Sadie got flustered again and fumbled her way off her seat. I had no idea what was causing it. I pretended to ignore it for her sake, and mine.

"I'm sorry about Amber," Sadie whispered before she opened the door.

"I'm sorry about Richard." We shared forced smiles. At least we understood each other that far.

Embarrassment was my main emotion as I surfed the web for the first time in a week. My fame was fading, as all digital fads do, but I had shined brightly for a few days. I couldn't watch the video, not out of shame, but out of fear of the pain returning. Amber had always said I had a lovely voice, I had just assumed she was biased. I sang for her because she got a kick out of it. For us, it was like foreplay. I never had a desire to share it with the world. I made up songs for her and her alone. The words were sometimes silly and sometimes drivel from my heart. Loud pillow talk and nothing more. Now the world knew because of a dying promise I could not deny. I loved her too much for that.

The blogs were the worst. Half had me as an insane idiot and the others thought me some kind of love god. Offers of marriage and psychiatric help were abundant. It was just a promise, it wasn't meant to go this far. I was going to have to hide for a while. The story would die a quick death as all things internet-related do. Amber would have gotten a kick out of the whole thing, but then I would have had her at my side. I could have weathered any storm with her there.

I went back to work and finished the last tax year. Like the rest, no errors. That, in and of itself, was amazing. Books this clean were usually done by professionals. The IRS can dig as deep as they desired, there was nothing to find. Sadie was pleased to hear my summary. I could still see a little fear behind her eyes, but the IRS had a tendency to do that.

"Do you remember Amber?" I asked pointing at the charity ball ledger.

"Sorry, there are lots of attendees and most of them bring checks from their friends." Sadie's eyes went sad. "I'm sure she was lovely, I can see her in you." I could only nod at that. Amber was certainly lovely.

Houser joined me for dinner once again. It was brownie night so he was an absolute pleasure to be around. I moved my brownie to his tray and he just nodded and kept telling me about his day. There was an accident on the bridge that screwed up his time keeping, but, other than that, it was the same day as always.

Maggie sat down next to me, her face all crinkly with her smile. I guessed I had become a regular and was considered safe. Houser placed my brownie on her tray. I gave him a confused look. I had never seen him give up a brownie. I thought maybe he was sweet on Maggie.

"Maggie got me new boots," Houser said, nearly bringing his leg and a construction boot up on the table.

"Nicely done, Maggie," I said as I admired the nearly new treads on the sole.

"Figured someone wanted 'em, don't fit me." Maggie was speaking with a mouth full of meatloaf. The boots did look warm and I knew Houser saw the value. It was strange how my priorities were changing. A month ago, I would have just run out and bought a pair if I wanted boots. Now, I was slightly envious. Sadie snuck up on us again. This time it wasn't to speak to Houser.

"Thank you for all your work, Frank" Sadie put a glass of jello on my tray. It had three layers, red, green and yellow. The layers were slanted, obviously she had spent some time putting it together. I had a strong feeling of déjà vu and Amber, sending a shudder down my back. I just stared at the glass, not knowing what to say.

"I thought you liked jello," Sadie said with pain in her voice. She started to reach out to take it back. She couldn't have known. I reached it before she did and pulled it close and forced a smile.

"It's perfect. It was just unexpected." I looked back at the glass, tilting it to examine the layers. "It's actually *q*uite beautiful. Thank you." I glanced back at her. She was wearing a grin that spanned the whole room. She turned and went back to her duties on the line, her blue flowered skirt floating across the floor as she moved. Maggie giggled and shared a stupid look with Houser.

"It's just a thank you," I said, exasperated. Maggie went back to eating. Houser just smiled at me. I spent a good five minutes examining the jello. Fond memories of Amber washed through me. I remember coming home from work with an arm full of flowers, we had fought that morning over something stupid. Amber had found letter molds and spelled out 'I AM SORRY' in different colors of jello on the kitchen table. We were like that, never seeking blame in the end, just sharing forgiveness. Amber was just uni*q*ue about it.

162

I REFUSED TO BE IN MOURNFUL MOOD WITH A GLASS OF JELLO

I refused to be in a mournful mood with a glass full of jello. I smiled at my memories and destroyed the jello's symmetry with a spoon. It was well chilled and tasted wonderful. The irony of the day was not lost on me, finding Amber's name in the journal and the three-layered jello. There was pain, but there were also good memories. I decided to concentrate on the memories that shown brightest. The pain would have to take a backseat.

"Thanks for the jello." Sadie was busy watching the hall as I spoke. She turned to me with an honest smile. She really needed to smile more and so did I.

"Your time is done here," Sadie said cheerfully, "what will you do with your day?" I looked around the room and felt a kind of affinity towards the place. I hadn't been here long, but I was comfortable here, for now.

"The work here is kind of therapeutic. I wouldn't mind staying on if you can use me." Sadie looked at me with curiosity. I could almost see her thinking. It wasn't the reaction I expected.

"Prep or the line?" Sadie asked when her mind was made up.

"The line. Might as well learn it all," I said honestly. Sadie laughed before she spoke.

"1:00, you'll just love the clean up." Sadie had a mischievous grin on her face. I had seen it on another woman before. I smiled graciously, somewhat wishing I would have said prep.

Clean up was a bitch. Sadie was adamant about sanitation. Nothing was clean until she inspected it and it usually didn't pass on the first inspection. Luckily, there were four of us slaves so the work wasn't totally oppressing. I washed hundreds of dishes, pots and pans, a lot of them more than once. The floor was done twice. Sadie would find the grime in places Sherlock Holmes would have missed. She seemed to relish finding issues when I thought I was done. I think she took my volunteerism as a challenge. I sucked it up and by the time we were done, I would have confidently eaten off the floor.

I spent the next four weeks learning the hard part of running a soup kitchen. Sadie began to trust me to manage the deliveries. She was hesitant at first and I don't believe she had ever allowed anyone else to do it in the past. The first time she watched me like a hawk. It was simple inventory control to me, but to her it was like lopping off an arm. Reluctantly, she began to trust I wasn't going to screw it all up.

We would receive both ordered goods and donated goods. The donated had a very short shelf life, the reason the grocery store donated them in the first place. It was priority that these short-lived items found a place on the next day's menu and everything was visibly marked so nothing expired would ever find its way onto a plate.

I watched Sadie develop menus. This was something she would never relinquish control over. It was as much art as science. The expiration dates drove some of it and experience drove the rest. She worked up to five days in advance, solidifying a day's menu as it drew near. It was not something you could easily automate. There were food clashes that needed to be avoided and last minute donations that needed to be squeezed in. She allowed me to watch, but laughed when I offered to help. This menu was her domain and it would take an army to drag it away.

164

The army arrived a week later in the form of microscopic soldiers. I walked into work to find Sadie, pale and sweating, slumped on stool trying to work on the menus. Her eyes were bloodshot and I could tell she hadn't slept the night before. She looked absolutely miserable.

"Go home," I said compassionately.

"Can't, too much to do." Sadie covered her mouth with her hand when she spoke. Her voice was raspy like something was stuck in her throat.

"Give me the keys," I said forcibly, "and go home. You're going to get everyone sick." I think it was the thought of contamination that finally convinced her. Reluctantly, she handed me the keys.

"I promised Richard," Sadie said softly while looking around. It was important to her that I understood why she was here, as sick as she was. I understood, maybe the only one who could.

"I will make sure the promise is kept." I said it with conviction because I meant it. When Sadie's hesitant red eyes meet mine, I added, "I promise." Her eyes sparkled for a moment as she held my gaze.

"Thank you." Sadie moved off hesitantly.

I ran the City Kitchen for the next three days. I had to send Sadie home every morning those three days. I made it easy for her to leave, everything was in perfect shape and I was the picture of confidence. It couldn't have been farther from the truth. I had no idea how Sadie did it seven days a week. I felt like I was being pulled in ten directions at once. Workers didn't show, deliveries were late, menus didn't fit supplies and clean up ran later than it should. I screwed up the prep list on the first day sending the next two days' menus into turmoil. The days were long and grueling. Sadie had made it look so easy. With the help of some of the more experienced volunteers, we were able to pull it together at the last minute. 'Sugar Magnolia' always played at 4:00 and people were fed. I was a stressed mess.

Sadie took back the reins on the fourth day. She smiled at the obvious relief on my face. I confessed it all, the problems, the botched menus and the overall mismanagement. She walked around inspecting the kitchen as I explained the problems that still needed solving. She ended in front of me as I explained about the lettuce I had to throw out because I didn't use it in time.

"Did anyone leave hungry?" Sadie asked calmly.

"Well no, but..." Sadie didn't let me finish. She went up on toes and kissed my forehead.

"Thank you, David. You did wonderfully." Sadie's smile burst through my misgivings. I let out the breath I was holding and stopped the tirade of my failures.

"I'm glad you're back," I admitted as I handed her the keys. It felt really good to put the place back on her shoulders. She was even stronger than I had given her credit for. The kiss was a little disturbing. I could still feel the impression her soft lips left. I was happy when she sent me to reset the tables for the day. Back to simple, completable tasks.

Three days later the IRS invaded. A black-suited field agent with two similarly-suited accountants descended on Sadie's books. It was a witch hunt. Normally, an auditor would look at significant transactions and a random sampling of others. These three did as I had done and checked every transaction and journal entry. Each, and every, bank statement for the last three years was scrutinized. The questions were insulting and bordered on acquisitions. My ire was already sky high when the audit came to a close.

"We will assemble our findings and you will be notified within two weeks of the results," the head field agent said. His name was Terrence Douglas and sported an obvious toupee. I could see the frustration on his face. I suspected he wanted to find glaring problems.

"You don't foresee any issues, do you?" I asked, thinking I already knew the answer.

"We will make a formal response only." Terrence's face was not friendly as he packed up his note pad and calculator. My anger was growing. The IRS was always a pain, but usually polite.

"You must have some idea," I added with my hands on my hips. Terrence looked at me from head to toe, then at Sadie with more than a bit of disdain.

"I recommend you secure proper guidance." Terrence closed his briefcase and started walking out. It was all I could do not to take a swing at the asshole. His words told me they intended to find problems. I couldn't imagine it would get anywhere in the long run, but they were going to pull Sadie through the ringer.

"What are they going to do?" Sadie asked. I saw fear in her eyes.

"I'm not sure, but it won't be good." I didn't have the heart to lie to her. "In the long run, nothing will come of it. I'm just not sure how long the long run is." Sadie looked ill. She seemed to be taking it as a personal failure.

"We'll get through this." I thought the words would be comforting. Sadie found them shocking.

"We!" It was the first time I had heard Sadie raise her voice. "There is no 'we.' It's me they are attacking. You're just some guy who dropped out. You risk nothing and then walk away clean." She raised a hand to shoo me away and returned to the kitchen. She returned to work, making sure not to look my way. It was time I left. I just didn't know where to go.

I left as quietly as I could, unseen. Sadie was right, I could just walk away. I walked for the rest of the evening, my stomach churning with bile. I thought I saw friendship in Sadie, I thought I could help. I had done nothing but raise her hopes, only to watch them get flung from a bridge

That night was cold. The seasons were changing and I wasn't ready. I huddled sleeplessly in a warehouse doorway, trying to avoid the wind. I closed my eyes and tried to see Amber, build her face in my mind. I saw only Sadie, hating me. I shivered with my knees tucked tightly to my chest. I wanted my wallet, keys and phone back. I wanted Amber and my life back. The shaking increased, memories of my first wet day under the bridge. The cement I was sitting on did me no favors. I nodded in and out.

"Move on." I awoke shivering. Above me was a cop dressed warmly. Around me I could see the rotating reflections of red and blue lights. "Can't loiter here; you have to move on." He gave my boot a little kick. I had trouble rising, my chest was having trouble bringing in the cold air. I stumbled a little, trying to wake up my cramped legs. "Next time buy some warm clothes instead of booze." He stood there making sure I was headed away. I heard a car door close; it sounded more hollow than it should. The rotating lights stopped and police car drove past me as I lumbered on.

The air tasted colder than it should. I realized my nose was nonfunctional and dripping mucus. My body had caught up with my soul -- both feeling lousy. The cop was right, I needed warmer clothes. Maybe it was time I went home. I didn't like the idea, not with all the memories, but I knew I wasn't built for the streets. I was no Houser, not strong enough. I needed sleep. Then, I could do what was needed, whatever that was. I tried to cough, but my lungs argued about it and decided to remain clogged. At least the shaking had stopped.

I stumbled forward for blocks. Directions were muddled and I wasn't sure if I was going the correct way. It was still dark and traffic was minimal. Houser would know what time it was. I laughed at that, me and my college degree easily shown up by an uneducated homeless man with bad teeth. My laughing didn't sound right, way too throaty. A laughing frog came to mind which made me laugh more. I had to stop with my hands on my knees to catch my breath. It felt good to laugh, but I knew it was sapping my energy. I had to find a place to sleep. I found another entryway, wood this time. I curled up against the corner away from the wind. It was better than the cement. I closed my eyes and Sadie's image formed in my mind. I was puzzled why it wasn't Amber's as I drifted off to sleep.

<<<<<>>>>>

It was music that woke me. It entered as a dream on the cusp of my memory and then the dream faded away. I was late, late for dinner. I sat up too quickly and ended up in a small coughing fit. When my eyes focused, I was in an office I knew well. Sadie's office. I could hear 'Sugar Magnolia' playing and the general din of food being served. It was muted by the closed door, but it was obvious it was 4:00. I was on a fold out cot with two thick blankets now bunched up on my lap.

I wasn't sure how I ended up at the City Kitchen. I remembered finally finding the wooden entryway and trying to get some sleep. In hindsight, it seemed like an asinine decision to sleep outside last night. I should have gone to the bridge to see Houser, or to the shelter. I still wasn't good at dealing with pain. I stood and coughed some more. My feet were steady, but my head felt like a brick. My nose was stuffed up and I could feel thickness in my eyes. I must have found my way back here. Sadie must be really pissed. I had to stop this stupid self-loathing homeless shit and get my life back.

The kitchen was in full swing. I was walking slowly with a foggy head. Trudy spotted me ambling toward the dining room and called out, "Sadie, Frank's awake." Sadie swung quickly around the corner, her green flowered skirt swaying with the momentum. Her long hair flowed just moments behind her, catching a small draft and flaring out for moment. I saw determination in her green eyes. I was ready for an earful so I preempted.

"I'm sorry." It came out hoarsely, my throat wasn't ready for words. So I cleared it with a cough quickly and continued, "I'll get out of here and leave you alone."

"What the hell were you thinking?" Sadie's voice was controlled, and I don't think it carried past me. She grabbed my hand and pulled me into the office. I followed, her will being stronger than my mushy brain could counter. "I had everyone looking for you." She pushed me back on the cot and began covering me with the blankets.

"I thought..." Sadie didn't let me finish.

"You didn't think," Sadie stated firmly, then her voice cracked, "if Houser hadn't found you...God... you were blue when he brought you back." There were tears running down her cheeks which she quickly wiped away. I was confused and my brain wasn't processing at full speed. She sat down on the floor next to the cot, spreading her skirt evenly around her. "I am so sorry." It sounded like she wanted to say more. She couldn't get it out and wiped away another tear.

"I don't understand," I said *q*uietly. One minute I thought she wanted me to leave and the next to stay.

"I don't either," Sadie said, her voice cracking, "it was ten degrees last night, I thought you were going to die." She dropped her head into her hands and sobbed.

"I didn't though." It was an obviously useless statement. I thought back to crawling into that wooden entry way. It was almost my grave. "My stupidity isn't your fault." Sadie tried to say something, then thought better of it. She stood, instead, wiping her eyes.

"I'm going to get you some food. You're not to leave." It wasn't a request. I watched her leave with her hair bouncing on her back. Something had changed and I couldn't completely wrap my head around it.

Sadie returned and allowed me to sit up. She placed a plate of roast beef and mashed potatoes on the desk. I hadn't realized how hungry I was until the smell hit me. She sat with me, watching me eat, smiling while I chewed. When I pushed the empty plate away, she spoke.

"I want to take back what I said." Sadie looked at me, then her eyes drifted toward the empty plate. "I was angry...I can't really explain it and it confuses me." She looked back at me with her clear, green eyes. "I don't want you to leave, although I know you might. I wouldn't blame you."

"I'm pretty messed up," I admitted. I tried to kill myself and then almost did it accidentally. "I'm not sure if I do more harm than good." Sadie put her hand over mine.

"I have been playing Richard's favorite song every day at 4:00 for nine years." Sadie smiled as she thought about it. "I've been hiding in a soup kitchen behind a promise. My acquaintances all live on the streets. I am the poster child of messed up and I am highly efficient at it." I didn't move my hand, thinking she might remove hers. I felt guilty enjoying the human touch. The last person I touched died in my arms. It felt nice to be close to someone again.

"I threw my life away to live in a cardboard box with Houser," I said to top Sadie's concept of messed up. She laughed as I smiled. It was nice to see her eyes crinkle and little dimples form on her cheeks. I was happy she didn't remove her hand.

"So you'll stay for a while?" Sadie's eyes were hopeful.

"I could use the distraction this place provides," I said honestly. "Those little solvable tasks are welcoming. I would also like to see this IRS thing through. I kind of pisses me off." Sadie's smile widened.

"You can sleep here until you find someplace better." Sadie rose and picked up the empty plate and silverware. I felt a small emptiness when she removed her hand from mine. The shelter had better beds, but this felt more like home. I could get used to the cot. "If you feel better in the morning, I'll put you to work." She started walking out, then stopped in the doorway and turned back toward me. "Thank you for not hating me." She spun back around and disappeared out the door before I could form a response. I had no idea where that came from. I was hating myself, not her.

I ate dinner with Houser the next day. I thanked him for finding me the other night. It turns out I actually walked back to the City Kitchen with his help. I remembered nothing of the walk. Houser's lecture on how to survive winter on the streets was long and disjointed. There was no lesson plan, so he verbally hopped around telling me things out of order then backtracking to fill in the holes. I listened patiently, knowing he was the reason I was there to learn it. I gave him my white cake, the first repayment of many.

Sadie and I began working closer together. I learned proper menu management and inventory control. The problems that plagued me during her brief sickness were the norm, not the exception. She just had the tools to deal with them without panicking. The management skills she taught me would put Harvard Business School to shame. There was a change in Sadie during my schooling. She would smile more and become more tolerant. I still had to do it right, without exception. She just identified the many errors in a pleasant, non-demanding way.

I was able to get into another Roma tomato coring contest with Sadie. I attacked with vigor and was handily beaten again. She had nine years on me, but I think I did a lot better than the first time. I suspected I could beat her given a few more tries. I loved her victory face. Maybe I would never win.

I really enjoyed the escape from my past. I also knew that staying forever wasn't much of a possibility. I had commitments I had been ignoring that would cause festering problems if I continued to neglect them. Using the office computer, I logged into my bank account. I had a few months of overdue bills and some of them mattered. A few clicks of the mouse and my mortgage and utility bills were brought up to date. I had to transfer cash from savings. I had enough to withstand nine months, maybe longer, if I ignored some things. Amber had always insisted on the buffer. She was my better mind.

I would lose my cable and the paper. Those bills were mailed. Nothing to really fret about, I wasn't using them anyway. I was a little concerned about my car. I had left it in the parking lot of the theater and I wondered if it was still there. I shrugged my shoulders and made the back payments hoping it wasn't already repossessed. It felt a little weird paying the bills. I had spent a lot of time these last weeks, trying to avoid real life. I was taking a step toward normalcy, and I still wasn't wholly comfortable with the move. I had already checked the boxes and hit 'pay' so I couldn't step back. I stroked my growing beard and logged out. It was just a step, I'll take the leap later.

Three weeks after the IRS audit, a letter arrived. Sadie was crushed and I was livid. The IRS had identified the fifteen dollar window cleaning payment as an undocumented cash disbursement. They claimed it indicated fraud and were notifying Sadie that a seven year audit of both the City Kitchen, and her personally, will commence in ninety days. It was the second time I had seen Sadie cry. This time it was on my shoulder. It took a few minutes to return to work.

The City Kitchen's fundraising banquet was a week prior to the new audit. The pressure mounting on Sadie showed in her face. She couldn't stall the banquet, its proceeds are necessary to keep the kitchen open.

"They're going to ruin me," Sadie said with surprisingly calm, "maybe this was all meant to end." I saw the signs of depression setting in. I knew them well.

"Only if you let them." I avoided the word 'we.' It was hard not to try to make it our problem. It felt like it was ours.

"I'm going to need you if I fight," Sadie said as she stopped chopping celery and looked up at me. I tied off the garbage bag I had just pulled it out of the can and smiled with confidence. She needed the support.

"I wouldn't miss it for the world." I watched her lips curve into a malicious grin as she went back to the celery. The knife moved with blazing speed. I think she was imagining IRS fingers as she chopped.

Sadie woke me early the next morning. She handed me the morning paper. There was a small article in the bottom right of the front page. 'Promise Keeper Alive?' was the heading.

"They say there were movements in your accounts," Sadie said *q*uietly. There was no one else here so I wasn't sure why she was almost whispering. "They are requesting you come forward."

"I paid some bills the other day," I whispered back. It was contagious, the whispering. "I guess they were monitoring the accounts." I read the article and, as Sadie had said, a detective Berkhard was asking me to come forward and claim my wallet. "I'm not ready to go back. Not with that singing thing." For some reason, I didn't like being forced back into society. I was planning to drift back slowly. Sadie sat on the edge of the cot.

"You can hide as long as you need." She took the newspaper back. "Forever if you need to." Amber would have loved Sadie. Amber never let the world tell her what to do. She made up her own mind and then steered the world to it. I saw a lot of that drive in Sadie. I just needed to get the IRS out of her way so she could live her life, her way.

"Thank you," I responded, and meant it. Sadie's eyes sparkled as she rose.

"We have work to do," Sadie stated. It wasn't lost on me that she used the word 'we.' I jumped out of bed. There were people to feed and an IRS audit to thwart.

A week before the banquet, my beard had finally come into its own. Sadie hated it, but endured it for my anonymity. She gave me a trimmer so I would at least keep it groomed. I had spent countless hours going over Sadie's tax returns. There were no glaring errors. Nothing that would even hint at fraud. I was confident the witch hunt would end the next week. The IRS has a lot of power, but would still have to defend themselves in court if need be.

Unfortunately, I was not prepared for the next bomb to drop. Sadie and I were standing at the head of the line, monitoring the dining hall when a large gentleman in jeans, red shirt and cowboy hat pushed his way to the front. Sadie moved quickly, her glare set to dagger mode.

"You must be new." Sadie stated the obvious and moved to block the cowboy from moving forward. I moved in next to her, thinking she looked awfully small next the large man.

"Sadie Millstead?" the man asked with little politeness.

"Yes, and your name?" Sadie responded with an equal lack of charm. The man handed her an envelope.

"You've been served." The cowboy smiled and headed out the door. Sadie's shoulders slumped, then her back straightened again. She moved back to allow the rest of the line through, gritting her teeth.

"Can you keep your eyes on things, Frank?" Sadie asked with false calm. I nodded and she headed off to the office. She didn't return.

When the meal ended I started the cleanup process without Sadie. When everyone was assigned a task I went to the office, my temporary home, looking for her. I found her asleep on the cot. Sadie's eye sockets were blushed red and sunken. I quietly moved to the desk where a stapled set of papers lay. The top sheet had a few small crinkled spots where wetness had dried. Tears.

I picked up the papers and read. I felt my throat knot at the first few paragraphs. A class action lawsuit filed by a donor claiming fraud. There were twenty some pages of legal language and the citing of precedents. Both the City Kitchen and Sadie were at risk. These people, whoever they were, were not going to stop with a fraudulent IRS audit. Sadie was right, they were going to ruin her.

I sat on the floor and watched Sadie sleep. I wanted to wake her and tell her it was going to be okay, but that would only make it worse for her. In the end, she was innocent and would prevail. I just didn't know when the end would arrive. The lawyers she needed to hire would most likely charge enough to send everything into a financial tailspin.

I rose, opened the file cabinet and retrieved the donor book for three years ago. I turned to the page with Amber's name and ran my finger across it. Amber saw something in this place, something in need of support. There was no way I was going to let Amber or Sadie down, not while I was breathing. Defense was no longer an option.

I left Sadie sleeping, and quietly left the room. She needed the sleep, and I needed to think. I cleaned and inspected, letting the helpers go once everything was to Sadie's standards. I locked up and sat in the dining hall, thinking. The rudiments of a plan developed, I knew the lawsuit wasn't the end. The timing was deliberate. They meant to kill the banquet and destroy the City Kitchen's funding.

Things would get worse before they got better. I would need help, and, to get it, I had to come out of hiding.

I woke to a pounding sound. I had fallen asleep, my head pillowed in my arms on the table. I wiped the drool from my lips and went to open the door. An elderly gentleman, one I had seen eat often, was there. I remembered his name as the dream fog cleared.

"Sadie said to be here at 9:00," Ralph said, rather surprised I wasn't Sadie.

"Come in and let's get started." I opened the door wider and stepped aside. I was worried about Sadie. It wasn't like her to let anything slide. I got Ralph into the shower room and went to check on Sadie.

I found her back at the desk, staring at the lawsuit. There were black circles around her eyes. I was thankful there weren't any tears. She must have run out last night.

"Ralph is here," I said as business-like as I could. Sadie looked up to me with a forlorn look.

"Does it matter?"

"Yes," I responded. I had a litany of reasons to go on and knew they would fall on deaf ears. Short and simple was the only good response.

"They are destroying me." I saw defeat in Sadie's eyes.

"The banquet will be next." I said it firmly. I didn't want to sugar coat it. Sadie's eyes widened with fear.

"It will bankrupt the Kitchen," Sadie said. I sat down on the cot as I watched her face go ashen.

"I won't let that happen." There was determination in my voice, hopefully something Sadie could latch onto.

"I don't think we can stop these people," Sadie said, holding up the stack of papers. I gave her a confident smile. The smile held more confidence than I felt, but she needed more.

"No one's going hungry, Sadie. I need to speak to some old friends to see if we can't turn this around." I pulled the donor book out again and turned to the page with Amber's name and pointed at it. "She thought this place was worth funding. I promise you, her donation won't go to waste. Ever." Sadie's face firmed up.

"What do you want me to do?"

"Make sure you open at 4:00." I needed to handle this alone. "And don't lose heart. It's going to be a very long week. Let me take care of the rest." Sadie stood up and nodded her head.

"I'll make sure we stay open," Sadie said, "whatever happens, thank you for trying." She moved past me *q*uickly. Her determination had returned, but not her confidence. I felt a little sorry for Ralph, he was bound to catch the brunt of her frustration. I sat down and made the first call.

"Herzog and Associates, this is Karen may I help you?" the receptionist greeted me. I knew Karen, but I really didn't want to explain myself.

"Doug Herzog, please," I said, trying to jump past the hurdle.

"Mr. Herzog is busy right now, would you like to leave a message?" It was bite the bullet time. I took a deep breath.

"Karen, it's David Thaxton. I really need to speak with Doug," I said it *q*uickly, hoping she would just let me through without an interrogation. No such luck.

"David, oh my god, are you alright?" There was concern in her voice that exceeded the relationship we had had in the past. I guess notoriety does that to a person.

"I'm fine Karen. It's really important that I speak with Doug," The secret was out. I needed to move forward at a *q*uick pace now.

"Alright, I'll see if I can't get him out of the meeting. Hold on a minute," Karen said, then added, "Amber was right, you sing wonderfully." I felt my throat knot a bit. I had forgotten she had known Amber. The two would talk during the company Christmas parties. I just sighed a 'thank you' and waited for Doug.

"Where the hell are you, David?" Doug asked when he came on the line, "The whole damn world is looking for you." I wanted to skip that part so I did.

"I have a problem Doug. I know I don't deserve your help, the way I quit and all." I knew he would help anyway, I just wanted him to know I knew I was a jerk, "It's just that you're the only one I could think to call."

"Your wife died, so skip the bull. What do you need." Doug had given me a pass. I had new respect for him.

"You know those pro bono hours your CPA requires? Do you think you can throw some to a friend of mine?"

"I'm listening," Doug responded. I told him everything. I did leave out some of my personal failures, like the bridge incident, but told him the rest. I told him about the City Kitchen and how its mission is to feed the homeless. I told him about Sadie and the IRS. I gave him the best guess as what was happening and ended with the class action lawsuit.

"Her books are clean?" Doug asked.

"Some of the best I have ever seen," I responded honestly. "Whoever is doing this, has strong connections. I promised Sadie I would do what I could to end this." Doug laughed.

"I would never stand between a promise and its keeper," Doug joked, "how many agents came the first time?"

"Three."

"I'll have six suits present and I need to see the books beforehand." Doug was all in. "Let me know when the banquet is and I'll make sure it's company policy."

"Thank you, Doug. You have no idea what this means to me," I said, trying to remain manly and not get all choked up. "I'll get you whatever you need. I know we're on the right side of this one." We ended the call with a lot of testosterone lingering across the line. Doug liked the idea of fighting the IRS, especially if he expects to win. To him, this was the accounting equivalent to a showdown at high noon.

"An auditor from my old firm will be here tomorrow," I said to Sadie who was cleaning some potatoes. She stopped scrubbing and looked up.

"You told someone you were here?" Sadie asked incredulously.

"It's war, honey, no holds barred." I blushed when I realized I had used a term of endearment. It just slipped out, as if I had been speaking with Amber. I moved quickly toward the door, hoping she wouldn't notice.

"Go get em, honey!" Sadie yelled. I heard her laughing, which sounded good. Ralph was giggling, which sounded bad.

I moved quickly now that my mind was made up. It took no time to walk the ten blocks to the sixth precinct. It was in an old three story brick building, probably a good fifty years old. It had a set of steep steps that I was sure wasn't to code anymore. I walked in and straight to the desk that was manned by a uniformed cop.

"I would like to see Detective Berkhard, please."

"Name, please," the cop asked, not looking up from the form he was filling out.

"David. He is expecting me." I answered. I really didn't want a scene at the front desk. The cop picked up the phone and dialed an extension. The brief interruption seemed to bother the man. Whatever he was working on was more important than my visit.

"I got a David out here for you." The cop looked up at me after a second, "David who?" I sighed.

"Thaxton," I whispered. The cop just smiled.

"Come on up, Tony. You definitely want to meet this man." The cop hung up the phone. "My wife thinks you're some kind of great romantic. I have you pegged as in idiot." His grin spread the room as he expressed his view.

"A bit of both, mostly the latter." I asked for this. I would have to deal with the results. The cop laughed and held out his hand. I shook it with a great deal of surprise. A short man sitting on the bench jumped up and headed to the desk.

"Who's this, Sergeant?" The man was wearing business casual with a long sleeve polo shirt. Nothing expensive, but not street duds.

"Leach,mind your own business," the sergeant responded sharply. He looked back at me and used his eyes to direct me down the hall. I was grateful for the fence he put up. This was going to be hard enough to weather.

I met Detective Berkhard about twenty feet down the hall. He wore a brown suit with a dull yellow shirt and a golden-shaded amoeba tie. His hair was cut military style with zero sideburns sitting on a six foot frame. He looked like the type of guy you want standing next to you in a dark alley.

"You David?"

"Yes." I held out my hand and the detective shook it. I saw his expression change as he saw past my beard.

"David Thaxton," he said, and shook my hand harder, "Tony

178

Berkhard." I added my smile to his and nodded. He lead me to a small conference room and indicated I should take a seat.

"I understand you have my wallet," I said. It would sure save me a lot of time if I didn't need to replace the IDs and credit cards. It would also be a convenient way to end the speculation of my death.

"Yes we do." Tony was still smiling. "My wife thinks you are some kind of super husband." His expression changed quickly when he realized what he said. "I am sorry about your wife."

"Thank you," I said in my practiced, ignore the painful memory, tone. "I don't really deserve the myth that seems to have developed."

"Well, obviously you're not dead," Tony said, returning to a subdued cheerfulness, "can you tell me where you were or do I have to read it in the paper?" It didn't sound like an official request. I don't think I was obliged to tell him anything. He just had one of those trusting faces and a pleasant attitude that was difficult to deny. I spilled the beans for the second time that day. I wasn't sure if he could help with the attacks on Sadie and the City Kitchen, but I let him know that was why I finally decided to end the hiding.

"You haven't seen the paper?" Tony asked.

"Nope."

Tony pulled out the paper from the trash can next to his desk. He turned a few pages on the front section, folded it over and handed it to me. The title of the article was "City Kitchen Sued For Fraud." The speed at which these people were operating was phenomenal.

"Shit!" I said as I read. I especially liked the part where they claimed that Sadie Millstead had no comment. "They are moving faster than I thought. This is going to kill the banquet."

"You could fill ten banquets if you just let people know you will be there," Tony claimed, "my wife would demand tickets. I could get half the force to show up." I smiled at the thought. Maybe my five minutes of fame would be worth one banquet.

"I don't have much time. These guys are a few steps ahead of me," I said. I could call the press, but I didn't know anyone I could trust. The story could spiral out of my control and become about me.

"I think I can help you with that." Tony picked up the phone and dialed. "Rick, Leach out there? Okay, send him to my office." He hung up. "Leach is our resident freelance journalist. He follows us out to crime scenes and sells the stories to the paper. I think you two can use each other." He smiled conspiratorially. Leach walked in.

"David, this is Bob Townsend. We affectionately call him Leach." I rose and shook the hand of the confused-looking man.

"What's this about, Tony?" Leach asked.

A STORY FOR A STORY, LEACH

"A story for a story, Leach," Tony, said indicating an empty seat to Bob, "David needs some press and in exchange you get an exclusive." Realization washed across Bob's face.

"David Thaxton?" Bob asked, looking at me. I nodded. He smiled from ear to ear. "Deal!"

For the third time that day, I explained what had happened. Leach was taking copious notes as I spoke, and asking questions to clarify what I said. Tony seemed proud of himself for putting us together. He excused himself to get my wallet.

"So you want me to let everyone know you will be at the banquet. That's it?" Leach asked.

"Yep and I would prefer they don't know where to find me prior to the banquet," I responded.

"You'll talk to no other reporters?" Leach was bursting at the seams. Tony returned with a plastic bag containing my wallet and some kind of form.

"No one but you," I agreed, "at least until you get a chance to print the story." Bob smiled and rubbed his hands together.

"After all this time, why are you coming out now?" Bob asked. I thought I just explained it all to him.

"I just told you, to help Sadie and the City Kitchen," I said, obviously frustrated.

"You don't owe them anything, why would you risk it?" Bob was pushing me. I had no idea why, but I was edging on angry.

"Look, I promised her I would help. So I'm helping." This time I made it sound final. Bob's pen went into hyperdrive.

"You just can't make this stuff up," Bob said absently, "another promise." Tony laughed and I sighed. Bob was going to blow it out of proportion. The banquet needed it so I let it go. "Is it okay for me to bring a cameraman to the banquet?"

"I thought you were newspaper," I replied.

"Freelance. With this story I'll be a media superstar." Bob celebrated with his hands in the air.

"Okay, but keep it low-key. I don't want this to be circus." Bob laughed at my remark.

"Too late for that. I'll just try to make sure you don't look too clownish." Bob was cleaning up his notebook as he spoke. "I'll need another interview the day after the banquet. It shouldn't take more than thirty minutes or so." I nodded my head. "I have to get this out if I am going to make the paper tomorrow. I won't leak your location, but some will guess it. I would stay hidden if I were you." He shook my hand and scurried off.

"You've been 'Leached,'" Tony said sarcastically. He pushed over a form for me to sign. It allowed me to get my wallet back. "You know it's going to be a madhouse, right?"

"If that's what it takes, so be it." I signed my name and retrieved my wallet. "I have to break into my condo, think I will get arrested?"

"Come on, I'll drive you." Tony laughed as he grabbed his jacket.

It was strange being back in my home. It was comforting and alien at the same time. Everything reminded me of Amber, not as strongly as before, but just as depressing. It was hardest in the closet, where her clothes collided into mine. My section kept getting smaller over the years. Fond memories of joking with her about being a pack rat burned through my thoughts. I couldn't live here anymore. Even if I would pack away everything of hers, the walls would still bleed her passing. It was just too much love to lose.

My pants were too big in the waist and I had to drop two notches on my belt. I had lost a lot of weight since I jumped off that bridge. I looked in the mirror and couldn't tell whether it was a good loss or an unhealthy one. I wondered if my beard hid an emaciated visage or a strong jaw. I wouldn't shave it today, I would save that for the banquet. I packed some toiletries and filled a suitcase with more clothes. I was done living like a beggar.

I put together a new set of keys from my spares and grabbed my warm jacket out of the closet. It was sitting next to Amber's parka. A person could survive the North Pole in that parka. Amber hated the cold, and loved how the parka would shield her against it. I always thought it was overkill. I grabbed it and brought it with me. No need to let it rot on a hanger. It was time to start letting the past go.

Tony drove me to my car. It stood, lonely, in the vast parking lot next to the venue I had sung in so long ago. It argued with me, trying not to start, but eventually kicked into a nice idle. I thanked Tony for all his help. He thanked me for promising to make an appearance at the annual Guns and Hoses boxing match next month. I couldn't say no after all he had done. I wasn't sure what I could offer a bunch of police officers and firefighters, but I agreed. I returned to the City Kitchen, this time with a car and a full wallet. I felt more normal, although I wasn't confident it was a good thing.

Dinner was in full swing when I arrived. I left my bags in the car, but brought in the parka. Sadie did not look good. I could see the strain in her eyes, and knew it had been a difficult day. She was stoic at the head of the line, but I knew she just wanted to collapse and let it all go. I smiled at her as I entered and got a bit of a surprised look at my slight transformation.

"The caterer for the banquet canceled," Sadie said quietly when I moved next to her. "There was an article in the paper and they didn't want to be part of it."

"I think they will reconsider tomorrow," I said confidently. I would have to move heaven and earth if they didn't, but I didn't want Sadie to know that. She needed my confidence. I needed her confident.

"What did you do?" Sadie asked, looking at me, confused.

"Everything I could," I responded, "where's Maggie?" Sadie pointed to the end table in the back. Maggie was eating with Houser. "I'll be right back." I walked over to the two of them.

"See if this fits you, Maggie," I said, holding up the parka. Maggie's eyes went wide as she stood up and removed her old jacket. I held the parka up like a gentleman and let her step into it. It fit her wonderfully.

"I ain't never had anything this nice." Maggie said, as she ran her hands along the fake fur lining.

"You do now." Amber would be pleased. She would have loved to know the parka was keeping someone warm. "Payment for the boots," I added, nodding over to Houser. He gave me one of his ugly toothy smiles.

"I owe you, Frank," Maggie said, "I owe you a lot."

"You owe me nothing and my real name is David." I was done hiding. "I had something I didn't need and you needed it. Simple as that." Maggie surprised me with a hug. It wasn't the first time I was hugged by that parka. I fought the tears and hugged her back. At least Maggie would be warm this winter.

I walked back to Sadie, clearing my eyes with the back of my hand. That was a little harder than I had expected.

"That was nice of you," Sadie said as I approached.

"It was Amber's," I said nodding back at Maggie and the parka. I saw concern form on Sadie's face.

"You went home?"

"Yes, I can't stay there, though."

"You're welcome to stay here," Sadie said, "as Frank or David."

"It's David and I would like to stay for now," I said honestly.

"I'm glad," Sadie said and quickly went to deal with an issue on the serving line. I watched her skirt swirl with her hips as she moved and realized I was glad also.

It was at the tail end of cleanup when a well-dressed lady entered. She was wearing a tailored dark gray business suit with a silk blouse. She was carrying an expensive black briefcase case as if it was part of her. Her black hair was pulled back severely and secured tightly with a tiny black bow. She walked like she owned the place. I disliked her immediately.

"Sadie Millstead?" the woman asked, holding her hand out to Sadie. Sadie nodded and shook her hand. "I'm Barbara Cane, a lawyer at Helick, Cane and Walters. I wonder if we could talk for a moment." Sadie led her to one of the dining tables. I hovered, re-cleaning part of the floor in the dining room.

"I represent a party who is interested in resolving the predicament you find yourself in." Barbara held a half grin while she talked. I suspected it was always there, but I found it rude.

"What predicament would that be?" Sadie asked, acting so innocent I almost believed her.

"I am speaking of the charges that have been leveled against you and the City Kitchen. I assume you have seen the paper." Barbara didn't let Sadie's act fool her. It seemed to be a game she liked to play.

"I don't concern myself with the idle chatter in the paper," Sadie said, waving her hand in dismissal. "My accountants assure me I have been more than forthright and all the issues will disappear in time." Barbara lost her grin. I don't think she was expecting Sadie's strength. In truth, I didn't expect it either.

"Things could get worse," Barbara stated. Sadie's face was turning red and I could see fire in her eyes.

"Who is this party you represent?" Sadie asked, holding back her sting.

"The party wishes to remain anonymous," Barbara smiled.

"Then we are done here," Sadie said calmly and rose. Barbara just smiled and stayed seated.

"I don't think you are considering the possible ramifications," Barbara threatened. Sadie exploded and shocked me.

"Bring it, bitch!" Sadie said loudly and pointed to the door. Barbara tried to hold her own, but fumbled her briefcase standing up. I guessed she was used to more decorum when she threatened people. I had to stifle a laugh as I stopped the phoney cleaning to watch Barbara scamper out.

"Tell me I didn't just destroy my life," Sadie said, moving toward me. She was shaking with the release of adrenaline. I folded her into my arms. She seemed a natural fit as she wrapped her arms around me.

"Bring it, bitch?" I questioned softly.

"It's all I could think of. She was threatening me in my own place." Sadie looked up to me. "Did I overdo it?"

"I was kind of proud of it. I just never heard you use a bad word before," I said with a smile. Sadie tucked her head back into my shoulder.

"I hope I didn't make it worse," Sadie whispered.

"Doesn't matter. We will get through this." I wanted to take back the 'we' as soon as I said it.

"You said 'we' again," Sadie responded without moving from my arms.

"I meant it." I wasn't in control of that word any more. I might as well own it. Sadie squeezed me harder. I was glad I did.

The next day we got a taste of the madhouse to come. Bob, true to his word, made the front page. An exclusive interview with the living Promise Keeper was big news. Without making any direct accusations, he detailed Sadie's plight and the possible demise of the City Kitchen. How I promised to save it and vanquish the bad guys was implied in every word he wrote. He promised articles to follow that detailed my exploits since my singing debut. The time and place of the banquet was clearly written. He used poetic license to rename it the 'Save the Kitchen' banquet. It was over the top and the public sucked it up.

Calls started pouring in. The caterer was one of the first with an apology. They were willing to cater the event for free, as a donation to the cause. The banquet venue called and asked if we needed more room. They moved us to their largest room at no additional cost. Best of all, Sadie was Sadie again. She was moving like a woman possessed. Everything was happening on schedule and everyone knew their job. With every phone call she received, her confidence spiked.

The mayor's office called and asked if it was okay for the mayor to attend the banquet. He would like to say a few words of support. It seems the police and firefighters union reps were going to be there, so the mayor felt obliged. I saw it as a win. The mayor certainly couldn't endorse the City Kitchen and then allow a developer to destroy it.

That afternoon, an auditor for Herzog and Associates showed. Tom Brandon, a man I had worked with in the past. We had a quick reunion and I took him to the office. We spent the afternoon going over the initial data and supporting documents. Like me, he was impressed with Sadie's books. Tom called Doug just before we opened for dinner.

"David's correct, these are clean and easy," Tom said over the phone, "I'll need two guys and two days to go through it all, but I doubt I'll find anything." He nodded and said yes a few times then handed the phone to me.

"You stirred up a hornets nest, David," Doug said pleasantly, "I got a call from a Barbara Cane this morning. After the article, I guess she assumed you would come to me for help. She tried to convince me it would be in my best interest not to help."

"I met her yesterday. Sadie told her, and I *q*uote, 'Bring it, bitch.'" I said it with a grin in my tone. Doug burst out laughing.

"I like Sadie already," Doug responded, "I told Barbara much the same thing, just in a more civil-minded manner. I did find out that your developer is the one and only Patrick Abernathy. You certainly don't pick small opponents, David."

"Mr. Abernathy picked us," I said. At least I could now put a name to the slimeball.

"Well Barbara pissed me off so I put in a call to Sarah Ferguson. Her firm is willing to defend the class action, pro bono of course, if Sadie will agree." I put my hand over the phone speaker and leaned out the office door.

"Doug Herzog found you a good lawyer, pro bono," I called out to Sadie, "you accept?" She laughed and nodded her head. I really didn't need to ask, but felt it was appropriate.

"Of course she accepts," I answered, "Doug, you have gone way beyond the line of duty here. I'm not sure if I can ever pay you back."

"I'll get it back in spades," Doug said lightly, "the firm that backed the Promise Keeper. It has to be worth a ton of billable hours. You going to sing at the ban*q*uet? My wife is expecting it."

"I wasn't planning on it. I was hoping the talent show was the last time I had to sing," I said honestly. I didn't really like the fear associated with being on stage.

"Well that will give me a leg up on the pool," Doug said, "right now it is two to one for you singing. No worries, Tom will bring a team out early tomorrow and get started. Tell Sadie to let us worry about the IRS. She just needs to get you to sing." Doug hung up before I could respond. It didn't occur to me that people would want me to sing. The Leach was planning on bringing a camera. There was no way I could sing for the world, much less another audience.

"Doug said you should let him worry about the IRS," I informed Sadie, leaving out the singing part.

"I can do that," Sadie said as she removed her latex gloves.

"Sarah Ferguson is going to take care of the class action," I added. I was full of good news. Sadie threw the gloves in the garbage, wrapped her hands around the back of my neck and kissed me on my lips. I wasn't sure how to respond. They were soft lips and slightly moist. She pulled back an inch and looked me in the eyes.

"My apologies to Amber, but you had that coming." Sadie smiled and headed out of the kitchen. It was 4:00 and people needed to be fed. It was the snickers from the crew that broke my trance. In my defense, they were really nice lips. I heard 'Sugar Magnolia' over the speakers and headed out to join Sadie on the line.

Surprisingly, the first person in the line was a uniformed police officer.

"You must be Sadie Millstead," the officer said, "and you must be David Thaxton." He smiled and held out his hand. I shook it as he explained. "There are two officers outside making sure the press and fans stay out. I'm supposed to stay down here in case they screw up. Unless you want to be on camera, you'll probably want to stay inside. It is a madhouse out there. I'm officer Brennan by the way."

"Thank you, officer," Sadie said, "I hope this won't be necessary for too long."

"Just until the frenzy dies down," the officer said, "your car caused most of it." He looked and smiled at me when he said it. I guess everyone knows I'm here. Should have taken a cab.

The night went without incident. We fed officer Brennan who also took some desert to the cops outside. No unauthorized homeless look-a-likes made it into the City Kitchen, but we were kind of in a prison of our own making. Sadie decided to spend the night on site. I chivalrously gave up the cot. To her, it was a foregone conclusion -- it was her cot anyway. I made do on a dining table. It was a little hard, but a couple of blankets made it tolerable.

The next two days saw the auditors hard at work. Sarah Ferguson stopped by the second day with a copy of the class action suit. She and Sadie talked strategy while I helped the auditors with data demands. In the middle of it all, we prepped the kitchen for the night's dinner. The Leach showed up just before 'Sugar Magnolia' to get some background on the City Kitchen. His articles had created a frenzy and he needed more information to keep them going. I took him to Houser, the resident expert on the subject. Bob had no trouble fitting in and making friends. He liked to listen and Houser liked being the expert. It also helped that I slipped Bob a brownie to grease the wheels.

The media spent those days camped out in front of the City Kitchen. Detective Berkhard made sure there were enough police that the media kept their distance. A couple of reporters tried to sneak through as homeless and were caught. Maggie pointed them out and looked good doing it in her new parka. It was a zoo, but no one left hungry so Sadie was happy.

The day of the banquet brought with it a wonderful surprise. In the past, Sadie would run the kitchen as normal then rush to the banquet site leaving a crew to clean. It made for an extremely hectic day. Before noon, two men and a woman, all dressed in white chef attire met with Sadie.

"Mr. Morgan sent us," the tall blond man said with an air of authority, "I'm Tom Flounder and this is Randy and Karen. We're here to replace you for the day and let you concentrate on the banquet." Morgan Catering was the firm catering the banquet. I guessed they wanted to make sure Sadie wasn't upset with their flip flop. Sadie looked them up and down and decided they could handle it.

"That would be lovely," Sadie said with a grin.

"Do you think we could meet David Thaxton?" Karen asked. I

blushed at the request. I was not used to my fleeting fame. Sadie laughed and introduced me.

"The beard makes you look older," Karen said as she shook my hand. I could see undeserved admiration in her eyes.

"It was just a disguise," I informed her, "I'll shave it soon."

"I sure hope so," Sadie interjected, "I've hated that thing since the first day." I suddenly hated the beard myself.

"And you could use a haircut," Karen added, "have you thought about what you're going to wear tonight." I tried to say something, but Sadie jumped in.

"I was thinking black pants and shirt. It would look dashing with his frame." Sadie had obviously put some thought into it. I was going to try to tell her I didn't have anything like that when Karen jumped back in.

"He would need black wingtips, short heeled with a matching leather belt." Karen examined me closer. "Maybe the shirt should be collarless with a hint of gray to offset the pants."

"Ladies," I said, a little exasperated, "I don't own anything like that. I was just going to wear some khakis with a polo shirt." Sadie shook her head and smiled.

"We're going shopping, David. There's no way I am going let you look like a dork." Karen giggled at Sadie's demand. I just sighed and agreed.

Sadie spent the better part of an hour with the crew, explaining the planned menu and how things worked. She explained the 'Sugar Magnolia' dinner bell and was adamant about the 4:00 time. Tom took notes and complemented Sadie on the cleanliness of the facility. He put her mind at ease and guaranteed her no one would leave hungry. He certainly seemed competent and I could tell Sadie thought so as well.

It took four police officers to get us out of the City Kitchen. We were able to make it out the back with limited exposure. A plain cloths officer, Roger Cummings, was assigned to drive us where we needed to go.

"So, you're really going to sing at the Guns and Hoses?" Roger asked, after we escaped in his unmarked car.

"I never said I was going to sing," I answered, trying not to sound ungrateful for the force's help. Sadie looked at me, a little surprised. I had forgotten to tell her about the event.

"You got to," Roger went on, "it's the only reason my girlfriend is going to come. She hates the fights, but she adores you." A felt my face flush again. It was only one talent contest. This was getting a little out of hand. I certainly didn't deserve anyone's admiration.

"You agreed to this?" Sadie asked. I looked over to her.

"Tony asked. I couldn't say no, not with everything he was doing to help us out," I explained. Sadie took my hand in hers.

"Us," Sadie said softly. Some guilt leaked into my mind, memories of Amber. Sadie's hand felt good in mine. I wasn't sure if I should like it. My heart was beating faster than it should. "I'll be there with you, singing or not." She squeezed my hand with affection. God help me, I squeezed back.

Roger took us to a men's shop downtown. An older woman waited on us, her hair turning gray in a classy manner, with name tag that said Sally. I felt like a mannequin as the ladies had me try on different pants and shirts. They discussed the results as if I wasn't present and pretty much ignored my likes and dislikes. I tried on six pairs of shoes before Sadie was happy. Comfort was not one of the criteria she considered. I would have just picked a pair of nice brown cloth shoes if I had a choice in the matter. I had to admit, I did look pretty sharp in the mirror. I just didn't think I could live up to the image staring back at me. Sadie was pleased so I agreed, as if I had much of a choice.

I pulled out my card as we approached the register. Sally spent some time ringing it all up and I wondered if I would need a second mortgage to pay for it all. She shook her head and smiled when I tried to hand her the credit card.

"We would like to donate the clothes Mr. Thaxton," Sally said calmly, "for the City Kitchen."

"You recognized us?" Sadie said with big smile.

"Not at first, that beard kinda threw me for a loop," Sally said, matching Sadie's smile.

"Thank you, and please call me David," I said, genuinely touched by her generosity.

"You're so welcome, David," Sally said, "I really hope you remember us next time you shop." The offer was laced with a fondness I didn't deserve. I was happy my beard covered a good portion of my reddening cheeks. I was not designed for fame.

"Of course," I stuttered. Sadie stifled a giggle and led me out the door.

The next stop was a hair salon. The beard was going to go, and with it, whatever I had left of my anonymity. Sadie was excited. I would have preferred if she just handed me a razor. My hair was long, but I had become comfortable with it. She wasn't having any of it. For some reason, I was letting her run all over me. She was a formidable woman. I was sure Amber would have liked her. Amber would have never let me get so shaggy.

Cindy was my stylist, or so she said. She looked too young to be anything but an amateur. She had dyed blond hair combed incredibly straight with a sharp part on the left side. The hair stood in stark contrast to her dark black eyebrows.

"What are we doing to your hair today?" Cindy asked. Again, before I had a chance to answer, Sadie jumped in.

"First, let's lose the beard and then..." I raised my hand sharply and gave Sadie a look. I didn't want to, but I kind of felt I was losing myself. It was my head after all. "Sorry," she said and covered her smile with her hand. I gathered my thoughts and realized I screwed up.

"Um...shave off the beard and..." I had no idea how I wanted my hair. I turned my head sideways and looked at it in the mirror. The shaggy dog look might be comfortable, but it looked like crap. I rolled my eyes, "and however she wants it." I nodded my head weakly toward Sadie who was no longer covering her silly grin. I had put my foot down, directly into dog shit.

"Get it off the collar and ears," Sadie kicked back in without missing a beat, "leave the sideburns down to about here." She touched just in front of my ear sending an unexpected shiver down my neck, "Can you use a trimmer to layer it a bit, you know, business-like, but with a little modern style." She had some kind of vision for my head. It had to be better than my vision. Suddenly, I had two women touching my head all over, discussing trimmer sizes and part positions. I was a mannequin again.

I am not ashamed to mention the fear I felt when Cindy came at me with the straight razor. I was white knuckling the arms of the chair and gritting my teeth as the her hand approached. The blade looked hellishly sharp and she looked virginally young. I didn't move a millimeter as she dragged the blade up my neck. It was an agonizingly slow process and I prayed the whole time I wouldn't see bright spurts of red liquid shooting up.

"I'm really quite good at this," Cindy commented, when I inadvertently sucked in my breath, "it's been a long time since I have cut off anyone's nose." Sadie laughed. I remained perfectly still. It turns out Cindy was right, she was very good at it. Not a nick or even a bad scrape. My nose was where it belonged when Cindy applied a hot towel to clean off the excess shaving cream. Cindy's eyes went wide when she removed the towel.

"I know you." Cindy's smile grew. "You're that promise guy." I think my face was already red from the hot towel. At least I hoped so. I raised my finger to my lips and formed the international quiet symbol. "You're the promise guy," she repeated in a whisper. I nodded my head. "Can I get an autograph?" she asked. I rolled my eyes. Sadie thought the whole thing was hilarious. Cindy didn't wait for an answer, she grabbed a marker and I ended up signing her blow dryer. It was my first autograph, and hopefully my last.

Cindy went to work on my hair. Large clumps were falling down onto the cape she had covered me with. I felt she was touching me more than necessary. Her fingers would slide along my neck and up behind my ear. She would lightly fluff my hair as she cut, her fingers not flicking, but combing along my scalp, almost petting me. At first I thought they were accidental. Their frequency increased and it began to feel like foreplay.

Sadie moved closer to me, examining the length being cut off. She absently placed her hand over mine. Like magic, Cindy stopped the stroking. It was some kind of secret female nonverbal communication. Sadie stepped back again, but Cindy never returned to the caressing. It was strictly hair cutting from then on and I was thankful for it.

I was able to stop the hair gel. Both ladies thought it would be perfect finale. I thought it would be a pain in the ass. I didn't want to spend my mornings fussing with my hair. If my hair wanted to jump out of place, well that's everyone else's problem. I can't see it anyway.

"You really have to stop flirting with every girl you meet," Sadie said once we had returned to the car. I heard Roger snicker up front.

"I didn't do anything to encourage her," I claimed, "I'm just happy it stopped."

"You look a lot younger without the beard," Roger stated in the rear view mirror. I rubbed my hand along my newly shaved face. I had to admit it was nice to finally get rid of the beard. Sadie ran the back of her hand softly along my jaw.

"It certainly feels a lot younger," Sadie commented. Roger's eyes whipped back to the road in embarrassed reflex. The hand was an intimate gesture. It didn't seem like it affected Sadie that way. She just smiled and turned her head to look out the window. My thoughts turned to Amber, then back to Sadie and the back of her hand. I closed my eyes and tried to see Amber. It was hard, the image imperfect and my thoughts were muddling it up. My memory was such a weak tool.

Roger brought the car to the back of the hotel, the venue for the banquet. We entered through an employee only door where a tall brunette in a business skirt and white blouse greeted us.

"Welcome Ms. Millstead, Mr. Thaxton," the woman said confidently, "I'm Tammy Kardigan, the manager. We have adjoining rooms prepared for you on the seventh floor. I think it's best we head up there to discuss the preparations. It's a madhouse out front." She didn't wait for a response as she took us to the service elevator.

"There are numerous camera crews outside," Tammy said as the elevator doors closed, "we were prepared for crowds, but this is exceeding our expectations. We have opened the two adjoining ballrooms to give you more space. It may still not be enough." She was confident, but I sensed a bit of frustration in her voice.

"I am sure it's perfect," Sadie said, smiling. She wrapped her hand around mine. "We appreciate all you have done." I felt a tinge of guilt when I gave her hand a small squeeze. Her hand shouldn't feel so comfortable -- it just shouldn't.

Tammy gave us each a key card, 701 for Sadie and 703 for me. I followed Sadie and Tammy into Sadie's room. It was fairly large room with a small sitting area with four leather chairs surrounding a short, round coffee table. There was a bucket containing ice with and a bottle of what looked like champagne nestled inside. The bucket was ringed by a four-piece flute set.

"From the mayor's office," Tammy said, pointing at the champagne. We each took a leather seat and Tammy unfolded a piece of paper she had pulled out of her skirt pocket. "The caterer is already here, they are expecting to begin serving at six. The mayor would like five minutes, if you wouldn't mind. His chief of staff said it would be strictly in support of the City Kitchen." Tammy stopped there and looked at Sadie."

"That will be fine." Sadie shrugged. This was all getting bigger than we had expected.

"How long will you need?" Tammy asked Sadie.

"Pardon?"

"Your speech, how long do you need?" Tammy repeated. I don't think Sadie was planning on more than a thank you. I could see her thinking within herself, trying to put something together.

"You can tell them about Richard, how it all started," I said helpfully, "'Sugar Magnolia' and the number of people that get fed. They might as well know what it means to you." Sadie smiled at me.

"Five minutes would be fine," Sadie answered with confidence.

"And you Mr. Thaxton?" Tammy looked at me and I looked at Sadie.

"I am just here to support Sadie," I said, "I wasn't planning on saying anything."

Tammy gave a small grunt of surprise. "You're going to disappoint a lot of people," Tammy said with a condescending tone. "A lot of people are expecting a song." I looked between Tammy's grim expression and Sadie's suppressed grin.

"I guess I could say a few words. Maybe talk about the people I met and how the kitchen helps them." I was thinking about Houser. "I could come up with a few minutes."

Tammy scribbled something down on her paper and looked back

up to Sadie. "I spoke with a Bob Townsend and he told me about 'Sugar Magnolia.' We are prepared to play it when the buffet opens if you like."

"That would be wonderful. Thank you, Tammy." Sadie looked very pleased and I thought it would be a wonderful addition. Everything seemed to have a nice flow to it. Sadie could explain 'Sugar Magnolia's' significance and it would lead right into it getting played. The only thing that could disturb that flow would be me saying a few words.

"I think 'Sugar Magnolia' should come right after Sadie's speech, you know, right after she explains its meaning," I offered.

"That makes sense," Tammy agreed, "but when would you speak." I wouldn't, I thought. I threw that wonderful thought away.

"Maybe during dinner I could say a few words." Maybe everyone would forget I exist by then. If not, I could just give everyone a great big thank you. Short and sweet. Sadie laughed. She knew exactly what I was thinking. Amber would have really liked her.

"I think they are expecting more than a thank you," Sadie said. She knew me as well as I knew myself. It was unsettling to hear her divine my thoughts.

"I can talk about Houser and Maggie," I offered, "how much it all means to them. How much it means to me that they have a warm meal." It was off the top of my head, but would be easy to talk about. The truth usually is.

"Perfect," Sadie said, her face going compassionate, "they need to know why they are donating and I can't think of a better way." I smiled. It wasn't a smile I could control. Pleasing Sadie was becoming important.

"I'll make sure everything is set, and someone will come to get you around 5:30," Tammy said, "sure you won't sing?"

"I haven't prepared anything," I said with a sorrowful shrug. Tammy left, promising the night will go smoothly as possible. Her confidence left us feeling pretty good about the event.

"I'm sorry you had to come out of hiding," Sadie said once we were alone.

"You're worth it." I meant to say the City Kitchen was worth it. My mouth was moving faster than my brain. I stood *q*uickly and headed for the door, "I'm going to get cleaned up," I offered as an excuse. I didn't want to look back, blood had flooded my face again. It took a few deep breaths behind the closed door of my room to calm myself. I sat on the bed and stared at the wall, wondering how Sadie mixed with all my guilt. I closed my eyes and fell back on the bed. I lay there until there was a knock on the door. It was 5:30.

I met Sadie in the hall. She looked at me with kind eyes. The kind that didn't look away from the shame I was feeling. The kind that begged to share the guilt. Those kinds of kind eyes. She held out her hand and I took it. This time she pulled me close as we headed toward the elevator. She raised on her tip toes.

"You're worth it too," Sadie whispered in my ear. I didn't feel like I was. I lightly kissed her forehead for the thought. She leaned into my shoulder and we rode the elevator down, more comfortable than I deserved.

The elevator opened on the first floor to a row of police officers and firefighters in their dress uniforms. A smiling official escort. The whole thing was way out of proportion. We entered the huge ball-room to a round of applause. Sadie took it stoically; I cringed. She turned to me, smiled and mouthed "thank you." The place was packed. Every table was full and many were standing along the walls. There were three buffet lines and we walked along the one in the center, toward the stage. I saw Tony Berkhard looking good in his dress blues with his wife on his arm. I felt ridiculous, but I stepped over to him as we passed and shook his hand. He had done a lot and at least my thanks were in order.

"This is my wife, Rebecca," Tony introduced his overly excited red-haired wife. I still didn't understand what women expected from my unexpected fame. More than I obviously knew how to deliver.

"It's wonderful to meet you," I said holding out my hand. Rebecca laughed and wrapped her arms around me and kissed my cheek. A cheer arose and suddenly I had to shake everyone's hand all the way to the stage. I also had to endure a few more kisses. I was beet red when I arrived at the stage. Sadie stood waiting, obviously enjoying my embarrassment.

I went to stand next to Sadie, just to the right of the podium. I turned to see a sea of people, all out of their chairs. The police officers and firefighters made up half the attendees. In the middle, off to the left, there were two tables filled with my ex-coworkers and boss, Doug Herzog. Some of them waving. Out of habit, I waved back. There were more cheers and I thought 'screw it' and waved to everyone. Up front, I noticed the Leach with his cameraman filming it all. My smile felt fake, it was hard to leave it on my face. I would never make a good politician.

I saw the mayor make his way onto the stage. His smile looked real as he approached Sadie and me. He shook my hand with his other on my shoulder like we were best friends. I was being used, but it was worth it if it helped the City Kitchen. He moved over to Sadie and kind of pulled her closer to me when he shook her hand.

"I understand Patrick Abernathy is causing you some grief," the mayor said just loud enough for only the two of us to hear, "let's see if we can put an end to that." He winked at us. Both Sadie and I lit up with large, honest grins. I am sure it played well for the camera and made the mayor look good. I had no problem paying the price. Sadie just loved the support. The mayor took the podium.

"It looks like half the city is here," the mayor yelled when he reached the microphone. The crowd cheered and the applause continued until the mayor asked it to stop with his hands. "Do you know what makes this city great?" He paused for effect, then answered his own question while pointing at Sadie, "it's people like Sadie Millstead. The City Kitchen provides a safety net for all those wonderful souls who fall through the cracks of our great society. She doesn't do it with tax dollars or by demanding concessions. She's there every day unselfishly giving of herself with one mission in mind." The mayor dramatically cast his eyes across the crowd. He was a speaker and damn good at it. "No one leaves the City Kitchen hungry," he said it with gusto and pounded his fist on podium. The crowd ate it up. The applause was deafening and Sadie looked awfully cute with red cheeks. I didn't need to fake my smile any more. I was proud standing next to her.

"Our proud police officers and firefighters know this. I see most of them right here." The mayor cast his arm across the crowd to more hefty applause. "I see it in all your eyes as you open your wallets to support the City Kitchen. I am proud to be among you, to call you fellow citizens. I want you to know my office and I stand with you. As long as I am mayor, the institution Sadie Millstead and her late husband created will stand strong right where it is. No one will interfere with the support it provides." The crowd went nuts again. I am not sure how many in the crowd knew what was going on, but the mayor just shut down Patrick Abernathy, on the record.

"I would like to introduce you to the driving force behind the City Kitchen," the mayor said, still in his excited speaking voice, "a role model for us all, Sadie Millstead." I smiled at her as she headed to the podium and once again shook the mayor's hand. The mayor spent a few seconds patting my shoulder and smiling with me as he exited the stage. At least my fame had bought Sadie a strong defender.

SADIE WAS A COMPETENT SPEAKER

Sadie was a competent speaker. Not the vibrant, play to the crowd type like the mayor, but she was confident. She spoke about how she and Richard started the kitchen. At the time it was mostly Richard driving the dream. How it became her dream as well. The crowd became **q**uiet as she mentioned Richard's passing and her promise to make sure the kitchen continued. She spoke well of the progress and future of the kitchen.

"I have kept one tradition as a tribute to my late husband," Sadie said calmly, "every day at 4:00 a song is played. It was his favorite and substitutes for our dinner bell. We will play it now to open the buffet." The silence permeated the room as we waited for the music to start. It didn't come and Sadie started looking around anxiously. I saw Tammy moving **q**uickly to the stage with a worried look on her face. I happened to glance down at the Leach. He was smiling, an awfully sneaky smile. There was a gleam in his eye. I knew then; he had set me up.

My heart started pounding and I closed my eyes. There were way too many people here. I heard Tammy whispering something about a missing thumb drive to Sadie. 'Sugar Magnolia' was too fast for me. I knew the words; I've heard them every day for months. The tune had melted into my brain long ago. If I could just slow it down, sing it at my pace. I tried to pull Amber together in my mind. I could always sing to her. The images were fleeting, my weak memory failing. My hands began to shake as I opened my eyes to a bewildered crowd. I turned toward Sadie. She was flustered and confused when she looked at me. Her eyes met mine and her face shifted to concern.

I sang. I sang to her.

The words just flowed as I memorized every facet of Sadie's face. I saw her eyes swell, a tear run down her cheek. I sang the song at my pace. Our pace. Sadie held my eyes and I drew confidence from her and sang stronger. She took a step toward me as I came to the end. When I finished, she jumped into my arms and I didn't want her anywhere else. I turned her face away from the crowd so they wouldn't see her tears. They saw mine instead. The applause was deafening.

I pulled away slightly when my heart began to slow. My mouth moved as fast at my guilt, "I love Amber." I don't know what I expected, but a smile wasn't it. Sadie raised her mouth to my ear and whispered..

"And I'll always love Richard." Sadie kissed my cheek softly and slowly separated from me, her hands following my arms down until she was holding both my hands. "We have guests to thank," she said, her smile defying the tears on her cheeks. I nodded and we headed down the stage stairs and began going from table to table.

I stopped when I passed by the Leach who was trying to follow me around with his cameraman. Smiling for the rest of the world, I leaned into his ear. "You're supposed to report the news, not create it." He laughed and handed me the missing thumb drive.

"I didn't report everything Houser told me," Bob said conspiratorially, "consider it payment for keeping my pen quiet." I thought about it. He was a slime, but a compassionate one.

We spent the rest of the buffet thanking the hundreds of people who showed up. We thanked the mayor for his speech and he made sure the Leach got a good shot of him with us. I have no idea how it would play with everyone else, I just know he had my vote.

I was never any good at accepting public praise. The constant comments about my singing were embarrassing me. I was lucky Sadie was there to buffer some of the praise. She had a way of allowing me to accept it without having to come up with too many verbal responses beyond the occasional thank you. I just let her do most of the talking. Some of the women were a little aggressive, but Sadie always seemed to slide between them and me. For some reason, my cheeks were open season for kissing and I was expected to hug closely. My clothes had absorbed a hundred perfumes by the time we finished.

The police officers and firefighters were ecstatic I was coming to the Guns and Hoses event. I had no choice but to seem excited. They were here for us, so I would be there for them. I really didn't want to sing again. It just seemed to draw more unwanted attention and the stage fright was slightly debilitating. I would be there though, hopefully increasing the attendance as they had for us. They were good friends to have. I thanked detective Berkhard heartily again, since he is the one who put it in motion.

I was called up to the stage once again. I had almost forgotten I would have to say a few words. Sadie came up with me and I welcomed her company. The stage was a lonely place to be. I spoke briefly about the City Kitchen, about the people I met and how much the kitchen meant to them. We were one link in a support structure for those who had lost their traditional ones. I spoke of Houser and how his warped view of life helped me endure the death of my wife. I thought about Houser as I spoke and I wondered how much he had lost. There had to be a reason he had given up and chosen his strange freedom. I closed, pledging my support and thanking all those in attendance. The applause was warm and everyone stood up. I was uncomfortable with it and glad Sadie was there with me, her hand taking hold of my fidgety one.

I felt the Leach owed me one after the stunt he pulled. There were things I needed to know. When I came down from the stage I asked him quietly for help. He said he would try. Now I owed him again.

It was 10:00 when I finally made it to the seventh floor and collapsed backward onto the bed. It had been a long day and it took its toll. I had promised myself I would consider the future once the banquet was over. Technically, this night wasn't truly over, but I knew I couldn't put the decisions off much longer. I relaxed my muscles; they had been taut all day. I felt the stress leave as I closed my eyes. An image of Sadie formed, 'and I'll always love Richard.' It echoed in my skull. I tried to see Amber, but her image kept getting replaced. I remembered how it felt to hold Sadie. I sang to her. I snapped up to a sitting position, eyes wide, my muscles tense again, loaded with guilt.

I was startled by a quiet knock at the door. I shook my head to clear my thoughts and headed to the door. I was about to open it when I heard another knock, but not from the hall door as I had originally thought. It was the door between Sadie's room and mine. My heart pounded hard and my throat thickened. I was hoping I wouldn't see her until morning. Too much was going through my head and I didn't particularly like myself right now. I was crapping all over what Amber and I had built. I opened the door slowly and kind of blocked the entry with my body. Sadie didn't attempt to enter.

"Hi," Sadie said kindly. Her hands came together loosely in front of her. It looked defensive in response to me blocking the door. I felt worse. My first impulse was to yell at her, my second was to the slam the door closed. Instead, I took a step back and let her in. My problems were not hers.

"Hi," I returned. My greeting was more generic. Sadie entered and I closed the door. I should have left it open. With it closed I felt trapped. I fidgeted until I decided to fold my arms in front of me and lean against the wall.

"Guilt?" Sadie asked softly. My arms fell down at her question. I put my hands in my pockets as I tried to come up with some kind of response. I had to look away. Her eyes were too caring.

"I'm sorry." It was a shitty response. It was packed full of cop out. I should have just told her to leave.

"I'm not," Sadie said and sat on my bed. She wasn't leaving. I had to look back at her or kick her out. One or the other. I looked back and shame filled me. "Amber was incredible. I can see it in everything you do. The way you care, the way you make my problems your own. She nurtured that in you. I wouldn't have you any other way."

"It hurts," I said truthfully, "I'm forgetting what she looks like. What does that make me?"

"Human," Sadie answered.

"I see you instead," I said, "it's tearing me up, dishonoring her like that."

"You sang for me," Sadie said, nodding. My eyes swelled and I closed them to hold it all in. "It was lovely," she added.

"Bob set me up," I said stupidly. Sadie laughed which made me smile.

"You sang to me," Sadie clarified.

"Yes," I sighed, "why did it feel like I was insulting her?"

"Because you love her," Sadie said simply, "you will always love her. I don't want you to ever stop loving her." Sadie stood and stepped toward me. "I want you to make room for me too."

"I already have," I said quietly.

"Good," Sadie smiled, "I've made room for you." Her hand softly found the back of my neck and gently pulled my lips down to hers. 'I love you Amber,' I thought as Sadie's lips met mine. 'I love you Sadie,' I thought as Sadie's tenderness engulfed me. I wrapped my hands around her and pulled her closer and returned the kiss as passion invaded. It was a different passion, Sadie's passion. Separate from what I had felt with Amber. Amber would always have my past, I decided to give Sadie my future.

I lifted Sadie into my arms, she was lighter than I had expected. Her giggle tickled my ears. I laid her on the bed and crawled up her body and kissed her again. She tentatively licked my lower lip and our passion grew. Our tongues entwined as we enjoyed each other's desire. I fumbled with the buttons on the front of her blouse, trying desperately not to break away from her soft lips. We ended up laughing as we got all tangled up in each other's clothes.

Sadie pushed me off her and stood up smiling, her clothes all askew. I watched as her blouse hit the floor, followed quickly by her flowery blue skirt. She stood before me confidently in white panties and bra. I realized I was staring, and started to quickly undress. I threw my shirt over the bed and a bra hit me in the face. Sadie had a sly smile as I took in her perky breasts. They were small, and incredibly cute. I tossed her bra after my shirt, and raised my hips to remove my pants. Sadie laughed and I glanced down to see my manhood poking proudly though my boxers.

Sadie reached over and shut off the light and crawled onto the bed as I lost the boxers. I felt a small tinge of guilt when her naked body folded into mine. I think she felt the tension and she slowed down.

"Second thoughts?" Sadie asked compassionately. I think she would have stopped right then and there if I had asked her.

"It's just hard," I said catching my breath. I wanted this and I wanted it to be with Sadie. I needed to move Amber out of the way without losing her.

"I was hoping it was," Sadie joked as her hand wrapped around my arousal.

"That's not what I meant," I said with humor in my voice. Her hand slammed the passion back into me. I groaned a bit.

"I know what you meant," Sadie whispered in my ear as she removed her hand, "I'll wait if you want me to. I'll wait as long as you need."

"I don't want to wait," I said and kissed her lips. I felt them smile and my heart jumped at her joy. She rose and straddled me. Her hand positioned me between her legs and she lowered herself. My moan matched hers as I entered her. She didn't stop until her butt was sitting on my thighs. We fit well together. She leaned forward with me inside her. Her hands cradled my face, my hands caressed her sides.

"I loved when you sang to me," Sadie cooed as she moved her hips slowly, "it was so beautiful. I knew then, I wanted to be right where I am now." She kissed me, then placed her forehead on mine, and concentrated on her movements, her breathing increasing. I lowered my hands, finding her little butt and helping her move. The sensations were burning into me, her need forcing mine forward. Unexpectedly, her body went rigid and she breathed a low moan onto my lips. I held her as she collapsed into me, little tremors forcing her legs taut, then loose. I lifted her slightly and rolled her onto her back, while remaining coupled. She gave a sated sigh, and I could feel her smile in the dark.

"I'm sorry," Sadie said languorously, "that was kind of greedy." I felt her suppressing a chuckle which forced me to smile.

"It was beautiful," I said truthfully, "feeling you let go like that." She laughed lightly, reaching up and stroking my cheek.

"It took nine years." I stroked the side of her cheek as Sadie spoke. I felt a slight wetness there. I felt her hips move, exciting me again. "I won't let you wait that long." Our lips met, passion flooding me again. My hips raised then lowered slowly, her arms pulling me deeper. Her moans, as I complied, brought me back to the cusp. Her breathing increased and I felt her tremors building again. I dropped my lips to her shoulder and lost myself in her. My whole body trembled as I gave myself to her, her body responding like mine. For a brief moment, there was nothing but us. It was a heaven I wasn't sure I deserved, but I greedily took.

When my mind returned, I rolled onto my side taking Sadie with me. I ran my hand across her cheek, pushing the sweaty hair I found there behind her ear. I kissed her forehead.

"I was contemplating my future before you came in," I said softly. I ran my hand down her arm and entwined my fingers in hers.

"What are you planning?" Sadie asked.

"I thought I was going to run," I answered, "now...I could become a nuisance, you know." Sadie's hand ran down my side and stopped on my ass, which she squeezed lightly.

"Stay," was all Sadie said. She was the only one who understood. I wasn't going anywhere. I had made room for her. It wasn't fair to make Sadie share, but I was bit jealous of Richard as well. I was comfortable in her arms. We fit well together.

"I plan to," I said, and then smiled, "greed is not necessarily a bad thing." I loved making her laugh.

We awoke early the next morning. We played lovingly in the early morning light before the time brought Sadie back to reality. We showered quickly. Well, as quickly as two people who weren't done exploring each other could. The City Kitchen needed to be opened so I tamped down on my passion. We dressed in yesterday's clothes and headed out looking for a cab. Tammy tried to stop us as the front doors opened, but her warning came too late.

A small cheer went up, cameras flashed and reporters armed with microphones ran toward us. The Leach had been busy. We smiled and waved as we tried desperately to break away. Finally, I stopped and grabbed Sadie's hand. The crowd quieted down.

"For twelve years the City Kitchen has never missed a day," I said, raising our hands, "please, we're late." Some of the reporters stepped back, others did not. Police broke through the throng and I couldn't be happier to see them. They led us to an unmarked vehicle and made sure we got out of there. I watched the reporters packing up to follow. No, fame did not sit well with me.

There were two reporters at the City Kitchen. Luckily, the main force was still en route. The cameras and questions were more cordial since they didn't have to fight with anyone. We were cordial in return, and answered some easy questions. A well-dressed man in an expensive long coat was standing by the door as we approached. He was older, but had an air of sophistication that offset it with confidence.

"Ms. Millstead," the man bowed his head slightly, "I wonder if I might have a word with you and Mr. Thaxton." I moved forward. I didn't like the way he carried himself. Way too authoritative.

"And you are?" Sadie asked from behind me. This was her place and she reeked the same confidence back at the man. The man smiled contritely.

"I would prefer we spoke inside," he nodded to the reporters. "I suspect it would cause a scene neither of us could afford out here." I knew exactly who he was. He wasn't hiding behind lawyers this time.

"I believe this is Mr. Abernathy," I said quietly. Sadie clenched her teeth and unlocked the door.

"Thank you," Abernathy said as he entered following Sadie. She moved quickly into the dining room, and turned, wearing a less than friendly expression.

"You're trying to ruin me," Sadie said. You could almost smell the poison in the air. I moved again to position myself slightly between the two. I wasn't sure who I was protecting anymore. Sadie looked like she might go for his eyes.

"Actually," Abernathy said calmly "I was trying to make you cave. I would have never taken it too far. I must admit, I didn't expect the retaliation." I was about ready to hold him down and let Sadie scratch his eyes out. He shook his head and held up his hand when he saw our anger brewing.

"I'm done," Abernathy said, trying to cool us down, "to me, business is life." He looked around the dining room. "I see you two have a different view."

"Why?" Sadie asked with her anger still at the forefront.

"Simple answer. You thwarted my rezoning." Abernathy shrugged his shoulders. "It's the equivalent of throwing down a gauntlet. I fought back." He chuckled. "I just completely underestimated you. The amount of support you two gathered was impressive."

"You could have sent your lawyer to concede," I said with disdain. I wasn't sure why he was here. I worried this was just another play.

"I am here to grovel, Mr. Thaxton." Abernathy was smiling as he spoke. He found the situation humorous. "You two have me by the balls. I wouldn't blame you if you decided to finish me off, but I have learned my lesson. I apologize." He bowed to Sadie whose expression changed to one of bewilderment.

"We haven't touched you." My confusion was apparent. "You've had us jumping through hoops the whole time." Abernathy laughed and had to cover his mouth to squelch it.

"It's your friends who have been thrusting the knives." Abernathy seemed generally surprised at our ignorance. "I have thirteen company vehicles in impound lots due to questionable parking violations, and three of my larger construction projects have had their permits revoked due to fire hazard concerns. At this rate, I will be out of business by the end of the quarter. I won't even tell you what the mayor's office thinks of me right now." Sadie was trying to hide a smile.

"Look, I wouldn't blame you if you buried me." Abernathy had lost his smile. "I'm rich. I'll survive. I have people who work for me who aren't rich. I would rather not hand out pink slips, not to mention having to tell my wife why." He looked at me. "She thinks you're something special. God only knows why," he said, shaking his head. Sadie let out a suppressed chuckle. I just cringed.

"Apology accepted, " Sadie said. The loss of jobs would have hurt her more than Abernathy.

"Good," Abernathy said. "I sent the deed to the adjoining property with a transfer agreement to a Sarah Ferguson. If you agree to the donation, you will control the block. Consider it atonement."

"And a tax write-off, " I said gruffly.

"There is that." Abernathy was smiling again. "Or, I could sell it to another developer."

"No!" both Sadie and I said at the same time.

"Then it's settled, you call off the dogs and I make sure you stay open." Abernathy turned to go, then stopped and turned back. "The mayor won't be in office forever, you could have worse friends than me." He was offering more than an olive branch. He was offering long-term stability. I looked at Sadie and she shrugged her shoulders to defer to me. Abernathy was one hell of an enemy -- I suspected he was one hell of a friend also.

"This doesn't mean I like you," I said as I walked toward the door. Abernathy smiled and followed me out. I had a feeling he always came out smelling like roses. The full press corps had caught up with us, and cameras were flashing as we exited. Microphones were shoved in my face and I answered a few simple *q*uestions. I put up my hands to stall more -- I was surprised when it worked. I pulled Abernathy next to me.

"Mr. Abernathy has just generously donated the property adjoining the City Kitchen." I was getting a little better at this. "This ensures the long-term viability of the Kitchen. I can't tell you how much his donation means to us and the people we feed. Truly a remarkable gift from the heart." The microphones shifted to Abernathy and he humbly answered *q*uestions. He was much better at it than I. He tied himself to the Kitchen's survival and guaranteed it all in public. Definitely a better friend than enemy.

I snuck away as soon as I could. Sadie was busy starting prep. I jumped in and another day began. I brought down all the chairs and realigned the tables. Last night's clean up crew didn't *q*uite grasp Sadie's anal tendencies. There were a couple of spots on the tables, which Sadie seemed to spot from the kitchen. She looked like she meant to toss me a rag, then thought better and brought it out. She put it in my hand and then kissed me hard. I had to admit, it was better than a rag toss. She smiled and headed back into the kitchen, silent and very confident I knew what to do with the towel. I did.

"You know you're going to have to sing for them," Sadie said when I pulled a box of lettuce out of the walk in. I knew she meant the police officers and firefighters. "I know you did it for me, but they went above and beyond." I opened the box and started unloading heads. I've sung twice, I could do it once more.

"If you're there, I will sing to you," I reasoned, "they can listen if they want." I loved making Sadie laugh.

"You have such a lovely voice. You should share it." Sadie moved toward me.

"Is it okay with you if I don't?" I asked honestly. She answered by kissing me again. Then she made me wash my hands. She had a way of making bossy seem so sexy.

The days that followed were wonderful. We spent our days running the kitchen and our nights, well the nights were simply more wonderful. I told Sadie about Amber and she, in turn, told me about Richard. It was uncomfortable at first, but that faded quickly. We learned to share each other's pasts. With the IRS and class action in the rear view mirror, it made everything easier. Well, almost everything. Sadie and I took a risk with Houser after Bob "Leach" Townsend got back to me with the information I asked him to find.

I sat down with Houser. I put a brownie on his tray and he smiled. I did not. Sadie sat down next to me and did the same. Houser looked up at our serious faces, and I could see he felt uncomfortable.

"I found your niece," I said *q*uietly. Houser lost his smile and his eyes swelled. He almost got up to leave. Sadie covered his hand with hers and held him there. I could see him suffering and wondered if we had chosen wrong.

"She wants to see you," Sadie said gripping his hand. I could see the panic in Houser's eyes.

"She'll hate me," Houser stuttered, "I couldn't...I have to go." Houser stood, Sadie held his hand and stood with him. I was afraid he would leave and never come back.

"Please don't leave," Sadie pleaded.

"I owe you Houser," I said while I remained seated, "you can't live without helping each other out here." I repeated his words to him. Some of the first he told me after yanking me from the water. Sadie gently pulled him back to his seat. His hands were shaking.

"You don't understand," Houser said, "I couldn't...I left her." I understood more than he knew, Bob saw to that. His sister died, then he lost his job. His world collapsed in on him.

"You left me with the Washingtons," a soft voice behind him said, "they are a wonderful family." Houser turned quickly, his eyes meeting his niece's.

"I'm sorry, I'm so sorry," Houser cried. Sadie had to let go of his hand. He rose and I thought he was going to run. Natalie Washington smiled at her uncle.

"Forgiven," Natalie said softly, "for what, I don't know, but you're forgiven." She took Houser's hand in hers. "Can you tell me about my mother?" Houser's eyes were tearing and he wiped them on his sleeve.

"Yes," Houser choked out.

"No one else can," Natalie said, "you're my only link to her. Can we just sit and talk?"

Houser sat, and Sadie and I drifted away. We watched as Natalie and Houser talked. His smile began to appear as the conversation continued. I wrapped my arm around Sadie and pulled her close.

"That went better than I expected," I said, "maybe she can talk him into going to a dentist." Sadie smiled up at me.

"I love that you did that." Sadie's eyes told me she loved more than what I did. It was the middle of dinner, the dining room was full with more hungry coming in. It was not the place, but it was the time.

"I love you," I said. I had thought it, and I had showen it. Now I said it without fear or guilt.

<<<<< Sadie >>>>>

"I love you," David said, with his eyes glued to mine. I knew he did, but it was the words that made my heart explode. I smiled up at him.

"I love you, too" I repeated to David. The way he shouldered the problems, making them his own. The way he made my pulse quicken by looking at me like he was right then. He was my future. He pulled me close and kissed me, the dining room disappeared and I barely heard the well-meaning gibes flowing from the tables. I loved the strength he didn't know he had.

Richard had that type of strength. He made me promise him before he died. A promise I thought I would fail to keep. Not anymore. 'Richard, I kept my promise -- I found love again.'

Manufactured by Amazon.ca
Acheson, AB